LOST EVERYTHING

TOR BOOKS BY BRIAN FRANCIS SLATTERY

Spaceman Blues
Liberation
Lost Everything

LOST EVERYTHING

Brian Francis Slattery

A TOM DOHERTY ASSOCIATES BOOK

NEW YORK

This is a work of fiction. All of the characters, organizations, and events portrayed in this novel are either products of the author's imagination or are used fictitiously.

LOST EVERYTHING

Copyright © 2012 by Brian Francis Slattery

All rights reserved.

A Tor Book
Published by Tom Doherty Associates, LLC
175 Fifth Avenue
New York, NY 10010

www.tor-forge.com

Tor® is a registered trademark of Tom Doherty Associates, LLC.

Library of Congress Cataloging-in-Publication Data

Slattery, Brian Francis.
  Lost everything / Brian Francis Slattery. — 1st ed.
      p. cm.
  "A Tom Doherty Associates book."
  ISBN 978-0-7653-2912-7(hardcover)
  ISBN 978-1-4299-8655-7(e-book)
  1. Regression (Civilization)—Fiction.   I. Title.
  PS3619.L375L67 2012
  813'.6—dc23

                                          2011033204

First Edition: April 2012

Printed in the United States of America

D 0 9 8 7 6 5 4 3 2

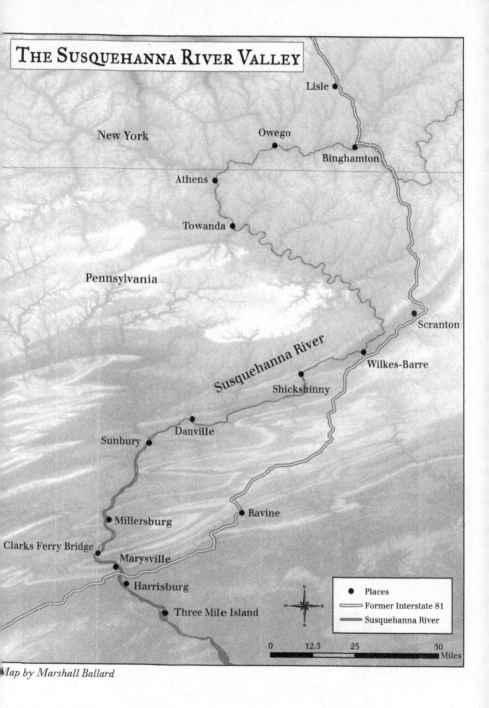

THE SUSQUEHANNA RIVER VALLEY

Lisle

New York

Owego

Binghamton

Athens

Towanda

Pennsylvania

Scranton

Susquehanna River

Wilkes-Barre

Shickshinny

Danville

Sunbury

Ravine

Millersburg

Clarks Ferry Bridge

Marysville

Harrisburg

Three Mile Island

● Places
▭ Former Interstate 81
▬ Susquehanna River

0   12.5   25   50
Miles

Map by Marshall Ballard

❖ ❖ LOST EVERYTHING ❖ ❖ ❖

HE WAS ON THE river with Reverend Bauxite when the dream descended upon him, of the mountains and hills melting into the sky. The wrinkles of the land smoothed and rose, the air thickened and fell to meet it, until everything was gray, dull yet luminous, as if there was a sun behind it, though he knew there was no sun there. The whisper of the atmosphere through his ears, the reverberations of the earth, the last echoes of voices all came together in a fading thrum, the final sigh before silence. It lasted no more than a minute, but the image, the sound, would not leave him. Downstream, the ruins of the Market Street Bridge were a tangle of twisted iron, shards of bony concrete jutting from the water. If the bridge goes down, you'll know we tried, Aline had said. Ten pounds of plastic explosive tied around her chest with a purple scarf. Upstream, the spindles of other bridges, the dark hills sliding into the water, the water itself a field of slate, the same color as the sky, promising storms. He looked down into the current, leaned over and let it wrap around his knuckles. The river was a rope, pulling him through the last hills, the submerged towns and factories, the stunted fields lined with sparse trees, all softened by rain. The leaning house where he was raised. The dead in the driveway. His sister in the window with a rifle, eyes closed and listening, as though she could hear it all. The cries and rumbles of the ruins of the coastal cities, the heads of the buildings on fire while the seawater surged around their knees. The roads snapping between the stony fingers of the shifting hills. The last houses groaning as the roots of the trees pulled them off their foundations, then rushed over the roofs and chimneys, pushing the walls down. Everyone, all of us, trying to speak at once. We are here. We are all here. Even after everything, we are all still here.

Aaron, my baby boy. I never should have let you go.

Sunny Jim's oar slackened in the Susquehanna's current. Reverend Bauxite, in the yellow boat with him, thought to say something, but did not. He could tell by the angle of Sunny Jim's shoulders, his wrists. Something had visited him, Aline for sure. They were so close to where she left them. Reverend Bauxite was on the opposite shore when it happened, saw the snake of fire slither along the bridge. A chain of bombs, a tail of oily flames. When the wind drew the flames away, the bridge was gone. Too much like a magic trick. Aline was in the other hand. Under the hat. She was behind Sunny Jim the whole time, one step away. She was under the water, hugging the bottom of the boat. Putting words in Sunny Jim's ear, talking to him as I am talking to you now.

Greasy smoke rose on the shore in front of them, over the blasted trees, the sandbags keeping the river back. There was commotion there, figures coming to frantic life in front of the small brick buildings. A new plume of fire, a gas can going up. The low thud of its ignition reached them a second later. There was no other sound until they reached the land and Sunny Jim leapt over the sandbags as Reverend Bauxite churned the water with his oar, fixing the yellow boat in the current. Then they could hear the wailing and shouting, the cries of agitated animals. A voice through a bullhorn. Reverend Bauxite stood and stepped to shore. They brought the boat over together.

"Just then, on the river," Reverend Bauxite said. "What did you see?" But Sunny Jim was already moving beyond him. The line to Aline, the line to Aaron, pulling him in opposed directions. These cords that God makes, Reverend Bauxite thought, we stand holding one end while they run taut into the darkness. We are connected, to what, we do not know. But if we put the frayed ends up to our ears, we can hear voices.

On the frontage road next to the river, a bomb had made a truck bloom into a metal lily, the sides peeled back and out. Tires melted into asphalt. Things on fire around it. A few old, dark trees, bright with flame. The wooden poles and tarps from vegetable stands, charred and ashen. The vegetables themselves. Twenty-seven corpses, four of them horses, three children. A line of cars, flames painting them gray. The occupying army's outpost was blackened, but not enough to take the graffito off the side: THERE'S NO PLACE LIKE HARRISBURG, PA. A mustachioed captain tried to restore order with the bullhorn. Calm down, everyone, please calm down. But they would not be calmed, for their families were dead.

The front of the war had come to Harrisburg and stayed for months, a malevolent hurricane, beyond what they thought nature would ever allow, before it moved on. They had survived all of that, thought after it ended that they would be safe. Thought that once they had lived to see it go, they would keep on living.

Sunny Jim and Reverend Bauxite found a crate of food, unwatched, unmolested enough to eat. Picked it up, heads down. Tried not to draw the soldiers' attention. But the grief around them was too much. Reverend Bauxite approached the families, bowed over the bodies, covered them with cloth. Closed his eyes, uttered words of general benediction. Rest eternal grant to them, O Lord, and let light perpetual shine upon them. May their souls, and the souls of all the departed, through the mercy of God, rest in peace. He did not know what the grieving believed, did not wish to send the dead where they did not want to go. But he believed that his deity was generous, would be a guide. A dim flame in dark woods. He bowed his head again as the faces of the families turned skyward, listening for news, for the last thoughts in the heads of the dead, set free and swirling around them like leaves. They never really go. They are always here. With me. And now with you.

The River

THEY SET THE CRATE in the belly of the boat, pointed the bow south, and floated on the thick current, under the broken arches of the bridges. Passed City Island, the flooded marina. The stadium overgrown with trees and split by shells. The baseball field now a cratered forest. Depressions filled with water from the rain, the river pushing out of the ground, flooding the roots of monumental maples. The whole place, the whole city, going under, for too much at last had been asked of it.

Reverend Bauxite looked away, then forced himself to look back. Smacked his lips and pulled a pipe from his jacket. Packed it with bits of dried apple, scraps of tobacco. He had not lit it in fifteen months. He missed the smoke, but the smell and taste of it were still there, a tang in his mouth. The feel of the bone against his teeth and tongue, and he was in his rectory again, years ago. The stained brick, the stone stairs. The dusty scent in the hallway, a hint of impending mildew. He could never figure out where it came from. In his office, blue carpeting, white linen curtains for the bay window. He was leaning against his desk, his fingers following the deep scratches in the top. Talia sat in a faded pink wingback chair, legs crossed, examining her nails. Speaking to him in a singsong voice, a lilt of minor thirds. Reverend, she said, your parishioners, myself included, think you should do more services around Lent. She was in the third row on the aisle every Sunday, fixed her eyes on him from the first word of his sermon to the last, closed her eyes when she sang. Always looked at him as if she already knew a truth that would take him years to discover.

The war was so distant from him then. Reports of small calamities from people moving north on the river. There's been some blood down there, they'd say. A couple towns burned in Georgia, North Carolina. Outside the rectory, they were celebrating the end of the monsoon. Boys beating on boxes and trash cans. Sixteen of the people in the choir singing and clapping their hands. A small mob in the street, shaking and shuffling, just glad for the sun. The church rising behind them, straight and serene. The light falling all over the city, taking the water away. It rose in columns of steam, as if Harrisburg was on fire, but when the mist dispersed, the city was still whole. That day, it was possible to imagine it always would be. For the city was weathered and sparking, a place of chipped houses on narrow streets, and you could read on its face what it had seen. During the Civil War, it saw soldiers and munitions heading south on the trains, corpses heading north, while young men trained for more slaughter in a camp on the edge of town, parading with bayonets before rows of white tents, as if they thought the war would be orderly. During the Cold War, it got a small dose of what everyone else was so afraid of. Not an explosion, but a meltdown, emptying the streets and houses, the people thinking about giving up on the place. But they didn't, not yet. Once, before Reverend Bauxite was born, even before the rivers rose and the trees came to swallow everything, when the last factories were not quite dead and the capital was still the capital, Pennsylvania still Pennsylvania, old men in wool jackets smoked in the bars of hotels with wrought-iron porches. On a sunny summer evening the streets teemed with people. A handsome couple rode in a red convertible with whitewall tires, a cooler of beer hanging open in the backseat. On a night of torrential rain, a slack teenager with long oily hair served Middle Eastern food to three out-of-towners, who could not keep a straight face at the things he said. Is the food any good? Because I've never eaten here. Here—bringing some fruit on a platter at the end of the meal—he told me to give these to you. The out-of-towners talked about him for years afterward, wrote it down in their diaries, and it fixed the city in their minds. Kept it alive for as long as they were, and after they were gone. Had the Confederate army come to Harrisburg instead of Gettysburg, had Three Mile Island been worse, Harrisburg might have died sooner, and I would not be able to tell you anything about it. It is gone now, and my memory of it, from before the war, before everything else, is all I have. If I had known when I was there that it would be gone so soon—if I had known all that was coming—I would have tried harder to remember more. To write it down then, instead of now, when I have forgotten so much.

They drifted past the islands off Steelton, under the broken span of the Pennsylvania Turnpike. Rounded the bend in the river near the blasted runway of the airport, Sunny Jim steering in the back. The destruction all seemed remote from them. Reverend Bauxite was always seeing it, the world without the war. Had to believe it would end, for all things passed, did they not, save one? On the land were burnt houses, the remains of firefights. Women kneeling in the street before a relative, bleeding away. Scorched trees, black vines, hanging over the current on the shore. Dogs in the leafy darkness at night. And in the river, fish hovered, water striders rode the surface. Herons stalked the shallows. As if the war had never begun.

Reverend Bauxite had seen it even the night Aline left. All along the Harrisburg shore, human screams and the roar of explosions. The end of the world for them, an end in fire. But all around him, mayflies rose in the air, trout leapt to catch them before their flight. He waded into the water, lifted his arms, and the flow of the Susquehanna whispered around his calves. It flowed as the bridge fell into it. Flowed as it put the fires out. We put our dead into it, our dead and mountains of slag, and still it flowed, Reverend Bauxite thought. We dug tunnels beneath it and it broke its way in, filled them, and flowed. It could wash away anything in time, without hurry or judgment, as it did before we ever saw it, as it would when we could not see anymore. But he was not consoled.

Evening was falling into night by the time they reached Three Mile Island. The river, a thin skin over the drowned causeway. Plants pulling down the rusted fence at the periphery. The road in the facility cracked by grass and saplings. A huge pine had burst through the pavement and shot for the sky, half its head knocked off by an errant shell, but still alive. The cooling towers spilled over with vines that ran in veins down their hourglass sides. Once they had been the house of the angel of death, who spread its wings over the city, getting ready to sweep everything up into it. Now they were filling with soil that trees took root in, braiding their branches together, competing for light. The cries of animals echoed inside. Keening bats, chirping birds. The hoots of small mammals. Someday, Reverend Bauxite thought, the towers would fill up all the way, the vines would cover all of them. Or the soil would be too much for the concrete to bear, and the towers would crack in two, the earth rumble out. Turn this island into a hill. He could not decide if that would be the end of us or the beginning. The glimpse of a revelation.

They lay down to sleep in the towers' shadows, in a rusting trailer crawling with honeysuckle. A single copper cable, insulated with green plastic, jumped from a hole in the side, slithered into the river. Inside the trailer, two bunks, a big blue phone. A plastic bag with three changes of clothes. They had been moving ever since the resistance lost Harrisburg and the occupying army moved in. No more than two nights in any one place, stringing up a pirated telephone line in twenty minutes that could be taken down in ten. Floors of wet concrete, warping walls losing their plaster, spun with jagged cracks. They stared at the water damage, squinting their eyes. Played a game with each other that they used to play with Aaron. It looks like a big maple, Reverend Bauxite said. No, like a bunch of lightning bolts, said Sunny Jim. Like an old hairbrush. Like a dried-out spider. Both of them missed the boy so much, though the games brought him closer. Then Sunny Jim slept. Almost every night, Reverend Bauxite lay awake for too long after that, returning to the day his church fell. He had been outside when it happened, saw three holes appear in the tiled roof, a fourth in the wall. Heard the incoming whines of artillery a beat later. Then a bright light from within, a tremulous roar, and the church folded in on itself, became a pile of burning stone. There were forty-eight people in there, his parishioners, who had come to him for refuge. He did not know how to get them out.

When he had celebrated with his congregation before the war, their voices had multiplied on the ceiling in song. The echo when they were finished never sounded like dying, only like the sound was moving away from them, out into the world. Their voices must be moving still, Reverend Bauxite thought. Understood that believing in their persistence was a matter of faith. But he still longed to see his people, to know that they had lifted themselves from the fire. He had asked his God to grant him this, even though it meant that his faith was wavering. That he was not as strong a vessel as he wanted to be.

The toes of animals tapped on the metal roof in the dark. You should go get your boy, Jim, Reverend Bauxite wanted to say. Aline is not coming back. But Sunny Jim was asleep then, listening only for her.

▨ ▨ ▨ ▨

REVEREND BAUXITE MET ALINE two months before the front came to Harrisburg. A meeting in the capitol building, with the mayor, several clergy, and four resistance leaders talking about what had happened in Baltimore. Horror stories. A vision of hell, Biblical violence, a village burned to nothing, people suffering an angry God's wrath. Brother will betray brother to death, Reverend Bauxite thought, and a father his child, and children will rise against parents and have them put to death, and you will be hated by all because of my name. But the one who endures to the end will be saved. When they persecute you in one town, flee to the next. For truly I tell you, you will not have gone through all the towns of Israel before the Son of Man comes. Gray light poured through the windows. The pulsing wind rattled at a crack in the glass. The light bulbs in the ceiling had burned out long ago. After the speeches, Aline came over to Bauxite, smiling her sideways smile, her hand extended.

Her palm a pad of callus. Something sharp embedded in the skin, a stone, an erratic jewel of shrapnel. She did not even know it was there.

"The war's coming this way," Aline had said. "You planning on taking a side, Father?"

"I'm on the Lord's side."

"And what side's He on?"

"The one that helps those who suffer, and causes the least of the suffering."

"And where was He in Baltimore?"

"I told you I'm on His side. I don't pretend to know His mind."

"You're making God sound like my husband."

Sunny Jim seemed half gone already when Reverend Bauxite met him, a stained photograph of another man. Said little. Never made eye contact. His thin fingers working. Reverend Bauxite thought maybe he was sick. Then he met the three of them together—Aline, Jim, and their boy—and understood. Aline and Aaron, flush with color. Aline's big voice, Aaron's shout. A spindly kid hopping up the stoop on one foot, jumping back down in a single leap. A run at the telephone pole to shimmy up it. He could bite electrical wire in half, Reverend Bauxite thought, send off sparks and swing out over the rooftop. Aline laughed, her elbow resting on the butt of a machine gun. Then Sunny Jim smiled and Reverend Bauxite saw it, a ray of warmth passing from husband to wife, father to son. Sunny Jim drew it from somewhere else, took just enough to keep him here, gave the rest to them. Did not mind the cold that came after.

"That's why I'm here," Sunny Jim had said. "I don't care who wins the war. I just want it to end. I just want to get them through it."

"And then what?" Reverend Bauxite had said.

"Does it matter? As long as I'm with them?"

They split a bottle of bitter whiskey that night in the kitchen of a brick house near the shell of an old factory. A candle on the table, the flame burning low and slow. The smell of a fire outside seeping under the front door. Aline out. Aaron asleep in the dark room above them. The talk between the two men was easy and expansive. It was talk before wartime, but something else, too, the sense of a common soul between them so strong that, after only an hour or two, they were telling each other things they had never told anyone. Sunny Jim had been looking for the man to replace him if the bullet, the shell, came for him, knew they were both staying out of the fight. Decided there was no time to waste.

"You'll take care of my boy with me?" he said.

"Of course," Reverend Bauxite said.

"Until Aline can do it?"

"Yes. I promise."

Two days before the war came to Harrisburg, the resistance was massing weapons in the street in front of the church. Stacks of rifles, jumbled boxes of ammunition. The guerrillas working in eerie quiet. All thinking of the noise to come. Of crouching in a ditch while the earth exploded. Clothes wet with blood, urine, gastric fluid. Reverend Bauxite and Sunny Jim stood on the steps with Aaron. The boy wanted to carry one of the rifles, wanted to know how to shoot one. Sunny Jim's hands were on his shoulders, fingers tight.

"I don't want any part of this," Sunny Jim said.

"Me neither," Reverend Bauxite said.

But then the church fell, and Reverend Bauxite found Sunny Jim and Aaron in a slumping apartment on Agate Street. The son playing with a yo-yo that the father made from a spool. The father watching the street for violence. Reverend Bauxite gray with ash, on his face and hands, worked into his clothes.

"They knocked my church down," he said.

"Sit," Sunny Jim said. Shook his head. Thought for a few minutes without moving, because he did not want to lose this man. Could not afford to.

"I guess you have to do something about it," he said.

"Yes," Reverend Bauxite said. "If only to end the fighting sooner."

"I understand." Then: "No guns," he said. "There are enough already."

But there was so much else to do. Engineering and sabotage. Said they were there to install a generator, robbed power from battalions. Clipped cables. Filled frequencies with noise. Kept lines open for guerrillas huddled in apartments carpeted with shattered glass, rifles angling from empty window frames chipped by enemy fire. Listened on headphones so Sunny Jim could hear Aline's voice, know she was alive. They worked in the day amid fires, the rush of falling shells, rising smoke. At night, under the stripes of tracers, pink arcs of flares. They always took Aaron with them. Kept him where they could see him. We need to keep him safe, they kept telling each other. But even Grendel Jones, their commander, noticed how the boy seemed to be good luck, how the fighting never touched him, like a blind giant groping for a wily insect.

"The war can't find that kid," Grendel Jones told Sunny Jim one night. "Won't find you or the priest either, as long as you're with him." She did not finish the thought out loud, how Aline would have to fend for herself. For Sunny Jim would never take his son to the front's annihilating edge, and Aline would almost never leave it. There was so much about Aline that Grendel Jones could not understand. Why, when the fighting started, a spark lit inside her. Why she had a family. Why her family wanted her. She could not see into that, or get Sunny Jim to explain. So she never learned how Sunny Jim and Aline had pulled each other through and away from the leanest years of their lives. How, when the war came and everyone else panicked, they looked at each other and nodded, recognized the shapes of their own pasts in the face of the war's violence, knew what it was, even as it began to pull them apart.

Perhaps that was why the boy was the charm he was. He was the best of both of them. He warded off the mayhem, just by breathing, that his parents had taken years to learn how to survive. Aaron, Sunny Jim, and Reverend Bauxite had shacked up one night in a burned-out apartment building near the state capitol, moved out at dawn. That afternoon, a flurry of mortars leveled the building. A firefight broke out on a busy street only twenty minutes after Aaron left it, killed forty-seven people, too many of them children, but left him unharmed. The boy played amid cracking masonry while his father strung wire to a satellite dish on a factory roof. Sat in the bottom of the boat when they crossed the river. Slept through bombing raids and firefights, woke up hours later, blinking and yawning. He did not know what power he had.

Didn't, until six months ago on North Second Street. There had been a market there in full bloom, vegetables and animals amok. The sweetness of picked fruit, sourness of butchered flesh, tang of hay, flowing together in the air. Reverend Bauxite and Sunny Jim passing through, cable slung from Jim's hip. Aaron zigging and zagging, curb to curb. Then a shell, a bomb—they argued later, for they never went back—and everything was quiet but for the moaning. They were far enough away to only be thrown, knocked down. By the time Reverend Bauxite could see, Sunny Jim was already cradling his son, a dirty hand over the boy's eyes.

"Dad, come on, let me see."

"No. No."

Soot was snowing on a wide wound in the pavement. The skin of people blown back and away. A slurry of blood and dirt. A knee on the sidewalk, disconnected from everything else, a scrap of denim wrapped around it.

"We have to get Aaron out of this place," Sunny Jim said.

"Where can he go?" Reverend Bauxite said.

"My sister'll take him."

"Your sister can protect him?"

Sunny Jim just looked at him. Ended the discussion. Reverend Bauxite acquiesced, and Sunny Jim sent the word up the highway to Lisle, thirty miles over the border into New York. Merry was there within two days for the boy.

"We won't be able to talk," she said. "Just come and get him when you're ready." They turned to go, but not before Aaron hugged both men. It was then that Reverend Bauxite understood how the past few weeks had changed him, how the duty Sunny Jim had given him had become a mission. He thought he had begun to see a tiny fragment of God's plan in the boy, let himself hope that maybe there was one, even if he could not say what it was. Aaron had given him some of his church back, and now he was losing it again.

Merry and Aaron were gone before Aline returned. The mother railed when she found out, screamed for three hours.

"How could you leave him with her?" she said.

"The reverend and I talked about it. It's the best we could do."

"The reverend is not his mother. I am. You should have asked me first."

He glared at her. You should have been around to be asked. Why the hell are you doing this, anyway? When Aaron was born, when the war began, he'd thought that both their fighting years were done. She'd known all along that only his were. He was so angry at her for that, yet still loved her so much. The two were chained together. Then: "You're right. I'm sorry," he said. The apology offered only because it did not matter anymore—Aaron had been sent away, and there was no getting him back unless they went for him themselves—and Aline knew it. What Sunny Jim said next, he would regret for the rest of his life, for it was as if he had been given powers of prophecy for that moment and failed to see it, could not hear his own message.

"We'll go and get Aaron when you and the war are done with each other," he said.

And since the Market Street Bridge, since Aline left, Reverend Bauxite and Sunny Jim had been having the same conversation in their heads again and again.

We should go get your boy.

No. I have to wait until she comes back. Then we'll go get Aaron together.

She's not coming back.

Yes she is.

How do you know?

I just know.

Nothing of it spoken between them. They could read it on each other, their faces wrinkled pages. Words hiding in the folds of their clothes. She was made of letters then, as all of us are now. Here, in these words. Us and the city and the towns and river, and everything else, too. All that we know, and everything—everyone—we wish we knew.

ALONG THE RIVER, THE market was already coming back, growing up around the ruins of the day before. The singsong calls of vendors, the shrieks of birds, gutter talk of larger animals, goats, cows. A troop of monkeys patrolled the dark, dank aisles, turning wares in their hands. The occupying soldiers were off the ground, standing in the backs of jeeps, behind weapons of comical size. The vehicles verging on tipping over. Propaganda barking from a loudspeaker planted on the roof. We are a force of peace. It is the resistance that fights us. Sunny Jim was already watching the soldiers' eyes, was gone before Reverend Bauxite knew it. Sunny Jim's gift, he thought, was to become invisible, granted because there was so little keeping him here. He watched a soldier watching him, a woman with a ponytail sneaking out from under her helmet. The helmet too big, the jacket too small. The soldier turned to Reverend Bauxite, eyebrows raised. Seemed to see in him, then, all that he had done, for he was not like Sunny Jim. He was an open man, his passions playing in the air around him. The same thing that made him a fire, a beacon, in the pulpit, made him a failure at espionage. They should have left days ago, he thought. Gone north and found Aaron, then west, across all that land. The war could not have broken it all. They still could go, he thought. Change their clothes, their hair, their names, until Reverend Bauxite and Sunny Jim were just two more men who died somewhere back in all that fighting, and their new selves were free.

That night they hid in the last building standing on the block of Peffer and North Seventh, a red brick house that used to lean on its neighbors, but had nothing to lean on now. The stairs falling off the porch. Window frames angling with rain and gravity. A kitchen half-gutted by rot, a gas stove with no gas. Across North Seventh, the railroad tracks were torn up in twelve places. They could see the remains of the capitol from the roof, burned down again. They drew the place where the building's dome had been in the air with their fingers. They listened to the howling of monkeys in the houses near them, sirens from the other side of the bridge. There were alarms all over the city that night. Neither of them knew why.

Their phone rang again after midnight. Reverend Bauxite had his speech prepared. We can't do your work anymore. Aaron can't lose a father, too. But Grendel Jones's voice on the other end was small. Something has happened to the west and north of us, she said. No. Something is happening to the west and north.

"What do you mean?" Reverend Bauxite said.

"You won't believe me when I tell you," Grendel Jones said. She was right. Reverend Bauxite argued and shook his head. There must be some mistake. Nothing like that can be happening. Nothing.

"What are you talking about?" Sunny Jim said.

There will be signs in the sun, the moon, and the stars, and on the earth, distress among nations confused by the roaring of the sea and the waves, Reverend Bauxite thought. People will faint from fear and foreboding of what is coming upon the world, for the powers of the heavens will be shaken. Then they will see the Son of Man coming in a cloud with power and great glory. Now when these things begin to take place, stand up and raise your heads, because your redemption is drawing near.

"You won't believe me," Reverend Bauxite said.

But Jim believed every word. He stood there nodding and frowning. Aaron. My favorite boy. Why did I ever let you leave me?

"We can get on the highway now," he said. "Get there as fast as we can."

"No, we can't," Reverend Bauxite said. "The war is there. And the army is looking for you. They're looking for both of us."

All because of Aline. We never should have gotten involved.

We didn't have a choice, Jim. Not a real one. Not one that was right.

There is always a choice, and we chose.

"How are we going to do this, then?" Sunny Jim said.

Reverend Bauxite looked out the window, toward the Susquehanna. The long meandering stripe through the Pennsylvania hills that drowned the railroad track, spread into valleys. It could take them all the way to Scranton, ahead of the war, without the army ever seeing them. Maybe all the way to Binghamton. Lose a few days, but it was worth it if it meant staying invisible. They would get there just in time, before the storm hit. The Big One, Grendel Jones was already calling it. A storm as wide as the horizon. Maybe as wide as the sea.

"We could go up the river," he said.

"Nobody's going up the river now," Sunny Jim said.

"Someone must be."

"How do you know?"

"I don't," Reverend Bauxite said. "But someone has to be. Don't they?"

His faith again, shaking. He tried to keep his voice from doing the same.

⸎ ⸎ ⸎ ⸎

DO YOU SEE? HOW the world is now? Nobody can say quite how it came to be this way. There is too much. There is not enough. It started generations ago, and so much has been lost, and even all that I found does not help. You wake up and the country is on fire, as far as you can see. How can you find the match that started it?

Our great-grandparents told our grandparents that things were different once, when they were children. A little colder. Simpler. Not as many people were dying. That the change was slow, slow enough to argue about it. A gradual, creeping shift. A field full of cars, grown over with grass and stalks of trees. The plants tipping the cars over, breaking them apart. A massacre three decades long. In West Virginia, we had leveled a green range of peaks into a gray waste, spotted with the rusting yellow metal of abandoned machinery. In Pennsylvania and New York, we had drilled for gas until the rock broke and the water went bad, and the towns that used to drink it died. We burned and we burned, until there was more smoke than fuel, and then things started to come apart. The roads breaking into rifts of jutting asphalt. Libraries with caved-in roofs, full of decaying books and dead monitors. We saw these things and yelled at each other. The system had been built on argument, believing that any problem could be fixed, explained, weaseled out of, with enough money, the right words. Until the problem was physics, and then there was only what we did and how the planet responded. It did not matter what we said after that, though we kept talking anyway. As if it was all we had.

There must have been a day, a single day, when it was too late, when we could not go back, but nobody can remember when it was. The storms started coming, more and more of them. A typhoon walloped in from the ocean, put an entire city underwater, and the water tore half the place down when it receded. Tornadoes swept across towns that could have lasted for centuries more, turned houses, fences, and cars into giant fields of shredded wood and metal strewn with the dead and everything they had loved. The bare trunks of dead trees that the wind had snapped in half and stripped of bark reached for the sky like scorched hands. The survivors staggered through the broken streets, stunned and shouting. Far away, there was news of entire countries flooded. Places where people had been for thousands of years, gone. In Richmond, Virginia, I found photographs in the basement of an apartment building showing a massive fleet of dilapidated ships arriving at a port, maybe in New Jersey, maybe Maryland. Maybe everywhere. Old cruise ships streaked with oil and smoke, tankers of rust, dropping sheets of corroded metal into the sea when they shuddered to a stop. Filled with people with clothes rotting off their backs. In those pictures, the seawalls our great-grandparents had put around the cities were still there. The ocean knocking on the door, about to let itself in. It took maybe seventy years. A growing beat, they say, of stronger and stronger storms, a long chain of hurricanes, until the walls gave way and the streets went under, buildings fell. Savannah. Atlantic City. A freak storm in Boston. A ragged swath carved out of New York. The remaining cities cringing with every change of season, every gathering of clouds, waiting for the Big One. A tide of survivors inland, looking for things that were not there. The government able to do less and less, until it was just men in frayed suits, arguing in buildings where the power kept going out, whose surroundings were turning back to swampland. The borders on the maps of America getting hazy, the names and the boundaries becoming lines and letters of no significance. Then there were just the cities and the towns, and the land all around. As though the planet was taking it all back from us. You could almost see it happening before your eyes, our grandparents said. The trees rushing over empty fields, year after year. Jumping from one dead farm to the next. The diseases followed, one after the other.

The war, the war. There was no Fort Sumter, no Pearl Harbor, no moment that we all understood at once that we were fighting. No one to tell us things had changed. There must have been a first shot fired, perhaps two men—it must have been men—arguing over where one's land began and another's ended, a first bullet flinging a ribbon of heat through the air. Another one shot back. But I have to believe they did not know what they were starting. If they knew, why would they have shot? An army was raised, a resistance arose. By the time Charlotte, North Carolina, burned, nobody was asking what it was about anymore. It was about territory. It was about food and water: who had it, who did not. The old fights, the ones we had fought since we got here, the ones our ancestors brought with them when they came here, all those bitter old things becoming new again. It was about how much we had done to the planet, and the way the planet, at last, had turned its great eye to us in anger. You have done enough. The war was about everything, it was everything, and the question of where it came from was meaningless. There was only the question of how to live through it.

The war came for us, my daughter and I, four years ago, in Charleston, West Virginia. We had moved six times, on a ragged diagonal across the South, from a washed-out beach house in South Carolina into the mountains. Slept in a garage outside of Roanoke, listened to the flood of rain find its way through the roof. Sat against the wall of a freight car with thirty other people, my arms around my little girl, while the train screamed and banged along the old Winchester and Western rails, too loud to rest. In Charleston, we heard the war was coming up the Kanawha river valley, talked about moving again. But the trees all around Charleston were in bloom, and we had a house, just big enough for us both, with a small yard behind it, a cinder-block wall. We were so tired of moving. Always thought we had more time. Three days later I was howling in the bottom of a metal boat with a man who had lost both his arms, shells exploding all around us. Then we drifted toward the Ohio, away from the war. He died when everything got quiet.

Do you see? The story I have left to tell is so small, of the people who stayed when everyone else fled. Two men going upriver to get a boy. Four soldiers going up the highway after them. Then the house where everything converged. But I had a child, too, strong and small. I lost her when I lost that house in Charleston, and I do not know where she has gone. And since then, I have been to Baltimore, to New York. I saw what happened to Philadelphia. I stood at the edge of a mass grave in Maryland, next to the parking lot of an abandoned shopping center. I walked through the windows of a fallen bell tower in Delaware that had crashed into the street after the bombs came for it. I was in a firefight in West Virginia, all oil and darkness and screaming animals, and when it was over, nothing but moans and crying, the ground swampy and fetid with blood and pieces of men. A tree hung with human limbs. I want to tell you their names, all those people who died around me, but I cannot say who they were.

I even went west to see the Big One coming in, because I needed to see it, to tell you. I stood on the ridge of the Appalachians and looked toward where the sun was supposed to be, toward the north, too, and saw no sky at all. Just a boiling wall of clouds, gray and green and sparked with red lightning, and underneath it, a curtain of flying black rain, rippling with wild wind from one end of the earth to the other. The sound of constant thunder. I watched it take a town in the valley, far away below, and it was as though a wave were rolling across the ground, lifting houses, roads, trees, and all—anything that was still there—up into the air, into the mouth of the storm. It was still rising, into the darkness, when I lost sight of it. It must have been so loud on the ground, the earth and rain and sky all screaming together, but I could not hear any of it. I wanted to say something then, but I did not have the words. There are no words for so much loss, not right after it happens. They come in time, but sometimes it takes years, and we do not always have years. My great-grandfather did not have them when he tried to speak of the towns all over upstate New York, the way the people seemed to dwindle year after year, the old ones falling into the earth, the young ones just not there the next day, as if plucked away. The decay of the houses moving across the villages and cities. Windows broken, then boarded. The lawns tangling with twisting young maples, black walnut, until the main roads were just strips of dying buildings, rusting bridges, sidewalks breaking apart. He loved it all so much. How would it ever come back? He would say these things, get that far, then try to tell you what had been lost, what he had seen himself. Then he'd just shake his head, put his hand over his eyes instead. It was the same thing for us as for them. Just much faster for us. For us, even less time.

We do not know what is on the other side of the storm. We cannot get around it, and the few who have tried to go over it say it never seems to end. We have heard that it came in from the Pacific like a tsunami, that it ate the coast. It crashed into the Rockies and crested them, then charged across the plains, tearing up towns and crops, roads and telephone lines. Pulling us all off the land, us and all we had built there. All the people who could not run, did not want to, we have not heard from since the storm passed over them. No letters, no signals, no photographs. No messages crackling across the wires. A veil is falling across the country, one long shattering shriek at its edge, and behind it, nothing but darkness and silence.

Though perhaps you are not silent. Maybe you can see things that I cannot, see them with utter clarity. Maybe you walked up to the storm and passed through it, because you were not as afraid as we were. Did you leave us behind, then, or take us with you? Or were we on the other side when you got there, lost and waiting?

❋ ❋ ❋ ❋

WHEN WE ALL LEARNED what was coming, there were reports of desertions, from the army, from the resistance. Soldiers just disappearing into the woods. Others found outside their camps with entrance wounds in the back of their heads, caught trying to leave by an officer the war had gotten the better of. A small string of suicides. A town somewhere upriver had, in a few days, lost all its citizens. In Harrisburg, the occupying army drove a van armed with loudspeakers through the tight downtown blocks around the state capital. Do not listen to the news today. It is full of lies. The sky over the city was enough like it had always been that they could say that and get away with it.

Sunny Jim and Reverend Bauxite rowed north, past the high-water marks on Rockville Bridge, up through the rapids at Marysville, to a herd of islands on a ten-thousand-year drift across the river's width. One of the islands' rocky spits had split in two with the effort, and Sunny Jim and Reverend Bauxite followed the channel up its course through a crevasse of dense vines, animals hooting in the shadows. For a few minutes, they were the only people left in the world. It was just them and the yellow boat, the water beneath. The trees closing around them. Roots walking into the water. Branches above their heads taking away the sky. Then the channel opened and the trees pulled back around an island smaller than a house, a single linden, gnarled and gigantic, hanging by its roots over the rippling water. A man with a rifle crouched in the tree's crook, the barrel following them as they entered. Two people stood in the gravel on the inside of the channel's curve. One of them Grendel Jones. Reverend Bauxite and Sunny Jim had seen her less than a month ago when the shells were falling, her hand on a radio, sending orders across the wires. She had caught their eyes and smiled, just once. Thought they were going to win. Now she was hobbling on a cane, scraggly hair tied back. Five parallel scratches striping her face from cheek to forehead. Her face rubbed in it. Your town and everything you loved. Let go of it all now before it hurts too much.

"Is it true?" Sunny Jim said. "About the north?"

"What do you want me to say?" Grendel Jones said. There was electricity between her and Sunny Jim that could have been mistaken for attraction, but was not. She was the war to him, embodied its rage. You stole my wife from me, Sunny Jim had told her once. Made me send my son away. Give me back my family. And that was before the Market Street Bridge went down.

She reached inside her frayed overcoat, brought out a battered envelope that looked like it had been sealed twenty years ago, though it was just the night before. The paper inside first being tacked to a plank of wood spongy with rot, so Grendel could write with her only hand, fingers stained with the dirty oil burning in the lamp. The light was a target for snipers, she knew. She was not so much careless as callous. Shoot me if you can, she thought. The war keeps taking pieces of me anyway. Makes the rest of me harder to hit.

"There's one boat still going upriver," she said. "Called the *Carthage*."

"How will we find it?" Sunny Jim said.

"You'll find it." Gave him the envelope. "You'll meet the boat at the Clarks Ferry Bridge. They'll let everyone on. Always do. But if you give them this, they'll take extra care of you. Take you as far as you need."

"Thanks," Sunny Jim said. She could tell how it hurt him to say it. In his grief, his anger, at Aline not being with him, he was making Grendel Jones complicit in her absence. The commanding officer felt it, too, the guilt and horror at her own power whenever she stopped to contemplate it. She gave an order, and people died. She could take lives just by speaking.

"Just get your boy," she said. Then caught his eye. I'm so sorry about Aline.

What do you want me to say?

That you forgive me.

I can't forgive you yet. Forgiving you would mean letting her go.

In Baltimore, the bones of Grendel Jones's left arm lay under a collapsed apartment building, softened by water. The rain was taking down all that was left of that city, the rain and the vines and trees, its accomplices. Wildflowers stormed along Falls Road. Tendrils of kudzu snaked around the Bromo Seltzer Tower. Plants and animals burying our dead for us. Turning us and all that we did into soil, then digging their roots in deep. They would never let us come back.

Grendel was not yet a soldier when she lost her arm. She was only there to care for her aunt, an invalid. After the first rocket attacks, they sat in her aunt's apartment, pushed the wheelchair up to the window. Watched a line of people leaving, a centipede of refugees. A family of five. The father with a coffee table and a rolled-up rug tied to his back. The mother with a bundle of clothes balanced on her head. Their children on leashes running from their waists to their parents' hands, staggering with the movement of drunken spiders. So little sound for so many people.

"They're overreacting," her aunt said, frowning. "This will all blow over soon." Her resolve never left her, even when the rockets came dozens a day and it seemed that someone was always firing a gun somewhere. Even when the flames turned the nights into the last minutes of evening for good, as though the sun were not allowed to set. When Grendel told her aunt about the massacres, she refused to believe it.

"People don't do that to each other," she said.

Fire, fire, I heard the cry, from every breeze that passes by. All the world was one sad cry of pity.

Grendel's arm left her as she stood in the doorway to the apartment building. It was wearing a blue sleeve with a white cuff, was holding cooking oil in a plastic bottle. The rocket's explosion threw the rest of her into the street, though she was already unconscious by then. When she woke up, she was lying on the deck of a barge in the Chesapeake Bay. A thin mat beneath her. The stump of her arm, bandaged, dirty. The Bay Bridge dim in the twilight. To the north and east, all of Baltimore consumed by fire or water, a long ragged band of orange light raging above the broken seawalls, the drowned streets, a mist of steam. Her aunt back there somewhere. On the barge with her, a small horde of survivors huddled under canvases, prone on the metal deck. A woman shaking with quiet sobs. A man sedated out of his head, still groaning on every pull of the saw that was taking off his right leg above the knee. A banjo and mandolin, two voices high and loose, their throats too smoky to get it quite right.

> *Oh Katy dear, go ask your mama*
> *If you can be a bride of mine.*
> *If she says yes, come back and tell me.*
> *If she says no, we'll run away.*

She was a glass jar dropped from a great height, then. No putting back together the past that had scattered from her head. Her life began again in that minute on the Chesapeake Bay, in ash and strained song. But her life before is back there somewhere, in the miles of her childhood before the war. Picnic tables rough from winter after winter. A biting insect clinging to a tree. Ankle-deep in a creek in early spring, her toes frozen already. A friend standing there with her, grimacing. You get out first. No, you. It all matters, it has to, even if she cannot remember it.

She became a guerrilla as soon as she could. Ascended through the ranks of the resistance until she was a field commander, ever in the calm land a mile or two ahead of the front. She learned to smell it, feel it, as animals sense weather, when it wavered and flexed. Spared some towns and destroyed others. She was ahead of it all through Maryland and into Pennsylvania. Knew what it meant when she got the orders to march to Harrisburg and settle in. They were going to be there a while, she thought, anyone could have guessed it. But she could even see it, in the way the city sat on the riverbank. The steps to the water. The bridges thrown across it, the stone arcades of their arches. A fortress already. The war would be fought in alleys. Window by window. Entire battles hinged on the turn of a staircase.

She met Aline a month before Harrisburg, after hearing about her two months before. The battle of Cumberland. Horses on fire, screaming, their manes trailing stripes of smoke. The resistance could never have turned the army back—it was ten to one—but they made them bleed for every brick of that old city in the steep valley, left them a smaller thing. The wounded lying under open sky in the shadow of the clock tower. Masonry cracked by concussion. Nothing to show for all that death.

"Somehow I thought you'd be taller," Aline said.

"Funny. I thought the same about you."

They both laughed, as if they were twins. Except

that Grendel never knew what to do with Sunny Jim, that wraith of a man. Their son under his arm, straining to run, the father refusing to set him free. It's not you, it's this, he said to his boy. All this. When the war is over, as soon as it's done, I'll let you go.

Sunny Jim turned the envelope over in his hand, eyed the stain running along its back. The folded paper inside pushing lines into its skin. As if Grendel Jones always knew it would come to this, the day they met.

"Why didn't you ever fight?" Grendel said.

"I didn't believe in it."

"Fighting."

"No. Just this war."

"Well, believe it. Because where you're going? It's going to get worse."

He knew that. He could feel it sometimes, in the dark. The front's gigantic edge, its claws, rusty and broken, tearing up the hide of the world. He had heard how it was along the highway from Wilkes-Barre to Scranton. Seen the debris in the Susquehanna. Tatters of clothes. A pair of eyeglasses. There were days that the river had changed color—bright orange, luminous purple—and he had thought of his boy and Merry, alone in the family house, almost two hundred miles upriver. The front howling behind the horizon to the south. And then the Big One coming in. When they were children, he remembered, his sister had told him this was coming as they stood on the ragged edge of a field. Watched the wind fall across the tall, dead grass, bright yellow under angry gray clouds. A desiccated red barn shaking on its beams. This earth, this sky, will come for us, she said, it'll get tired of us and come. And what comes after will be beautiful, even if we're not allowed to see it.

No wonder it was happening now, Sunny Jim thought. After what we had done.

❉ ❉ ❉ ❉

THEY WERE IN THE back of a delivery truck on the road out of Harrisburg with four other people, all down to what they could carry. The highway was broken by craters, clotted with the wrecked exoskeletons of military equipment. The remains of some hard miles. They passed a checkpoint after the sign for the Super 8, where the driver sweet-talked the soldiers into letting them go without inspection. They had nothing the soldiers wanted anyway. Across the river, they could see the lights from the army camp at Marysville, hear the murmur of a bullhorn across the water. The soldiers having to pacify themselves as much as the people they conquered. Soon the truck was swerving along the river valley's side. The hills to the right steep and jutting, a radio tower's single signal on one summit. The river to the left, slipping past dark clusters of islands. Betraying nothing of its strength. The southbound lane teemed with a long, unquiet line of people swinging torches and whipping animals. The chatter of confused children. In the places where the highway seemed to hang over the water, they could see up the valley, the refugees' lights drawing a chain across the foot of the slope. They were taking everything they could and going. The truck with Sunny Jim and Reverend Bauxite in it the only thing heading north. If either of them had glanced outside, they could have seen the looks. The shock and pity, the jokes and prayers. Why would anyone want to go up there?

They curved onto a long ramp over the water, where the islands fell away, the valley opened out, and the river swelled wide. It was cutting the hill in half, tearing the wound wide. The ridge was ragged with the river's assault, fell to the shore at steep angles. Covered in foliage, leaning trees. Rocks shaking loose from the bleeding wall. The highway, the giant Clarks Ferry Bridge, a toy amid all this violence. Once it had shot across the gap over the water, the river unperturbed around its monumental pilings. It would have pulled it all down in time. But the war got to it first, took down the bridge's middle third. The western end then fell all on its own, leaving the eastern end a jagged pier, its length ending in crumbling concrete, bubbled asphalt. Metal beams jutting below. The rubble from the explosion was gone. The river had made its bed with it, and the birds had returned already to the bridge's underside, built nests in the blackened steel. Their cries bouncing off the water's sleek surface. All the while, the river dug deeper. Bringing the mountain to its knees.

Up on the bridge, people waited on the pavement. Pairs, groups of three, of five, with small livestock muttering in cages. A dozen children wandering back and forth from the ramp to the bridge's edge, trying to make friends. They had a game with a ball of rags tied together until an errant throw sent it into the water. They watched the river take it away from them. Then started playing cards, rules involving slapping, punches in the arm. Evening brought fog that hung in suspense, threatening to become rain. Lanterns and small fires flared. Low voices. Someone humming. They huddled together for warmth as the river seemed to widen in the fading light, gather water far beyond what the Juniata brought in tribute less than a mile away. As if the whole world were water below them, rising into the air. They could smell it, taste it. The earthy musk of plants and soil, curdled by dead fish.

Near the end of the bridge, a woman had hung a tarp across plastic pipes to try to stay dry, started a tiny fire that writhed in a trash can lid. Two people joined her, beckoned others to join them, until there were eight of them standing in a semicircle, just out of the rain. Hands extended and open over the heat. The woman who started the fire giving everyone a faint smile, hesitant greetings. Looking for what is good in us.

"Do I know you?" a man in a top hat said to Sunny Jim.

"I don't think so. I'm not from here."

"No, no, I think I know you."

"I'm sorry," Sunny Jim said, "but I don't recognize you."

The man in the top hat peered at Sunny Jim, as if waiting for him to say something. He was a con artist, a professional, thought he read something in Sunny Jim's face. A vulnerability. A fragile man, he thought, who had much and was unaccustomed to losing. Pegging Sunny Jim all wrong.

"Then it's my turn to apologize," he said. "I thought you were someone else."

He was, Reverend Bauxite thought, not so long ago. A man tied to the planet by a thread of happiness and rage, his wife and child his only anchor. Now both were far away, beyond his sight, and his belief in them was all that was keeping him here. Reverend Bauxite began a small prayer, that his friend have the strength, the forbearance, not to lose his faith. Be granted a sign, a small thing, to tell him to hang on. He thought again of Talia, in the days before the war started. Picking at a hangnail in the pink wingback chair in his office, lips drawn tight with the concentration of it.

"You know," she had said, "I believe we are all given at least one moment in our lives when the world reveals itself to us, in all its workings. We comprehend everything at once, and then forget almost all of it a second later, because none of us could hold it all in our heads. But we are changed afterward," shaking her head, "in a most profound way."

"Has this ever happened to you?" Reverend Bauxite had said.

"Oh, yes." Eyes sliding upward to meet his. "Hundreds of times."

For Reverend Bauxite, it had happened only once,

not long after the death of his father, though he could not say that was what had caused it. Nothing he could see or comprehend had caused it. He was in the backyard of the house he had rented, and the yard ended at a line of trees, the fringe of a thick wood. The clouds above an exercise in stillness against a deep blue. Then the sunlight changed, and the clouds began to move, twisting against a graying sky. The wind made him look up, and he saw, for an instant, a movement among the trees. They were parting, in concert, as though they were a door opening, and though there was darkness beyond, he knew something was stepping through. Then the door closed, and the trees thrashed in the gathering wind as trees do, and it began to rain. He did not understand what he had seen, but he stopped being a bricklayer and instead became a priest. Read for orders under an Episcopalian minister with a shock of curly white hair, uneven glasses. Was ordained by the bishop in a ceremony by the Susquehanna's shores, with no walls to protect him. As if to warn him that he would have to build his church like that, wherever he went.

He had such conviction in his first years of ministry. Spoke as if through a golden horn, his voice wide and strong, enough to fill the old church he took up in Harrisburg. He had found it half-abandoned, stripped of all that was not stone. He hauled in metal chairs, a card table for an altar. His confidence his pulpit. Put out a sign on the church step for services every morning. Attracted first just the curious, but soon the devout. People who swayed when they sang. Eyes closed or lifted to the roof. Hands out, raised, clapping. His first extended families, the withering elders sitting on the aisle, the married ones standing without shifting from foot to foot. Backs straight when they knelt. The younger ones chasing the kids along the walls where the stations of the cross used to be. It's disrespectful for them to play in church, a clucking parishioner said. Not if you think God has a sense of humor, Reverend Bauxite said, and loves his children. He said it so fast, so gentle, so firm. Still filled with what he had seen before the storm.

He marveled at that now. The vision had to fade with time, he knew that. Knew, too, that when it did, the real work of his faith could begin, to believe when he could not see. But he had not counted on the war testing him so much. Making him ask the questions that he had seen kill the faith in others. The war could kill the faith in him, too, if he was not strong or careful enough. He could feel it fluttering within him some-times, a bird in a cage of knives. Its own blood on its face and wings. Let me go. He shook his head. No.

His hands over the fire were warm in the mist, and he squinted into the coals. Finished the prayer for Sunny Jim, but refused to pray for himself. Did not believe in doing himself any kindnesses.

Down the bridge, under the bent green sign for Hal-ifax, a man in a brown jacket fiddled with the latch on a wooden viola case. It was his cousin's. Her talent had been obvious early. She watched a guitar player from her stroller, her fingers shadowing the shapes his made. A song within a week of getting her first instrument.

By the age of eleven she played it for hours a day, with an emotional surety that most adults never feel. She could get it within minutes of starting to play, a direct line to somewhere else.

The war came upon her without warning. The man found her apartment in Hagerstown unblemished, but her not in it. Her viola lying on the kitchen table, next to a cutting board, a half-peeled onion. The case on the floor beneath it. He took the viola, left the rest, and headed north, where she must have gone, he thought. There was nothing left in the south for her. The cities burned, the families scattered. Better to go where it was cooler now, even if the rain never seemed to stop.

He kept the viola no more than a few feet from him. It was the thing he valued most in this world, as if he was tied to one end of its strings, his cousin to the other. He had this idea that he was going to find her and give it to her. Already worked out what he would say: You forgot something. Holding the case out. She would laugh, almost without a doubt. Know better than to ask where the rest of the family was. Push him like she did when they were kids, and their parents, their aunts and uncles, their blind grandfather, were all there. But he had not found her yet.

He unlatched the case and took the viola out. The fog settled on the surface, made the wood sweat. He tightened the hair on the bow a little too much, drew it across the damp strings. The metal, the horsehair, did not like the weather and scratched in protest. But he had heard all the songs she had played in the house a hundred thousand times. Just before dinner, on weekend mornings. Some very late nights, when he came stumbling home trying not to be too drunk. The tunes were humming in his head now, and her with them. He could almost get them into his fingers. The sound he made was unclean, but the melodies were simple and clear enough. He kept the viola out for longer than he should have, but he could not help himself. Every note brought her back to him.

❈ ❈ ❈ ❈

I MET THE MAN with the viola first, after he had left the *Carthage*, after Towanda. I was in my third house since Charleston by then, for we are always moving now. I saw him coming through the cloudy window of the kitchen, lit two candles, and put them on the sill so he would know someone was there, for all the houses around me were dark, everyone else gone. I fed him three eggs, boiled in water with a little salt. A little rice. Made him some tea, a few ancient bags that I strained the flavor from, sweetened with a spoon of honey. He leaned back in a rickety chair, took off his shoes, and put his legs up on the wooden table. So happy to rest them. He was the first person to tell me about Reverend Bauxite, a little about Sunny Jim. About the ship. How it was a sanctuary, a temporary shelter. Their camp on the road to Canterbury, their villa in the hills during the plague months. The place where they celebrated their survival. For him, it lasted until Towanda, and then left him at the edge of the storm. He knew so little, but it was enough for me to begin, to find everyone else—everyone I could—so that we might not be lost to you. For things are ending now, ending as none of us thought they could. But I have the people I met, the things they told me. I know them all. I have not seen the viola player since he left my house, cannot remember his face. But in an instant, I can recall his speech, its languid meter, half-chuckles for punctuation. His voice, what he said, remains, and it is here, all of those voices are here, in what I am telling you. If in the beginning there was the word, then perhaps, with humility at the smallness of our powers, in words a small part of us can return.

⊠ ⊠ ⊠ ⊠

THE DARKNESS WAS ALMOST complete when a sound came over the water. A long note from a horn, steady and strong. Turning upward at the end, asking a question. The note rolled along the valley, over the broken bridge, through the wound in the ridge. Then it came through the fog, a hallucination of a ship, a drawing of one, done by an artist slipping into schizophrenia. Every plank a different color, bearing pieces of language, fractured words, the edges of letters skittering across its wooden skin. A dozen half-remembered monikers fighting to baptize the ship, but the real name, *Carthage*, painted in bright yellow letters. Sunny Jim would learn later how the wood was taken—from a dozen ships on the verge of sinking, from buildings before the flames.

The two smokestacks stolen from two different factories before they collapsed on themselves. The paddle wheel from the last mill in Pennsylvania. The faces and animals carved along the rails, framing portholes, running all the way up the three masts, were the likenesses of living creatures the ship's crew had seen, seen and then climbed up the side of the ship with paint and chisels to replicate. The *Carthage* was a vessel, all right, a book with half its pages torn out, but the ones left were enough to piece together a history, a history always returning. The spark of a new city amid the ruins of an old one. They say you could see it in the warp of the floorboards, hear it in the creaking stairs. Smell it in the fat burning from the lanterns in the hallway, the grease from the galley. Feel it in the way the boat rocked on the waves. You could not take a step, open your eyes, without knowing how it all was falling, and rising, too.

The horn sounded again, chased by a sweeping cacophony of bells. A string of lanterns fired all along the rails, and the people on the Clarks Ferry Bridge crowded at the southern edge above them to watch it, shout, wave it down. Take us. Take us from this place. The boat seemed to swell as it approached, bulge at the bow. Too big to be there. The crew, dozens of them, swarmed the deck, busy with ropes and hooks. Long ladders. The people on the bridge jumped and yelled, panicking their animals in their cages, as the boat disappeared beneath the bridge and they saw only the tops of the naked masts passing by, the mouths of the stacks. Then, with a single shout, the crew threw their ropes from the rails, the hooks skittering and sparking across the bridge's pavement. Finding cracks, warps, bends. The ropes all went taut and the ship shuddered, groaned to a stop. Moved back into the gap until the deck was there, thirty feet below. Then the crew brought ladders to cross the distance, ladders and spiral staircases, up which four officers climbed, smiling.

As one, the people on the bridge ran for them, shouting entreaties, throwing coins. The officers put up their hands, began to reassure them. There is enough room for everyone. But the people had lost too much already to believe them. Reverend Bauxite put his shoulders to use, cut through the pressing crowd, holding the envelope over his head, fluttering it in his hand. The second mate, with an old trumpet horn for an ear, cocked her apparatus at the rattling paper. Pointed at Bauxite, beckoned with one finger. In the commotion around her, she closed her eyes, ran the envelope under her nose. Was transported, for a full seven seconds, to the printing press she'd run before the war. When everything depended on the arrangement of type, so that letters flowed together into words without impediment, arms joining arms, legs wrapping around legs, until no limbs were left behind, and a sentence could save the world.

She moved the letter from her nose with a flourish, stepped aside with a bow. "Captain Mendoza will want to see you," she said. "Before you even take a room. She knew Aline once, too, you know."

"Aline?" Sunny Jim said. "My wife? Have you seen her?"

"You're her husband?" the second mate said. "No, I haven't seen her." You poor man, she thought. She will never leave you.

※ ※ ※ ※

ON THE DECK OF the *Carthage*, the crew were lighting more lanterns and candles. Animals everywhere, horses, camels. A cow and three ponies suspended in the air in harnesses, screaming. A troop of monkeys occupying the bow. A llama, easing itself into slumber even as the humans clambered around it, shouting, hauling trunks across the wood. The roofs of the forecastle and the pilothouse were lined with brass birdcages, swaying. The birds in them a parade of luminous plumage, cracked talons. Ceding the evening to the bats swarming around the ship's masts. Below decks, a buzz of voices, as though a band was tuning. Fervent applause. Shouting, too loud, carrying the promise of violence. But Sunny Jim asked only where the captain was, followed the gesturing hands to the forecastle. Knocked on a door studded with dried guano.

"Go away."

"This is Aline's husband. I have a letter—"

The door opened and the captain's head peered out.

"You?" she said. "You're Aline's husband?"

"Yes I am."

Was, my friend, she wanted to say, but then saw it was no use.

"Come in."

The room much darker than they expected, crowded with furniture. A giant oak wardrobe. A stack of wooden chairs. Bolts of floral-print fabric leaning against a dresser missing all its knobs but one. A Victrola playing "Mal Hombre." A red carpet, woven medallions at the threshold. Paths forking away from them, forking again. All around a forest of curls and snarls. "It's a Sufi motif," Captain Mendoza was saying. "The paths to becoming one with Allah. The moment it happens, here." Her foot on the other end of the carpet. "This joining with Allah is also the point where the self is destroyed. It's like that with mystics everywhere, I think. Transcendence and dissolution, always the same thing."

Then I saw a new heaven and a new earth, Reverend Bauxite thought, for the first heaven and the first earth had passed away, and the sea was no more.

The captain laughed, and Sunny Jim heard a familiar thing in it. A tone, a rhythm, shared with Aline.

"I want to thank you for getting us on board," he said.

"It was the least I could do," the captain said. "I held Aline in the highest regard, sir. How far are you going?"

"Binghamton."

"What's there?"

"The road to Lisle. Our boy's there. Mine and Aline's."

"I see." She gave him and Reverend Bauxite a look, a trace of his wife in it again.

"She never mentioned you," Sunny Jim said.

"It was before your time." She laughed again, held out her hand. His fingers curled around hers, the grip dry and tight. Like vines that take years to choke a tree. Harder than she expected, to look at him. And the skins of their palms shared an understanding of whom they both had touched. A memory lying along the nerves, though the cells on the surface had been shed and replaced years ago.

The captain grew up in a trailer hitched to a pink pickup under a stand of scrappy maples at the end of a dirt road rutted with tire tracks. It was hard for her to remember it. In the winter, the rain pattered on the metal above her head, like flying dogs landing on the roof. Long rides across dark country to get to her aunt's house to learn reading and math. In the summer, the trailer walls sweated mildew. Mosquitoes at the screen, pumping their knees. They could smell the blood. Her father worked afternoons in a slanting shack that used to be the ticket booth for a drive-in, fixing tillers, small tractors. The stretch of asphalt in front of the tattered screen strewn with rusting machines being dismembered for parts. Her mother washed the floors of a clinic, around the feet of exhausted doctors who worked with fraying bandages, syringes used for years. They boiled the needles, dipped them in alcohol. Hoped for the best. Her father stood outside the trailer, chewing on the end of a stick. One of these days, he said, we'll get this pickup moving again. Find some gas and haul our life out of here. But when she left, at the age of sixteen, the truck was still there.

Between her last walk down the tire tracks and when she met Aline, she remembered even less, though it all changed her, she knew. A cigarette shared on a porch hanging over the river, it must have been in Owego. Somewhere else, Johnson City maybe, she spied a man through a broken window, sitting on a bed, naked but for a paper party hat, playing a purple plastic guitar. A woman in a green robe sitting behind him, back against the wall, drinking coffee from a yellow cup, her other hand tapping out the beat on her knee. Then there was a damp sleeping bag in a cave on the lip of Cayuga Lake, the graffiti from two hundred years of teenagers in love all around her. The railroad tracks running beneath, smelling of greased metal. A black dog barking on the ridge. By the time she met Aline, the miles were in her muscles. Her eyes not quite as wide, her head clearer.

She was working in a diner in Deposit when Aline walked in. A jacket sewn for a high school sports team long ago, blue and yellow fading together toward a gray pallor. Patches of pink bands sewn into it. Half her head shaved. Light brown work boots. All of her clothes at least fifty years old, smelling like a closet, though the woman beneath did not. They were in Binghamton when the Susquehanna swelled its banks in a heavy monsoon, put half the city underwater up to the second floor. A man fished from his bedroom on Seminary Avenue. Women with canoes full of ripening fruit rowed among the submerged houses, shouting their prices across the flood. They saw shoes in the water, ankles. The tips of fingers. The city lost five bridges, entire neighborhoods, never got them back. The places where Ukrainians had eaten pierogi in the social hall before the services in the domed wooden church. Where small mob bosses had counted earnings in downtown houses while boys dared each other to walk the sewer pipes suspended over the river like rusting tightropes. Where the bus from New York City had pulled in at three in the morning, and people got on, bound for Ithaca, only an hour away. Why they needed to get there by four, why it could not have waited until six, until nine, was a mystery. It was Binghamton, and there had been shooting sprees, yes, and a sweeping rush through the city as the manufacturing left it, of boards going up over windows, buildings emptied and staying that way. But there had been bakeries, too: Roma, Vestal, cannoli and bread. Arches over the roads into the city, built by unions, fraternal organizations. A night in a club downtown back when there was still snow, and a band full of high-school kids trying to pass for older played loud, ragged reggae to a throbbing throng that shouted for more, until the next group came on and hit them even harder, and kept going after the young players were dead on their feet, loading their gear into their cars, still learning. It was all under the mud now, under the stones. But on a quiet night, when the water and sky and hills between were all moving toward the same color, and we stood on the banks under black branches and waded into the current, we could feel the water talking about it all, the words moving around us, running up through our bones, until the city was in us, the city and all that had come before, even though it was almost gone. Almost.

The captain fell into awe of the river then. It was the nerve of the land, carrying the memory of the city along with the ghosts of the hundreds of miles of white pines on the Pennsylvania hills. The thick oaks and maples of upstate New York. A forest as big as a country, darkness on its floor at noon. They said they logged it for trade, ship masts and two-by-fours. But you could see the fear behind what they did, the way the giants drank the light while the houses quivered beneath them. They had to kill it, all of it, to chase the fear away, but it would never go. She could still feel it on the roads in the hills, in the towns where people went to bed early, left her standing on the sidewalk in the sudden dark. In the towns, they were afraid, but they could not tell her why. On the river, at least she knew.

"I want to stay on this river forever," Captain Mendoza had said, though she was not a captain yet, would not be for years. They were lying side by side on the deck of a barge, slipping by the last hills of New York, away from Waverly, into Athens, Pennsylvania. A candle weaving a scarf of smoke to keep the insects away. The spring flood silent beneath them. Aline got up on her elbows, looked to the banks. The trees up to their waists on the submerged shore. The river eating the houses beyond.

"Well, then you have a choice to make," Aline said, "because I'm leaving." She did not have to say how much she hated it. The captain could see how she stayed away from the rail. The kids on the barge tied yellow ropes to the stern and jumped in, rode the current on those tethers. Swinging wide on the river's turns, arms and legs brushing by trout under the surface. Aline never put her feet in the water. As if she knew then, the captain thought, had a premonition that she would be down there for good someday, and just wanted to stay in the air for now.

The *Carthage* was fifteen miles south of Harrisburg when Captain Mendoza got the news about the Market Street Bridge and who had been on it. She lowered anchor, did not leave her quarters for two days. Closed the windows and lay in bed, staring at the warped timbers across the ceiling. The afternoon air thickening around her. At night the rain rolled across the deck and the birds huddled in their swinging cages. Below, in the vaudeville theater she had salvaged from an old movie house, the evening was beginning. Voices rising, the slap of cards, the rolling of dice. The clicks and shouts of six young men playing Russian roulette with a two-hundred-year-old gun. Bottles breaking across the floor. A scattering of music, struggling to coalesce but coming apart again in a pile of dying notes and cantankerous percussion. Two fights beginning in hoarse names and ending with splintering furniture. It was chaos down there, unless the band prevailed, and it would end as every night did since the war had gotten so bad: with people hurt, ruined shoes, a photograph destroyed, a pocketknife that belonged to a grandfather gambled away and lost. The sanctuary that the boat gave unable to altogether shut out the country beyond and what it had become. But that night all the noise seemed to come together into wails and moans, swooping sobs. As if they had pulled Aline out of the water, hoisted her up through the floor, laid her on a table. Let the cry go out that she was gone. Hacked apart the floorboards to fashion her coffin, fixed it with screws and twine. Bore her over their heads, passed her from hand to hand. The body rocking on a sea of palms as the band played and the people sang, she is dead, she is dead, and dropped to their knees in submission to their grief, opened their lungs and shouted at the sky. The end of their misery lay in another country, a place they did not want to go yet. Not if it meant leaving her behind.

No. No, no. The truth is, I do not know what the captain was thinking. I never met her, never got to talk to her. She was gone, and the *Carthage*, too, before I ever knew they existed. But you must allow me these lies. The violence I do to all of them, when I put holes in their skulls to show you the thoughts in their heads. It is the only way I know how to bring them back for you— them, the boat, the cities, everything—and let them into your head. Maybe then we can live again, in you. As though it were the last day, and we were all risen from the dead.

The House

THEIR CABIN ON THE ship was dark and tiny, had a small window to the night outside. Reverend Bauxite closed the shutters, picked the hammock, and collapsed into it. He slept at once. Sunny Jim, on a mattress on the floor, could not. Lay awake clear through to the gray of the hour before the sun came. In the rocking of the boat, the walls flexed. There was shuffling, footsteps on the ceiling above him. Outside, a monkey screaming in a tree. Then the door to the hallway bowed, drifted open, and three boys shambled up it and across the ceiling, down the opposite wall, then across the floor, dragging their legs, pulling themselves into crouches around him. The past coming to visit.

"Long time no see, Jim," Henry Robinson said.

"Yeah. Been a little while," the Wallace brothers said, in unison. "Heading back our way?" One of them had his arms wrapped around his chest, trying to cover the hole on one side of his sternum. The other was missing his left eye, all the blood long gone.

"That's the plan," Sunny Jim said.

"Do you think you'll get there in time?" Henry Robinson said. He had two holes in him, one in his stomach, the other in his forehead, above his right eye.

"I have to," Sunny Jim said.

"It's not up to you, though, is it," Henry Robinson said.

"We have seen it," the Wallace brothers said. Turned their heads northward. "What's coming."

"What does it look like?" Sunny Jim said. "Tell me."

"Like the land and sky are going to sleep, and all their dreams are coming out."

"The good dreams or the bad dreams?"

". . ."

"You know what they're talking about, don't you?" Henry Robinson said.

"Yes. I do."

When Merry was eight and Sunny Jim was six, there was a double murder in the hills behind their house, in the place where a small plane had crashed decades ago. The bodies were found at least a week after it happened, lying side by side, legs and arms straight, heads angled until they were almost touching, eyes still open as if watching something moving in the trees above them. It took a day to remove them from the woods. Nine men bearing them in stretchers carried them down Owen Hill Road, past their house. The kids' mother told Sunny Jim and Merry it was rude to look, but Merry did it anyway. Could not stop staring, until they had turned the corner and were descending into the steep gully.

They had no idea how much had been lost already. Their elementary school in Whitney Point had caved in decades ago from water pooling on the roof. Rows of broken windows, shelves of rotting books. One part of the bus shelter in front of the school fallen over into the road. The parking lot overrun with spiky weeds. The doctors' offices in town on the other side of the river had been abandoned years before they were born, after the last doctor died of tetanus, his jaw locked, his body arched off the bed in a convulsive rictus. There were no more shots, no more antibiotics, for anyone. After that, children were delivered in their houses by a man whose father had trained him as a veterinarian. He could do stitches, fix splints. Little more. But had an intuition about Merry by the time she was two.

"There's a hospital in Binghamton that's still open," he had said then. "You might want to take her there." The mother had screamed at him until he left, then hugged her daughter too tight to notice that the girl did not hug her back.

There was violence in the house then, shouting, splintering wood. Four babies crying. Dozens of extended family members brawling up and down the stairs. They were all made of kindling and gasoline, needed the smallest spark to go up. A fight between Sunny Jim's father and one of his uncles ended with six planks of siding falling off the house, rattling together on the ground. It was too much, so many people living there, and they said how much they hated each other when they were angry, even though they were family and did not want to go. But they would in time, one by one, even if they had nowhere else to be. Two of the uncles, an aunt first. Just packed up three suitcases and walked down the hill, the aunt carrying her bag on her head. So long, old house. But that was not for a little while.

The siblings left the riot in the house and went out on the back porch. Moved into the grass gone to seed, the yard thick with summer's rain, over the crest of Owen Hill Road. Through the fields overgrown with clawing saplings, the line of trees beyond, the patches of pine, the bleached trunks of birches, all swarming with vines. They passed into the woods as deer would, following a trail in their heads. The trees shaped like men, like animals. The ravines that turned to streams every time it stormed. The mossy foundation of a ghost building. Sunny Jim thought Merry was taking him to the hill where the small plane was. The broken wings still at angles. The glass from the cockpit lying atop the soil. It had been a game of theirs to sit in the metal frames of the seats and reenact the crash in reverse, until the plane was safe on the runway again, a century ago, preparing for takeoff. But Merry did not take him to the crash that day. Her path veered off the slope, descended into a valley that Sunny Jim did not know well. All at once the light was almost gone. The trees changed into black trunks against a fading gray, all flowing together, the air dead already. His feet cold in the dusty leaves. Merry just a shade that stopped, turned.

"Do you feel him?" she said.

"No."

"The shadow man. He's so close."

" . . . "

" . . . "

"I want to go home," Sunny Jim said.

"Sh."

". . ."

"I love it so much here," she said. "I would live here if I could."

The River

IN THE MORNING, THE *Carthage*'s deck was heavy with the peaty reek of animal droppings, the sugar of their milk. Refugees cooking breakfast in pots over hot coals. The crew throwing shouts and hand signals from bow to stern. An argument between strangers ended with one of them almost overboard, his assailant catching him by his ankles, then pulling him back up and smacking him across the face. A man in a bow tie tried to sell camels' ears, for your dogs, for your kids, got no takers. Nine monkeys squatted on the tin roof of the pilothouse, brows furrowed, lips protruding. Surveying the chaos of human affairs with a wary detachment that preceded sorties for fruit. The skirmishes among themselves would come later.

Under the roof, Faisal Jenkins, the pilot, sat perched on a stool, fanning himself with a wanted poster folded like the bellows of an accordion. His bare feet on the pegs of the *Carthage*'s wheel. A thin cigarette rolled from a yellow receipt angling from two fingers. He eked out a drag, let the smoke waft from his mouth. Fanned himself seven times. Another drag, another fan. His vigilant feet moving on the pegs, responding to signals only he could feel.

"Do you ever sleep?" It was Judge Spleen Smiley, bandleader, with two cups of coffee.

"If I do," Faisal Jenkins said, "I'm unaware of it. Why? You don't sleep, do you?"

"I don't remember the last time I was awake," Judge Spleen Smiley said. "I'm only a musician in my dreams, see. In my real life, I'm a bookbinder. Denim apron, glue on my hands. The whole thing." He took Faisal's cigarette, put it to his lips, and dragged.

"Hey, I need that," the pilot said.

"You don't want this, too?" the judge said. Raised one of the cups he held.

"Real coffee?"

"Don't tell anyone."

"Where did you get it?"

"Wouldn't you like to know?"

The cup was warm even against the spring humidity. As if a living creature nestled in the pilot's hands. The liquid was like bitter chocolate. He tried to discipline himself, but he could not. Drank it all too fast, under the musician's smirk.

"To what do I owe the pleasure?" Faisal Jenkins said.

"I need a favor."

"I figured."

"It's not what you think."

"And what is it you think I think it is?"

"Whatever it is, it's not what you think."

"What is it then?"

The musician came in close. "Remember what you told me a couple nights ago?"

"No . . ."

"Well, you told me that when a ship is on a course

that it won't recover from—when its destruction is certain—the pilot is the first to know."

"I said that?" the pilot said. He must have been drunk then, said too many things, things that sober Faisal would punch him in the stomach for saying.

"You did."

"So what's the favor?"

"If it happens to you," Judge Spleen Smiley said, "if you know it's coming, will you tell me?"

"Judge, I don't know if I'll know."

"But if you do. Will you tell me?"

Faisal Jenkins's earliest memory was of his mother, making coffee in dim light. A faint lantern, a wan flame. The aluminum coffeemaker with a half-melted handle, balanced on a seething blue burner. The coffee's bitterness spiking the air. He liked the smell even then. He was an addict by the age of twelve. You'll be a pilot yet, his mother said. Like your grandmother. Like me.

His grandmother was not born to be a pilot. She said she could remember when summers used to be dry, grass burnt to blond. Acres of dirt on farms. The heat bleeding the green off the leaves in the woods. She remembered the last time it snowed, too. Not a big storm. A few flakes, none ever seeming to land. She was in a car, walked through the flurry to get to the house. She went out later and it was already over. The ground wet but not white with it. A lip of it dusting the house's gutters. If she had known it was the last snow, she used to say, she would have stayed out in it. Captured the flakes on the wool of her coat. Do as the smallest children do, fling out her arms, open her mouth, stick out her tongue. Snow tasted like ice, she said, like it and not like it. There was a tang in it, something brought down from the atmosphere. She never could recall what kept her inside that day. It never got that cold again.

The monsoons began, she said, not long after the snow stopped. First, a wet, warm spring. Then a spring and summer under clouds, two months of steady rain that dissolved houses, filled basements. The stairs from the kitchen dry only for the first two steps, the rest descending into brackish liquid. The rain seeped under the roof, around the chimney. Dripped into the fireplace that would never house a fire again. Crept across beams and under moldings. Poured down the walls of the living room until they shimmered.

There's going to be a war over this, Faisal's great-grandfather said. Outside their windows in western Pennsylvania, there was war in the forests already, old species flooded out, new ones flooding in, the trees from the south all moving northward year by year with the spreading warmth. Roads and sidewalks burst by them. A phalanx of flowers breaking up a highway. Great trunks growing in the middles of streets, hung with fiery flowers. Turning towns into woods, his great-grandfather said. You think this is forest? said his great-grandmother. Have you seen the forest? She had visited the day before. It was like humans had never been there. Like everything else was getting ready for us to leave.

"This place is becoming inhospitable," Faisal's great-grandfather said. Mopped his sweating brow. The great-grandmother looked out the window, into the dense flora. Heard the calls of large mammals, new fauna coming in.

"Just inhospitable to us," she said. "There's a big difference." But what was coming next? she thought. And was she being greedy for wanting to know?

Under the rain, the Susquehanna grew, year after year. The first few monsoons were warnings to the towns along its banks. The river stole docks off the shore, rose against embankments and bridge pilings up to the roads. Then, all at once, it jumped. Started taking whole bridges and dams. For a month, his grandmother said, the river was a monster, eating the land. When it was done, there were wounds, raw with mud and metal, in every town it ran through, from Binghamton to the Chesapeake Bay. They had to redraw the maps. Some towns gave up, let themselves slip into history, into myth. The corner where he held her for the first time. The porch of the bar where she left him. The plot where his great-aunt, who had raised him as her own, was buried. The stand of trees by the river's bank where she undid the buttons on her shirt after dark. Those places all taken by the river as it deepened, widened. Scoured out its channel.

The crews of the first boats sailed it with teeth clenched. Expecting to do as their predecessors had done, end in fire or drowning. But they made Binghamton, north of Binghamton, headed south again. Drifted past Owego, where children waved handkerchiefs from the porches hanging over the banks. There were strings of accidents, boats running aground and the river taking them apart. But the memory forgives, perhaps too much, and the Susquehanna at last became a highway. The days of a mile wide and knee deep are over, the captains told their passengers, we get so much more rain now—and that was the truth, but not all of it. Their pilots were special, had learned to read the water, its ripples and surges. Knew how to hear when it spoke of islands submerged just beneath the water's surface. So Faisal Jenkins's grandmother gave what she knew to Faisal's mother, who gave it to him. His most vivid memory.

He had been on the water all his life. A boy who balanced on the rails during storms. Never slept in a bed that did not move beneath him. Pitied those who did, the sad kids on the muddy shore. Swinging themselves over the water on a rope, dropping themselves in, then thrashing back to land. Not for me, Faisal thought. Dragged a huge striped bass from the river's belly and grilled it on the ship's boiler. Until the night his mother woke him with a sharp nudge in the ribs, poured coffee down his throat.

"I need to tell you something," she said.

"What?" he said.

"Everything," she said. "Now listen close, because I'm only going to say it once. Then tomorrow morning, when we stop in Towanda, you're getting off."

"Why?"

"Just pay attention." It took only a few hours for her

to tell it all, for she had thought about it for years, distilled it into short, sharp sentences that he would spend the rest of his life cutting himself on. What her own mother had taught her, what she had learned herself. The river's wicked ways. She was done before sunrise, and when the boat docked, she hustled him down the plank.

"You're a pilot now," she said. "Find your own boat."

"Aren't you coming back for me?"

"We'll see," she said. She died the next day in a boiler explosion. He was fifteen.

Judge Spleen Smiley was still looking at him, waiting. The coffee in his hands.

"Will you tell me?" he said again. "If you see it coming?"

"I'll try," the pilot said.

The Highway

WE KILLED HALF THE towns along the river's edge years ago when we put the highways through them, the ones we built in the second half of the twentieth century. We must have figured cars and trucks were better than railroads, and because we could not use the river for trade, we might as well not use it at all. Did we ask the people who lived in those towns if they needed the river? And did we apologize to their children? For the strip of pavement was a ravine, parting the town from the shore. Cutting off the roads and houses from the reason they had been put there in the first place. Making the towns places to pass through, pass over. When the war came to take everything, it found nothing to take. Nothing to eat. Progress had eaten everything already.

But in Marysville, just north of Harrisburg, there was a truce. The railroad and highway scarred the hill but left the town breathing. The houses leaning on each other in irregular blocks, as if they would all fall into the river together if the first one gave in. The church steeple tilting shy of vertical. A café with purple walls, a wood stove. The trains running through backyards, loud enough to crack foundations, but not enough to make the people who lived there leave. Then the war granted Marysville amnesty—it had spent itself at Harrisburg and its touch lightened for a time. It was regrouping, drawing strength for the towns and cities up the highway, turning Marysville into a scrappy garrison. But the army was bad for the town. The narrow streets choked with bivouacs, lanterns reeking of kerosene. Stalls on the church steps selling tobacco, cameras, plastic bags of sweet cheese. People without running water in their homes calling out to the soldiers in sharp voices: Buy this, buy this, you son of a bitch. Trash scurrying across the main road, lined with dim, smoking fires. Prostitutes calling to the soldiers in ragged, trilling voices. A row of tents made from men's clothes stitched together, mattresses on the ground inside. A navy blue van with the wheels off, candles inside bubbling the vinyl seats. Four poles with sheets of plastic for walls and a plywood roof. A filthy RV parked on an island of grass, a torn Astroturf rug under the awning, plastic lawn chairs. It looked as if it were brought there before the war, on vacation. Had not been told what happened, that its owner had changed. That the people who were using it did not sleep there.

From the water, on a barge paddling up from Harrisburg, Sergeant Foote could hear three soldiers on the shore making music. One beating on a guitar, another on a wooden crate. The third clapping his hands. Out-of-tune three-part harmony, trying to pull down some gospel.

This train is bound for glory
This train, all aboard.
This train is bound for glory,

This train, all aboard.
This train is bound for glory
Don't ride nothin' but the righteous and the holy
On this train.

They were all drunk. Flogging the song to death, the words coming out wet and slurry. Soon it would expire, and the soldiers flop over, mouths open, gone from the world.

The camp's dissipation began at the landing, got stronger along the street that led through the long stone tunnel under the highway, under the railroad tracks. Grand blocks of damp masonry. At the end of the tunnel, the street curved off and up to join the bigger road above. Rows of steel-framed hospital beds, cots on wooden frames, lined the tunnel's walls. Soldiers dying. The stench of urine. Two doctors, eight nurses, running out of painkillers, switching to whiskey. It made the infirm rambunctious, hollering and shaking the bed frames. Three weeks before, six of them sprang from their sheets, danced down the middle of the tunnel in a line, arms locked, legs kicking in unison while the invalids clapped and cheered. The staff powerless against them. They ended by the sewer outlet at the riverbank, their feet in the water, daring each other. Come on, drink it. What do you have to lose? One of them did, and died four days later.

The highway above boomed with trucks, one after the other in a steady beat. A diesel caravan moving north, toward the front, drawing a wake of shouting and engine trouble. The prostitutes all waving good-bye. Come back soon. They knew they would never see those boys again. Sergeant Foote almost missed the old train station, which was hunched in a hollow on the side of the road, bristling with wires, antennae. Soldiers bustling in and out, hollering orders. As if the news had not reached them about the Big One coming in—the war was calamity enough and their eyes were fixated on its hot edge, the place where people burned alive, where the world was always ending, over and over again. An apocalypse at the tip of a shell, a bayonet, a turning bullet. There were people leaving the world at the very moment Sergeant Foote stepped into the station, hundreds of souls departing as her boot swung through the air, tapped against the tile. The air swarming with the dead, and the war still on, torching gardens, pushing over buildings. Pointing its smoking finger at the unlucky few who would go next. You. You. And now you.

The inside of the depot was dust and dingy wood. Marks all over the ceiling, long scratches in the beams. It had been a train station, then empty, then a boat shop, then empty again. It seemed as though the screeches of the trains against the rails, the jokes of the boat jockeys behind the counter, still moved through the thick air among the rafters. But the field commander could not hear them, sitting in the dark space behind a wooden desk too large for him, surrounded by stacks of paper, the overwhelming records of death, to the south, to the north. The price of the campaign, of decisions he was making. He did not look at them for long. The tap of

Sergeant Foote's boot startled him. He saluted from his seat, beckoned with a gloved hand for her to approach.

"Counterintelligence," the field commander said. Pronounced it with such forceful precision that he broke the word in two. "Counter," he said, "intelligence. Is the nature of your assignment. Though not intelligence as you understand the phrase. Perhaps espionage would be better. In the sense that violence is not precluded from your options."

The field commander was a tiny man wearing very large circular glasses with such a heavy tint that Sergeant Foote wondered if he was blind. She was ten inches taller than he would be standing, and he was sitting down. She looked at the woodwork. The closed metal shutters over the windows, rattling with every passing truck. The beams. Anything but so far down at him.

"I understand," she said.

"These are your targets." He pushed a stack of twelve photographs toward her. They weighed too much, were printed on the wrong paper. Each of them shots of crowds. A mob on Union Street in Harrisburg. A demonstration near the capitol. The market near the river. Each one pocked with two red circles around out-of-focus faces. Desperate to catch up with their subjects. Heights. Stance. The curve of an eyebrow. They were Sunny Jim and Reverend Bauxite, but in the photographs, they were unrecognizable. Disappearing.

"This is the best you have?" she said.

"Afraid so."

For a moment the field commander froze, eyes squeezed

shut, shuddering. As if succumbing to a shock moving through his body. It took too long to pass. Then he moved three piles of papers to the floor, the last records of several hundred dead men. Brought out a tattered map, spread it across the desk. It was of central Pennsylvania, though that was not obvious. The ink was fading in places, smudged in others, and a giant hole had been burned away in the middle of the Alleghenies. The field commander's notes scrawled across the paper in a frantic hand, the ends of words vanishing into a thicket of scratches.

"As you know," he said, "the front is moving along here." A thin finger tracing the line of I-81 through the middle of the state, up from Harrisburg to Binghamton. "The reasoning is obvious, Sergeant. Our operations are at a critical juncture. After years at war, we are poised to strike a final, decisive blow to the enemy"—he said this as if he believed it, Sergeant Foote noted—"and so we are moving with great swiftness, through Scranton and Wilkes-Barre up to Binghamton, where, we believe, we can subdue the resistance at last. But it all depends on speed, momentum. We cannot have our plans disrupted."

His finger returned to Harrisburg, then followed the Susquehanna. Traced how the river bent from the highway for over a hundred miles, reconnected with it at Scranton and Wilkes-Barre, fled north into the mountains, then joined it again at Binghamton, sixty miles later. "We have conflicting reports as to where your targets might be. Some suggest that they are moving north on the highway, perhaps just ahead of the front, so they can receive support. Another report suggests that they are traveling by water, where our forces are under-represented. Now, your targets, these two men, are responsible for some of the most effective sabotage against us in the Central Pennsylvania campaign. Communications lines disrupted that cost us entire units of men. Spottier intelligence suggests that they were involved in a series of very effective bombing campaigns across the greater Harrisburg area. We do not know that this is true, but we have our suspicions. We believe that they may mean to do us more harm, and that we cannot tolerate. Not at such a crucial moment in our cause."

Foote found herself echoing his speech. "So I am to find them and figure out what their purpose for traveling north is. And if they intend malice toward us, I am to prevent them from acting upon it."

The commander frowned, seemed to grow almost wistful. "There was a time, Sergeant, when the men of our army could have covered the highway and the river, brought everything before us under our dominion. No more. We had to make a choice, and having made it, we have to live with the consequences. One of which involves you. We are sending four soldiers up the highway, to move ahead of the front and perhaps intercept our targets. But we are sending you, incognito, up the river itself. Only one craft we know of is still moving north now, for reasons that should be clear—" and here he faltered. So he knew about what was coming, Sergeant

Foote thought. Just could not get his head around it. She did not know that she could, either. It was too hard to imagine, a storm that would not pass, thunder that moved above your head and never left. "—and you are to board it," he continued, "and investigate for the presence of your targets. If they are present, ascertain their reasons for being there and assess the level of threat they pose."

He stopped, turned his head a little away from her. "Of course, the world is not a court, Sergeant," he said, "and we are not lawyers. What I mean is that establishing their motives beyond a doubt is not, in the strictest sense, necessary to the mission. Or to taking effective action. No one will know the difference."

"I understand."

"Do you accept?" the field commander said.

"Of course."

"Another question first."

"Sir."

Another surge of electricity seemed to move through him. His eyes clenched shut, his lips quivered. Then: "What are your thoughts on the meteorological phenomenon that may or may not be occurring to the north and west of our operations?" It was happening, it was coming.

"From a personal or a professional perspective?"

"Please speak with candor."

"I have no opinion."

"You must feel something."

"I do not, sir." She was lying. She felt everything.

". . ."

". . ."

"Well done," the field commander said. "Whether it's true affects nothing." A delusion, she could see it in the twitching of an eyelid. "You have shown yourself to be an exemplary soldier, Sergeant. There will almost certainly be a promotion for you when this is over." Another delusion. This one she saw, too, in a movement in his throat, the way he could not look at her when he said it.

She told herself she should not ask, should not push, but could not help herself. "When what is over, sir?" she said.

The field commander's lip began to quiver again, for a moment, and she saw that the war had taken it all from him, all that he was before it began. Hollowed him out and beaten him into a mimicry of its own shape, until he could not imagine living without it. Could not fathom a place where no bombs fell, where bridges were built over water unchoked with metal and corpses. Where no smoke hung over cities and fires were for warmth and food. It had all left him. The war had seen to that, and it would never let him go. He would walk around its tautology—we fight because we fight—for the rest of his days.

"The operation, of course," he said. "What did you think I meant?"

"Nothing," she said.

There had been times, she thought, when the war had come for her, too, commanding her to submit. Give herself to it. A hot finger running along her cheek. In Baltimore, when she saw what her fellow soldiers had done. Again, in a long fight with a sniper nested in a boarded-up gas station in Wilmington. She lost four people. The sniper was eight years old. Then in Harrisburg, over a simple thing: a man standing in the street in a tattered coat, crying. Kneeling and hugging himself, shaking with sobs. The war spoke to her then. Do not ask how he came to this place, or how you got here, either. Do not ask. But she remembered anyway, remembered being in a kitchen when the war began. An iron pan on a woodstove. Potatoes in hot bacon fat. Half an onion, facedown and browning at the edge. Cooking for her father, who was upstairs, bedridden with pneumonia. He would die within the month, leave her alone in the empty house. The crops she did not know how to keep, eaten by animals. She would enlist a few months later. But four years before that, she was on a plaid blanket in a field of milkweed, naked but for her shoes. Her boyfriend next to her, dozing in the sun. His arm flung over his face. His car in the gravel by the side of the road, on its second-to-last tank of gasoline. A mosquito biting her ankle. She wanted them never to leave that field, the blanket, told him that. Told him, too, about the children they could have, the little wonders. She could not wait. Two months later, he left her, because it was too much for him, too much at once and it scared him. But she kept that memory close now, because the war could not get to her in that place. When the fighting was over, she thought, she would find him and thank him for rescuing her. Tell him it was all right. Then she would leave him alone and go, wherever she wanted. Thus could her history save her, and all of us, from annihilation.

I found her fifty-five miles south of here, sick and limping from a bad ankle. Helped her prop it up on a broken chair. Placed a cold rag on her head to ease her fever while another man held her head, spoke to her in a voice unafraid of how much he cared for her. The next day, while it rained outside, enough to drown the world, she told me everything, everything she knew. I'm not sorry I didn't give up. I know it has to get better. I just wish I had children to see it for me.

She left the field commander's office. Outside, four soldiers were waiting for their audience. One was wearing only one boot, joshing with the others. Trying to get a rise out of them. The uniform of another was fastidious, tailored. Sergeant Foote had not seen such crisp lines since the war's very beginning, when such things had still seemed important.

"Ma'am? Are you Sergeant Foote?" the neat one said.

"I am."

"Lieutenant Tenenbaum. We are your backup, as I understand it."

"That's my understanding as well."

"Don't let what I just told you reflect on the faith that our superiors have in your ability to complete your mission," Tenenbaum said.

"I hadn't until you mentioned it," Foote said.

"I'm sorry?"

"I'm teasing you. Good luck on your mission."

"Thank you, Sergeant," she said. "I have some good people here."

Good enough, and up to their mission. But only one of the four would survive it.

The River

NIGHT FELL, AND IN the half light, the islands melted into the opposite shore, the river into the sky. All into simple shades of gray, as if everything had been replaced by its shadow. Faisal Jenkins whistled to the watchmen, and the *Carthage* dropped its anchor. Leaned back into the current and rested there. The pilot propped his legs against the wheel, folded his arms. Tilted back in his stool and closed his eyes. An astonishing mimicry of sleep. But his ears were open and listening to the river, listening for news. There. The march of troops toward Scranton and Wilkes-Barre, before the Susquehanna turned north and west, away from them. There. A tremor in the water, a first ripple, the first signal that the tip of the storm's finger had touched the source of a stream that fed the Susquehanna far to the north. That the long arm of the storm had arced across the Adirondacks, taken the towns in the mountains already. Was howling over the small farms in the foothills, tearing apart the rusting grain silos. Pulling the gigantic windmills off the ground while they spun into a blur in the gale. Descending on the houses to flay paint from wood, then render the wood to splinters. Those towns had survived hundreds of scouring squalls, weather systems that hurtled down from the Arctic. The slanting soil all around them could freeze solid, be covered in sheets of driving, whipping snow, and still accept seeds in the spring. The people who lived when there was still winter had endured the black flies, the deer flies, the sudden swamps when the snow melted. Accepted those glorious summers and falls as consolation. But they had watched their towns start to disappear around them, even then. People walked out of their doors, drove south along the thin highways, and never came back, and their houses fell into themselves, the trees moving in to feast on the remains. They left because there was no money there, they said, because the winters were too hard. But it seemed now as if they had seen into the future, seen the Big One coming. Thought of their great-grandchildren, and left while they had the chance, before the curtain of lightning fell on the place where they were born. In Utica, they could see it coming now, the black clouds spinning and twisting, the storm screaming down the long hill into the Mohawk Valley. They were turning and looking at the city they'd stayed for, its bricked-up factories and green copper church spires, all the people who had come there for refuge. So long, everyone. The river was trying to explain it, tell the pilot what he was heading toward. Maybe, at its headwaters, the Susquehanna could see what lay beyond the edge of the storm. But it did not know how to say it.

Inside the *Carthage*, all the cabins were empty, the long wooden hallways quiet. Everyone was in the theater, on the verge of riot, people shoving for seats at the tables arranged across the floor, packing into the boxes along the sides, sitting in huddles all across the aisles, roaming, running, skulking, sweltering, their breath thickening the air until the room seemed to swell beyond the ship's hull, the vessel expanding to fit them all. The boys playing Russian roulette decided to add another bullet, spun the chamber on the pistol. The fellow in the patched overcoat and impeccable top hat leaned over the shoulder of a woman who had just boarded. Showed her a card trick with his right hand while his left began to relieve her of her wallet, the object transfixed between long middle finger and angular thumb. A family of five occupied a table nearby, the parents in chairs, the three children fighting on the table-top. They had a long buck knife among them, dared each other to throw it in the air, catch it in their teeth. A woman on crutches, a purple line threading down her face from hairline to jawbone. A young couple with obvious love between them sat in a box in the rear of the room. He sat close to her, put his lips to her ear. She had a faint, smoky smile, her hands where no one could see. A party of twenty coursed to stage left, all whoops and clanking bottles. Toasts and cheers, threats of violence. To stage right, a woman with a black parasol and sunglasses sat in the highest box, unmoving. Surveying all she could see while the partiers shouted for the show, urged the house lights to go down. One could not become festive in such brightness. It was against nature.

At last the house lights dimmed and a spotlight played across the stage's ragged curtain. The violin and accordion began together, creeping along a chromatic line that first lilted upward, then swooned like fabric spilling from a drawer as the curtain rose and revealed the ensemble, the violinist and the accordion player seated side by side, breathing as one. A woman on bass, a woman on vibraphone, listening, waiting, for their notes to arrive. Judge Spleen Smiley slid on stage singing, an ascending minor line in Neapolitan dialect. At its height, the bass and vibraphone moved together, let out a pulse as the melody climbed higher, another as it fell away.

Vide 'o mare quant'è bello.
Spira tanta sentimento
Comme tu, a chi tiene mente
Ca, scetato, 'o faje sunnà.

They had caught the audience already. Heard a faint sob even before they climbed into a major key and the melody became unabashed, unafraid. A voice that shot across languages and decades, through a frayed wire bound in tattered cloth. It mattered not that they did not understand a word. Only that they were hearing it, that it had come so far, so long, to enter their heads. The woman in the box touched the frames of her glasses with a pale finger. The con artist's fingers froze in mid-theft. All the *Carthage* seemed held in suspension, until the last note fell away and the musicians' heads dropped to follow its descent. The applause should have begun then, but it did not. Nobody wanted to go. As if they knew what was coming, that this was all the peace they would have until morning.

Judge Spleen Smiley lifted his chin into the silence and hummed, three falling notes that the vibraphone caught at once. She covered the chords while the accordion player swapped her instrument for a guitar, the violinist put down his fiddle and picked up a lap steel. The bass player walked down to the five to follow the phrase out, and everyone hit the downbeat together, a different band. Swaying in a languid, bluesy swing that half the audience had been aboard long enough to recognize at once:

Mama bought a rooster, she thought it was a duck
Brought it to the table with the legs straight up
In came the children with a cup and a glass
To catch the liquor from the yass, yass, yass . . .

The judge mugged it up, elbows and knees out. Hand to the side of his mouth for the last line. A wink telegraphed to the next township, you know what I'm talking about. And the crowd did, waited through two verses, the Georgia Rub and the hoodoo women of Spain, to holler back at the singer when he told them how his gal caught the rheumatism in her feet—and the same thing struck her in the *yass, yass, yass*—then cover themselves in a sheet of laughter.

Until three bottles, end over end, flew toward the judge's head. The judge, a professional, saw them and spun away, let them break and the glass slide and spread across the stage, a pool of sharp light. The musicians felt fragments bounce off their shoes, looked down and regarded them without dropping a beat. Trying to supplicate the growing chaos. A rising scream went up from the darkest corner of the room. Something had gone wrong back there. A woman staggered forward with her cheek split open. Blood in a delta down her shirt. Cries, gasps, a sound of collective dread. Fights sparked across the floor. A man took a knife in his side. A woman was knocked down and kicked in the face. People began to run, jam the stairs out of the theater. Then Captain Mendoza was there, the crew spindling and flowing across the floors, walls, ceilings. Pinning down the people trying to hurt each other, pulling all the air out of the room to smother the flaring anger.

"Stop," the captain said, "stop. We can't live like this."

A few days later, the first woman who was hurt would die of a rampant infection that spread from her cheek into her bloodstream. Two people trampled and cut open in the rush out would lose limbs to gangrene. Another man curled around a chair in the theater, just dead, somehow, the life pushed out of him. Not a mark on the skin. They asked Reverend Bauxite to do a short service and he obliged, gave himself away. Could almost feel the walls of his church in the air, though he could not see them yet.

※ ※ ※ ※

SUNNY JIM EXCUSED HIMSELF from Reverend Bauxite's company after the service. On the deck, a light rain was washing the planks. Animals and humans huddled together under the wide roofs. Eight people in a tight cluster behind the pilothouse, cupping hands against the wind. Passing something lit around. One of them spotted Jim, threw him a quick nod. Come here.

"Can I help you?" Sunny Jim said.

"We were going to ask you the same thing," said the one with the joint in his mouth. Took it in his fingers, flipped it around. "Here. You look like you could use this." He had a green beard.

"That's all right," Sunny Jim said.

"You sure, now?"

"I'm sure."

The man with the green beard shrugged, passed the joint to a woman with four braids in her hair that began at her temples and seemed to join in the back. She did not smoke, passed it along. The talk among them was easy. So free that there was no rush. I had a dog once that licked its own nuts for hours. Died four days after my seventeenth birthday. I still have the collar. My first bicycle was a green-and-red thing with tassels streaming from the handles. My parents sold it later for six crates of vegetables. It was summer, so they lasted only five days. We ate as many as we could and boiled the rest for stock. Fed seventeen people for three more days on that. After every meal there was schnapps that someone had made in a glass jar in their basement. It tasted like rotting cherries to me but everyone said it was the best thing they'd ever had. I understand why now. I saw a man shot once, before the war. Just walking down the street. Then there was a hole in his head, and he fell as though he had been dropped. I went home and would not say what I had seen. Never did until this very minute.

They passed the rolled paper around again, musky smoke in their nostrils. They were making up for the years they spent carrying these weights. Could not figure out why it had seemed so important to harbor them. As if they thought they were defined by what they did not say. As if giving it away meant dissolution, not transcendence. They were not sure if they would know the difference. But they were hopeful, and were opening themselves up now, as wide as they could, feeling their lives quicken with it, the possibility that they could fit the years they thought they had left into what remained. No time for anything but the reaching for dreams. Not even time to wonder why they had not decided to live like this sooner.

They looked at Sunny Jim from time to time, expecting him to speak, too. But he said nothing. Did not want to tell them what he was thinking about. He had gotten the news that Aline was gone from Grendel Jones. Her weary voice over a fuzzy line, the alarm rising in his veins, up through his body. Setting his head on fire. Grendel had been on City Island, she and several other resistance leaders, she told him. Aline was protecting them, giving them a chance to get away. They could not have escaped without her, she said over the line, and they would never forget that, Jim. Jim?

Reverend Bauxite had told him not to go. Too risky, he said. Tried to soften the impact, give him a chance to escape, too. But Jim went anyway. Saw the wreck of the Market Street Bridge, the soldiers taking bodies, parts of bodies, out of the water. A man with a leg slung over his shoulder, not knowing how else to carry it. A woman cradling a helmet, half a head inside it. He kept waiting for them to take Aline out of the water, too. Saw it a hundred different ways. Three of them tugging her out of a tangle of driftwood and metal, her arm snapping in its socket. A boot stepping on a wad of her hair. Fishing her jacket out of the current, not a stain on it, not a tear. Blown clean off. He would have taken anything, then, that told him it was over. Anything to tell him what to do next.

"We should head back down soon," the man with the green beard said.

"Here, finish this," the braided woman said. Handed the joint to Sunny Jim. "I'm not smoking any more tonight. Let them know if you need some more, though. They're on the boat as far as Towanda, and they have more than enough to go around."

"What's in Towanda?" Sunny Jim said.

"It's not what's in Towanda. It's what Towanda is," the man with the green beard said. Then frowned, an appraiser. "Towanda's going to be huge. Because we think what's coming is nothing to be scared of."

". . ."

"You know, you can come with us. Everyone on this boat can, if they want."

"Thanks," Sunny Jim said. "But I've got someone I need to find."

The man with the green beard smiled. "That's what she keeps telling us, too." Patting the braided woman on the back.

"I'm Elise," she said.

"Jim."

"Good to meet you."

"You too."

"I need to go check on my boy," she said. "So we'll be downstairs? If you want to find us?"

"Thanks."

Then he was alone under the roof, smoking. The animals nearby pressing together, the birds nestled tight. The music straining through the rain, a distant machine breaking down. On the islands all around, the chirping of a million frogs. Sunny Jim closed his eyes—he did not know for how long—until a tap on his shoulder startled him, made him cough.

"Mind if I join you?"

The man in the overcoat, its patches dampened into different colors. The top hat showing a stain. Four long scratches hooked on his cheekbone, bright with blood.

"That looks like it hurts," Sunny Jim said.

"Nah. From a fight downstairs." His mark had caught him before he could complete his robbery, before the chaos began. Kicked him in the crotch, pounced atop him when he fell to the floor, hands between his legs. Clawing his face was an afterthought, unnecessary but satisfying. He backed into a table, pulled himself to his feet. Staggered backward while she yelled and pointed. He shouted his apologies over and over to cover up what she was accusing him of, until the real violence started, and he escaped. He stepped into the hallway a cipher. Brushed off his coat, straightened his hat. Climbed the stairs to follow his next mark, the one from the Clarks Ferry Bridge. He had picked out Sunny Jim in the crowd, again, as though the spotlight were on him. That one. Exploit that one. Misreading him all over again as a man who had something—money, a valuable object, anything at all—he might be able to steal.

Sunny Jim passed him the joint, and the con artist took a long pull.

"Thanks, brother."

"Don't mention it. It wasn't even mine."

"Whose was it?" the man said. Eyed the wet end.

"Does it really matter?"

"No."

"What are you going upriver for?" Sunny Jim said.

"Business opportunity. Up in Binghamton."

"Where the front is going to be?"

"That's right," he said. "Friend of mine up there pulled a scheme together. We should do all right." He told me later that he was cringing as he said it, even then. It made no sense.

"You mean make money," Sunny Jim said.

"Course. Or something like it. Human nature, you know?" He handed the joint back.

Sunny Jim squinted, pulled. "What's the point?" he said.

"Of making money?"

"Yeah."

"..."

"..."

"Between you and me?" the con artist said, "I don't believe what they're saying about the Big Blow, or whatever it is they're calling it."

"What do you mean?"

"That there's nothing left inside it, or after it. Everything has to go somewhere. Doesn't it?"

"..."

"Besides, what else are we supposed to do? We have to live our lives, don't we?"

Sunny Jim gave him the joint. The con artist looked at his mark's shoes, what he did with his hands when he was idle. This man was hiding something, the con artist was sure of it. Assets up north. Land, maybe. Heirlooms. He imagined Sunny Jim a week from then, in a cart frothing with furniture and linens, pulled by a pale mule. Unused pairs of boots. A knife that had never cut vegetables. Taking the tiny roads back down through Pennsylvania, twisting through valleys, over patient creeks burrowing into underbrush. Passing houses with warped vinyl siding. Whipping the beast into a commotion that carried a hundred yards ahead of him. He would never make it, wherever he was going. There would be looters, or soldiers. It would be a mercy, the con artist thought, to figure out how to rob him now.

He took a long drag and waited for Sunny Jim to answer him. But his mark was looking upriver. He was already in Lisle, arriving at the house too late. Finding it charred, eaten by fire. The bodies of soldiers in the gravel driveway. The corpses of his sister and son on the living room floor, hands extended toward each other. Or the whole town beyond the veil, beyond where he could go. He already knew what he would do if either of those things happened. Aaron, his boy, was everything. He did not know how to be without him.

The House

THE STRUCTURE'S CORNERS SKEWED to four different angles, none right, as if great hands had ripped the house from the earth, stretched and broken it, set it back on its foundations. One last flick of the finger, and it would fall into the basement. The porch hung from the front of the house on twenty-seven nails, bending from the weight. The window to the attic was already gone, broken years ago by who knew what. A bat, a bird. A branch in a storm. Merry knew only that the glass had shattered. She found the shards on the attic floor, let one of them slide its edge into the palm of her hand. Looked up at the empty window frame and shrugged. The town had not seen new glass in decades. She turned and looked across the attic. Almost nothing left in it by then. No more cribs, children's clothes. No books stacked and tied with twine. Just eleven boxes piled near the corroding bricks of the old chimney, labeled on the side in a neat cursive hand. The boxes were older than she was, left by the people who lived there before her family did. One of them had died in the house, she was sure of it. A peaceful thing. When she was five, she had wandered from room to room wondering where it had happened, but she could never decide. She could feel it everywhere.

Merry sat in one of the second-floor windows, a rifle

across her legs. Pointed toward the ground. She could hear Aaron playing on the first floor. Throwing blocks at a toy xylophone he was too old for. Then his feet creaking on the stairs. The whisper of his hand at the door.

"Can I go out?" he said.

She did not turn to look at him. "No."

"But I want to."

"You can't."

"Why not?"

"Because you can't."

"Why did you show me all those places in the woods if you won't let me go back there?"

"Because I can't let you go by yourself, okay?" She was trying to protect him, and keep him from thinking too much about why he was there, with her, in the house where his father was raised. Stalling him by giving him puzzles about the family, people long gone. The holes in the kitchen walls. The chips taken out of the banister. The gouges in the living room floor. How did they all get there? she asked him. His first stories were about pirates and Indians. Then ghosts, burglars. Fights with household objects, pieces of furniture. Always getting it half right, but never as brutal as what had happened. My brother raised him better than that, Merry thought. Never touched him in anger. Or maybe had, once, and never forgave himself, even as the boy forgot it. You broke the chain, Jim. But look down. It is still around your leg and mine. If there is a fire, we will not escape it. But at least he can get out.

She had already taken Aaron down the hill, to the road that swelled over the grassy dike that kept the river out, separated the town from its phantom half, its impatient past. The stream swollen from the last storm, but still seeming so innocuous. As if it could never have risen and taken half the town with it, as it did long ago. Put its grimy mark across everyone who survived and their unborn children, their children's children. Your town will never come back from this, the river told its people, and in time the rest of the country, all that you know, will follow. They bowed their heads and acquiesced. They would always know, even if they forgot. It was in the shape of the hills, the way they climbed into the night when it got dark. Speaking of what was coming. Merry could hear it, see it, even when she was small, the ghosts standing in the conspicuous emptiness between the water and the dike's rise. The people and the houses huddled on the other side. Thinking maybe if they kept quiet, the ghosts would go away. But they knew one day the river would crest high enough to finish what it started. Rise and take the Methodist church, the building with the old arcade sign hanging from it, what was left of the antique store. Just like the Lisle Inn had been taken by fire a couple generations ago. A town landmark, the last place to get a beer. Just gone one morning. Everyone went down Main Street to get a look. They could not believe the place had burned down, but in retrospect it seemed inevitable. All that cracked wood and peeling paint, the dirty old plastic sign. The kind of place that people driving through the town pitied, but people who lived there loved. Aaron played in the streets, oblivious.

When the news hit Lisle that the Big One was coming, Merry and Aaron stood on the railroad tracks on the shoulder of Route 79 and watched the parade of people moving out of town, toward Route 11, toward 81. Any road that pointed south or east. Wearing five layers of clothes. Bags taped to their backs, trailing children with dogs, giving them long stares as they shuffled past, then turning their heads away to concentrate on their feet, the approaching hills. The land that they could still see in front of them.

"Why aren't we going with them?" Aaron said.

"If we move, how will your dad find us? We can't talk to him anymore."

"What if it comes before he does?"

She did not say anything. Turned and smiled. Put a hand on his shoulder.

"He won't let that happen," she said.

She moved her hand to Aaron's head, curled her fingers into his hair. He looked up and smiled. He was lit from within, and she could see everything. See her brother, her brother's wife, though Merry had never met her. Everyone who had lived in the house, Merry's parents, her cousins, her aunts and uncles. The grandparents with their knives and rusty frying pans. All of them in the boy, looking out at her. As if the boy was the place where violence ended, where truces were made in soft voices and there was light and warmth all the time, and the only thing Merry had to do to stay there forever was to smile back.

The Highway

LIEUTENANT TENENBAUM'S SOLDIERS COULD not see out of the truck. The four of them were packed into its back with another, larger unit, bound for Binghamton, and they sat against the walls in tight rows, everyone's legs touching. The trailer had no windows. The doors had to be bolted shut from the inside. A crack between them let in a line of light and rain. A lantern hanging by a steel cable from the ceiling threw a wan orange glow over them. The highway beneath was slow, fractured into a web of fissures that turned the pavement into a long row of broken teeth, studded with stray rocks. When the truck hit a big pothole, the lantern jumped and smoking oil sputtered to the floor. The nearest soldier smothered the infant flames under his boot. No one else moved, as if they had agreed that they would let each other do as little as possible. In return, they did not have to speak to each other, try to be friends over the loud, shuddering ride, the heat, the sweat. They could each sink into themselves, walk back into their memories before the war, try to put back together who they were, but it was getting harder to do. Every bullet that moved the air near them, the sharp shock from every explosion, scattered their pasts. They could not always find all the pieces later, could not be sure whether their memories were true or pulled from what they wanted to be true, though some had decided that the difference did not matter.

Ketcher had all the files from the field commander on Sunny Jim and Reverend Bauxite in a leather satchel, dozens of sheets of wrinkled paper, a few blurry photographs, years old. He had not had the time to look at them, and no one else cared enough. Let Ketcher do the homework, Largeman had said. Just tell me what to shoot and I'll do it. A pause, then a long laugh that made Ketcher and Tenenbaum shiver. Jackson just shook his head. Largeman had been in Baltimore, they had heard. Had done a few things that the army chose to overlook. A good fighting man, they had opined, and said nothing more. And Ketcher did not like it. Even before the war, he had survived on his ability to see into his fellow man. Saw into Tenenbaum within hours of meeting the lieutenant, for she had opened herself to it. Believed being a leader meant being readable, predictable. The shining lines of law that governed the squad emanating from the clear edges of her personality, the things she would not hesitate to do. But Largeman was a blank, a hole in the air. A shark, Ketcher thought then. Soon, he will do something that horrifies us. What will we do then?

The truck hit something, bounced too hard, blew a tire. The lantern shook and two soldiers had to stamp out fires. The vehicle was limping off the road, heading for a stop, when there was a flash through the cracks between the doors. They did not so much hear the shell as feel it, a concussion that forced its way through their bodies, pushed air from their lungs, moved their bowels. The truck jumped, landed on its wheels again, stopped. Outside, they heard screaming metal, the truck in front of them falling over. Shouts and cries. A long string of shots that prompted more screams, drilled a wavering line of holes in the wall of the trailer above their heads. The soldiers scrambled, unbolted the doors and kicked them open, dropped to the ground as soon as they were out. A few became corpses. The others fired on the side of the highway, where the bullets, the rockets, were coming from. They could hear the guerrillas there shouting orders to each other, but could not make out the words. For Ketcher, it was as though he was trapped underwater in a churning sea. A hurricane breaking the sky in two over his head. He curled on the ground, a rope of mewling sobs uncoiling from his throat. Fumbled with his gun, could not get it or his hands to work. Could not see as well as he wanted, could not tell that it was because he was crying. Then the noise ended, and there was the sound of the guerrillas retreating along the bank of the highway. Shouting to each other, fading away. The stuttering moans of the wounded. From where he lay between the trucks, Ketcher could see soldiers moving along the rising land, shooting the wounded guerillas who could not get away. One of them turned just as the soldier reached her.

"Why are you doing this?" the guerrilla said.

"Why are you?" the soldier said.

"You burned down my town," she said.

The soldier paused, lowered his gun. Put his hand on

his helmet. Ketcher could not see his face, but he felt his resolve breaking. They both fought for family killed, land lost, farms razed and houses burned to ash. For animals butchered in the road. For cities brought to ruin. They were one step away from each other, the soldiers and the guerrillas, one side fighting to keep the small things they had left, the other fighting because they had already lost them.

"She knows the rules and so do you. Shoot her already." The commanding officer's voice. Ketcher could not tell where he was. Maybe back inside the truck already. The soldier raised his gun, and he and the guerrilla seemed to have a short conversation. She closed her eyes, and the soldier shot her in the forehead. Then the soldiers dragged all the bodies into a scorched hole left by a rocket and began dousing them with oil.

"Half hour," Lieutenant Tenenbaum called. She sounded tired. "Piss if you haven't already."

They milled along the side of the highway, a gray stripe of pavement that had been painted over stitched patches of small farms the monsoons later turned to mud. A haze of gray smoke all around them, a gauze thrown over the earth. Someone set the pile of bodies alight. Ahead of them, an upraised hand from a robed sleeve, a part of a bearded face, smiled from a half-burned billboard. The word JESUS, and then below it, IN YOUR TIME. The rest of the message obliterated by fire. The highway next to them broken by black craters, until it escaped and rose to execute a graceful curl up a long slope to the north. Ketcher had a feeble thought.

That was the resistance, putting holes in things, getting killed, and fleeing. It was easy to see that they were on their way out. If they felt their loss so hard, wouldn't it be best to surrender, kill the war? For it was the war that ate houses and towns, left the bodies of children in the street. The war, not the army. He could not bring himself to examine the connection between them too much, for it brought him closer to accepting his complicity.

He had joined the army to escape from a farm in Maryland that seemed to fade more and more into the air with each day. The weeks of training had been refreshing, even energizing, though they had been too short, with not enough firearms practice. We can't spare the bullets anymore, his officer had said. Preserving Ketcher's delusion that the war would never be dangerous for him. But now he was here, and moving northward, the stench of this place burrowing into his skin. He could feel the front ahead of him, a creature as wide as the horizon, and was terrified. Wanted to talk about it with someone. Knew it could not be Tenenbaum, who had no patience for such abstractions, the idea of the war as a singular entity, a monster. There is no war except in our heads, she would say, or in our commanders' heads. The reality is simpler. The bullets are flying or they aren't. Things are on fire or they aren't. That's all. Jackson had no interest in talking about the war, either, was only waiting for it to be over. This'll all blow over soon, I can tell, he had started to say. Had started smiling more, fooling around more, as if he knew, with great precision, what he was going to do the minute they discharged him, and nothing would stop him. And there was no talking to Largeman at all.

Ketcher left the road, climbed over the lip of a crater. Felt something small and hard under his boot. It was a finger. Tiny patches of hair between the knuckles. The nail ragged, bitten to the quick. At once, he could no longer look at the dirt he had just walked through, at the soles of his shoes. He had been headed to the top of the ridge, but he changed his mind. It was too easy to imagine what was on the other side: corpses, body parts, half-cooked by explosions. If he stepped wrong on the way back to the truck, the ground would seep around his feet. His stomach bucked, forced bile into his throat, his nose. He put his hands on his knees and spat. He was sure he was going to vomit.

"Hey," Largeman called. "What's the matter? You never smelled burnt people before?"

He had not. Had not seen combat until now, though the others did not know that.

"Hurry up," Tenenbaum said.

The bile was gone. He was an insect, detached, inquisitive. Picked up the finger, turned it over in his hand. Brought it back down the slope with him, almost put it in his pocket. Then he left it in the burnt grass on the side of the road, before anyone could see what he had done. Before they got back in the truck, Jackson patted him on the back, not so hard that anyone noticed, but firm enough to send a message. He had seen everything, and understood.

The River

JUST BELOW MILLERSBURG, THE Susquehanna flattened into a cool, expansive plain. The current loitered among submerged rocks while the *Carthage* threw its jagged reflection across the water's surface, the only waves arising in its wake. The pilot banked the boat west, then cut east, up to a channel that men had dug and the river widened, until the *Carthage* sidled up to the sloping town. Once there had been an idyll here, as if it was a hazy morning all the time. A park of long shadows, shimmering trees. Only a growl from the motor, the slapping paddles, of the little ferry that carried people, a few cars, across the river. On the shore, eight people waited to board with the unhurried calm of vacationers. Standing by plaid suitcases. Lounging on the grass beneath the trees, propped on elbows, legs crossed at the ankles. Four greasy canoeists out for a few days' float, making coffee on a camp stove on a picnic table, then ambling into town for water and ice. The canoes pulled up onto the shore, safe. The shaded houses conversing down the length of the river road, settling into their long decline.

But now the park was gone, the houses blanched and streaked with mud. On the dirty slope down to the water, in the lawns and in the streets all the way up the hill, a vast camp of hovels had been banged together from parts of cars and fences, tents of stained bed sheets sagging after days of rain. Encampments with no shelter at all. And people everywhere, thousands of them. A family of thirteen, six adults and seven children, huddled around a scrap pile. People sitting, standing, their heads down, bony fingers clasped in their laps. All with the same expression of stunned lethargy. In the air, the tang of rancid food and burning plastic, from dozens of fires that fogged the air with a blue-gray miasma. Murmuring voices, the weakening cries of children. Low wails whenever someone died of starvation, of dysentery, of pneumonia. It seemed to be happening every second, a life loosed from the flesh, the grieving survivors. They had seen it coming, but were still in shock. Did not know what to do with the bodies. Looked around at the town being killed. The trees among them stripped to poles, to stumps. The yards uprooted, the buildings peeled to their skeletons. Millersburg would not survive much longer this way, but it was not the refugees' fault. They had nowhere else to be. The war had driven them here. They had fled from it like animals before a forest fire. Left behind everything they could not wear, everyone they could not carry. They had lived like this for weeks, for months, their own bodies eating them alive. In a week, the war, moving with purpose up the river valley, would reach them at last, its hand falling upon them, and there would be a massacre. For what reason, none of them would ever know. They understood that the bullets that would take them were not far away—just a few miles south. They just couldn't run anymore.

As the *Carthage* drew close to the shore, they all raised their heads, stared at the people on the ship as one, all those faces and all that they had seen. Remember us, that we got this far. That we were still breathing when you saw us, though we did not get a chance to speak. Elise, the braided woman, stood at the *Carthage*'s rail, hands white around the smoothed wood. Up on tiptoes, scanning the shore. Her anxious brain making everyone on land familiar. Lost cousins, sisters she had not seen since childhood. Friends she had last seen eleven years ago, when she was sixteen, sitting in a car in February, the windows rolled up against a warm rain. The wipers screeching across the windshield. The vinyl sweating beneath her. Her boyfriend next to her in the car, saying Elise, you couldn't be any prettier. The headlights slicing a gleaming gash of a wet field from the darkness, dead stalks of corn snapped off at calf height. Her friends running toward her, clothes soaking, arms pinwheeling through the growing storm, as though they were on fire.

Elise grew up in Elmira, New York, but when she was seventeen, she fled south to Shickshinny, seventy-five miles north of Millersburg. Shickshinny huddled in a hollow among five peaks, houses scrambling up the steep hills along narrow streets not meant for cars. Stopping at walls of stone, the sheared toes of the mountains. She spent part of her pregnancy in a stolen car at the moldering remains of what used to be a gas station just north of town. The girl at the counter was fighting through the bulletproof glass with a man in a stained white T-shirt. Four people stood by a crate of overripe vegetables, watching, unmoving, one of them thinking he would break it up if it got too bad, one of them hoping it would get worse. A half a mile later she had the car on the shoulder, her door open, and she was vomiting into the gravel and crying. It was all catching up to her. Seven cars coughed by, a cart pulled by three horses. None of them slowed down. The ninth vehicle stopped, a green pickup too old to be running. A man with long stringy hair, a baseball cap, his beard tied with slim ribbons into four tails. An extended hand.

"Looks like you need somewhere to be."

"I'm pregnant," she said.

"I noticed. What's the name?"

"Elise."

"That your name or its name?"

"You a pervert?"

"No. No, just curious," he said.

"That's my name," she said.

"Pleased to meet you, Elise." He smiled. "Monkey Wrench."

"That's not your real name, is it?"

"Might as well be, around here. Come on."

They left her car to die. He siphoned off the oil, put her in the passenger seat of the truck, and started driving. She understood then that she had been hallucinating for fifty miles. The road swimming out from under a collapsing sky. The steering wheel going soft in her hands, turning to wet clay. The fetus singing to her in a language she could not comprehend, all the way down

Route 11 out of New York and into Pennsylvania, following the road as the road followed the river, the nerves along the spine. The last dozen miles, through Shickshinny and farther south, she remembered later only as a blur of gray and pale yellow, except for Monkey Wrench, who was in sharp focus. No. Just his hands. The right one on the wheel, the left hanging relaxed from his wrist, his elbow out the window. The hands were huge, knotted with veins, bolts of muscle and tendon. The web of creases and pores rubbed with dirt, turning his skin into tiny scales. A thin mat of fine dark hair from the cuff of his shirt to his knuckles. The tail of a tattoo that slept on his arm. Giant calluses on his fingertips. She thought he must work construction. Realized later it was small engines and the string bass, though he always joked he never could tell them apart. She fell asleep in the truck and Monkey Wrench carried her inside, lay her down on a mattress next to the stage. Put blankets on her and went outside, as quiet as he could. Told everyone else to shut the fuck up when they got back home.

Elise slept for a long time, longer than she had since her pregnancy had begun. Since she had met the father, just a boy himself. The afternoon after, her parents' anger. Alcohol stinging her face, her throat. All that felt like ages ago when she first woke up in the West Side Ballroom, just north of Berwick, as if another girl had died at the state border and she had inherited her soul and her child. It was not quite light out, and she could see nothing. Her hands moved across her belly, pushed down. There. The pressure of a foot, pushing back.

The sun crept into a tiny window and across a flat of bare red carpet. Others were sleeping like hills in the distance. Metal chairs with mottled vinyl cushions, stacked in towers. Folded card tables leaning against the wall. A stage of plywood risers. Bad speakers. Four spotlights, the ends wrapped in colored cellophane. The fetus kicked and Elise shifted, itched. The blankets she was wrapped in were scratchy, but warmed her. She saw that two people were sleeping on the bare floor in just their clothes, that the blankets were theirs. Understood that this was her family, the one that she had always been trying to find, though they had not yet spoken a word to each other.

In the next four months, before she gave birth, she got to know them all, the inhabitants of the West Side Ballroom, as it was called on the sign hanging off the building's front. The letters punched out of metal, tin silhouettes of instruments—shadow puppets of fiddles, guitars, and banjos—swinging below them. The building had a curling metal roof, looking more like a barn than a dance hall. The days and nights were filled with music and scavenging. Plucking weeds and boiling them for hours to make them edible. Seeing what the river might bring. A fat smallmouth that they salted and boiled whole, making chowder. A string of catfish. Sometimes ducks. They put on shows to get the rest. Little gigs on the risers that people came from a few towns over to hear, bringing potatoes and carrots, leeks pale and slender. A giant zucchini, grown for sustenance, not flavor. They boiled all of it, fed everyone. A small miracle every twelve hours: to always have enough, just because they believed they would.

Elise's son was born in the parking lot outside, beneath the birdhouses perched on stilts. The house band playing under six torches, while teenagers danced and five men got in a fight over a motorcycle. Her new tribe all around her, holding her back and shoulders, stroking her hair. Strong hands on her feet, calves, and knees every time she pushed. They put the boy to her naked breast the moment he was born, and he squirmed and screamed. She swooned so hard her breath left her. She had never been so in love, knew even then that she never would be again, except perhaps for her other children. Her heart grew larger for them already, but they never came. Never would, now.

Andre was eight when the war began. First it was a rumor, of floods, fires. A beast that ate men. It was east of them. It was south. Three buses trolled Route 11 shouting for recruits. Promised paychecks, a new pair of shoes. An officer with gold on his cap gave a speech on the steps of the marble bank building, in the shadow of the mountain. The people at the West Side Ballroom did not go to war. They saw enough of it in the people who came back to Shickshinny. Bandages covering half of someone's face. A man with no legs struggling by in a wheelchair built from the sawed-off end of a church pew and three bicycle tires. Others were bodily whole, but their minds were scrambled. Monkey Wrench broke up a fight between three of them at four in the morning, in the middle of the road that ran down to the fields by the river. Talked about it after the sun came up, shaking his head. Those men didn't fight like people, he said. They were snarling and howling, lunging, rolling, flipping on the pavement. Nails and teeth. After he separated them, they would not speak, just hacked and spat at each other from either side of the road. Monkey Wrench stood in the street with his big hands out, looking to one side, then the other. Trying to hold the town together by keeping them apart.

But the war was spreading. Recruiting turned to drafting. Taking the men younger and younger. Nothing but legal kidnapping, a woman said. The coal companies all over again. Throwing the children into the black pit. It made the town mean. At the West Side Ballroom shows, there were more fights than parties. At last, a killing. In the morning, a dead man curled around the post of the Zephyr Plaza sign. They buried him on the other side of the tracks, far enough down that the river might take him, carry him to the sea. Then they stood around the grave and argued, half for staying, half for going, away from the war. They could turn their back on it, the second half said, live as if it had never begun. And besides, Elise said, there is no way they can have my boy. Ever.

Monkey Wrench, who would never leave Shickshinny, smiled. Let the other half go, as long as they promised to come back before it was over.

"We promise," they said, and meant it. For the bond

they shared seemed to be stronger than the fighting all around them. It could abide. The fires would pass, and then they would return, as if nothing had happened to anyone, and they had been gone no more than a day, maybe three.

Andre was thirteen now. Skin, hair, clothes all the same tawny color, steeped in sun and river. He could remember the West Side Ballroom, the birdhouses, the cracks in the asphalt. Monkey Wrench throwing him in the air, his wide smile. The closest he had ever had to a father. He could recall, too, the string of houses and parties after they left. Then his first girlfriend, on the ladder of a water tower in Maryland. Her pink polyester shirt. Her hand on his bare shoulder, wet with dew and nervousness. He told people he was from Pennsylvania—or all over, he would say, tilting his head, sweeping his hand, taking in the world. But they had been on the *Carthage* long enough that Elise knew that the ship was the land that made him, the wooden planks from bow to stern the plains of his native country.

Elise looked at the refugees along the shore of Millersburg again. A man shambling through the mud, eyes pushed into his skull, skin stretched over his cheeks. Five children beating on each other, too hard to be play. She thought of the parents she ran from, the war all around them. They were sailing through it all as if they were ghosts already. As if they could reach the edge of the world, glide off into emptiness through a thick morning fog. The boat floating on nothing and everyone on board still together, music and violence and all.

Her son came up on deck, shirt off, shorts hanging off his hips. A swagger that had come with the first blond shadow of a mustache. He took a long look at what Millersburg had become and seemed to Elise, to accept it at once. He was better at that than she was, Elise thought. Tough in a way she would never be, so natural, so nonchalant it could be mistaken for gentleness. It made her so proud of him, so angry at everything else.

"How long are we here for?" he said.

"Tomorrow," she said. "Maybe two days more. Shickshinny's not far now."

"Are you sure we have to go?" There was a girl, the mother knew. One of his friends meant more to him than her now. She could not say when that had started. A few weeks ago, maybe. They were still trying to keep it secret, but she had seen them together. Knew what was happening inside her son, his life before discovering that girl already falling far away from him, the world receding. It was insanity at that age, the mother thought. A flash flood, a typhoon, dragging you out into the squall of the storm. It would drown you if you let it. It was impossible to imagine anything stronger. Until you had your first child.

She did not answer him, and he turned to the river. The ferry squatting in mid-current, still more than a half mile off.

"I'm going swimming," he said.

"Andre?" she said. "Are you sure it's safe?" But he was already crossing the deck, leaping over the rail with a whoop and letting out a caterwaul that lasted all the way into the water, legs moving as if pumping a bicycle. Six other kids were in the river already, splashing and taunting, kids from the camp on the shore, who would be dead within a week. They swam out of the river's current until the water was only up to their waists. The lighter ones mounting the heavier ones' shoulders, pairing off to conduct chicken fights.

She had protected him for so long. Saying, don't eat that. Get away from there. Had leveled guns four times at other human beings in service to him. Never had to shoot because the target could tell how serious she was. All to ensure that the boy would live, for the war could not last forever and he was young. He had decades to only half remember what he had seen, to bury it under years of peace. To have children of his own. But the night she heard about the Big One, she gave him a shot of whiskey. Let him smoke dirty cigarettes with the pilot. Turned away when she saw him approaching the revelers sitting in a circle on the deck, passing a pipe. For a few days, he was a dog that did not realize its leash had been taken off, moved as if he were still wearing it, walking to what used to be the end of its length and stopping. Then he put his foot out, saw that there was nothing holding him back, and started running. Now she could always find him in the throng in the theater before dawn. Passed out under the roof of the captain's quarters, feet hanging out in the rain. The best week of his life, he said, and she seethed with anger. It was supposed to be better than this. She promised her son then that she would do something about that.

Out on the river, the ferry's paddles slapped toward shore, toward the camp. On it, a man with two camels, ropes around their necks. A woman dressed in clothes made from blankets. Four children without an adult, the second-oldest bossing the oldest around, bickering as though they were married, while the youngest trailed her foot in the water and the second-youngest squinted at the pages of a water-warped book. Sergeant Foote, in a long dress, boots, and sun hat, a suitcase at her feet, watched the shore approach. The chaotic shape of the *Carthage,* the crew crawling across its skin. The refugee camp a strip of grays and browns, rising ashen smoke, sprawling across the shore. She turned to her reflection in the window of the ferry's pilothouse. The shape of a woman again. Almost believable that she had never seen an entire town on fire around her, animals bleeding in the street, the cries of dying horses. But the war was there to be noticed, in the eyes, in the hands. She would have to be careful, or look for the other ones who had the signs. Her targets must have them, after all they had been through. Had her commander been able to see into her head at that moment, he would have reprimanded her. Compassion has no place in your mission, he might have said. But she could not help it. Did not want to. She imagined sometimes that kindness would come as an annihilating flood. Drown the war and us with it, recede just when we were on the edge of death. Leave us lying faceup on the ground, staring into the brilliant sky. Thankful for every breath.

In Southern Pennsylvania there is now only a grayness

beyond the hills. A long line of people in the narrow road below, winding among the empty farms. Untied sheets floating above them like flags. They are half dead already, ash and sallow skin. Yet it takes so little to bring them back to life. I open the front door and bring out food, and the shuffling stops, necks turn. Parents push their kids forward, become happy to the brink of tears to see their children fed. As if it is enough to sustain them, too. They hug me, offer me something from what they have left. A mechanical eggbeater, a pair of leather shoes. Something for when I have to go, too. All of us linked in chains of small kindnesses, the length of the road, from town to town, city to city, stretched across the land, lashing us together. We should be killing each other now, and some of us are. But others of us are meeting under highways, exchanging news and small peaches. Asking how everyone is. There are children playing soccer in debris-strewn streets. People holding each other on the chipped steps of dusty churches. We are not done for yet. If I did not believe that, there would be no point in writing, in trying to find you, so that we might speak to each other, tell each other what we have to say.

※ ※ ※ ※

THAT NIGHT, VIOLENCE BROKE out on the shore at Millersburg. It began with grain alcohol and shouting. Fights in the street at the park's edge, a woman bleeding from the shoulder and forehead. A flash of fire, a house lighting up. The flames taking it faster than anyone expected. The man who had lived in it just standing there, shaking his head. He had refused to leave the town, even as his neighbors cleared out. No war, no refugees, no nothing, could chase him away. He had been born in that house, on the tiles of the bathroom floor. An only child. When he was seven, he had climbed up to the roof, did not know how to get back down. Did not understand why his parents were so upset with him, why they held him so tight after the neighbor got a long ladder and brought him back to the ground. When he was sixteen, he went up there again with a girl he knew his mother and father disapproved of. They stayed there all night while all four parents scoured the town for them. Watched the first glimmer of sun pour across the sky. She kissed him twice, fidgeted with a bra strap. Said she would come back, and shimmied down the gutter. He did not see her for a week, and when at last he found her, walking with her head down on the side of the road, passing the grocery store on the way out of town, she would not talk to him, say where she was going. Then he did not see her at all, and for months afterward, he did not know what to do. He took it hard, too hard. He hated the house, hated the town. Almost hated his parents, until he realized that they had taught him everything he needed to pull himself from the wreckage. They saved him, and for all the years they had left, he tried to show them how grateful he was, was never sure he succeeded. He got everything his parents had when they died. Always said he would trade it all in to have them back. But now the flames had his house. What would he trade now if his parents were to approach him, standing at the threshold, staring back at him? The guardians at the gate needing only a bribe to let them come back?

There was no time to think about it. All around the house, young men were gathering, staring into the flames. Kids that the war had entered. A boy with a brown shirt who had seen men with guns—he would never know who they were—come to his house, force his father to his knees in the living room and shoot him in the face, take fistfuls of his mother's hair and lead her to the front yard. An hour later, she was disemboweled, her pants off. Then the men picked the boy up by his legs and swung him against the wall until his head cracked and he was bleeding all over the floor. They left when they thought they had killed him. He did not know when it was that he came to. His head in shock. His father on the floor next to him, bent backward, his blood dark brown and dried into the carpet. Through the window, he could see only his mother's legs in the grass. There are people who live through that, with it. They put a hundred miles between themselves and the screaming memory of what happened to them—never far enough away that they cannot see it, hear it, but never so close that they cannot make themselves into something else. Not this boy. There was never the chance to walk the miles. His life was that living room, that yard, after the atrocities, for from Baltimore to Harrisburg, the country had shown him nothing else. Now he looked into the flames, grabbed the end of a burning timber, and spread them. Lit a rag on fire and threw it into the next camp. Destroyed a suitcase that had made it all the way from North Carolina to there. Four shirts. Six books tied with twine. The woman who owned these things came up to him, hollering, what the fuck are you doing? But there were already more boys throwing fire, the flames crawling across the park.

The crew pulled the alarm on the *Carthage*, a cascade of bells, and Captain Mendoza rushed from her cabin, looked at Millersburg, and spat orders. The lines were loosed, the ship pulling from the shore, and Sergeant Foote and twelve other refugees who had boarded hours ago watched the land recede. Twenty-two boys gone feral with violence who saw them trying to leave ran into the water, threw burning sticks that made spirals of fire in the air. Three of them bounced off the hull and fell, hissing, into the water. Then there was only the light from the flames on the shore, the heads of the children in silhouette. Their ragged howls carrying across the water, as loud as ever.

� ✶ ✶ ✶

SUNNY JIM AND REVEREND Bauxite lay in the smoldering dark, ears cocked to the screams outside. The tang of ash too strong to be a small fire. It was like Reverend Bauxite's church after the bombs. The charred pews, the broken windows. The stains on the stone. He had kneeled at the ruined altar, mumbling his prayers. Trying to give the building, the people who had gone with it, the best funeral he could. Talia, Talia, if only you were still here.

"Do you think we're all right?" Sunny Jim said.

"I think we're fine," Reverend Bauxite said. "They'll never let the violence aboard."

"Do you think they have a choice?"

"As long as we can move, they do."

Crashing splinters. A yelp, simian. No. The sound of all the birds on deck, frantic in their cages.

"I know you think I waited too long," Sunny Jim said. "To go get him."

"It doesn't matter what I think," Reverend Bauxite said. "I've never been married. Never had a child. And I have enough respect for both to know that I can't imagine it."

They both felt the untruth in what he was saying. It had been only a matter of months, but it was months of bombs and ruin, of running in the dark, both of them making sure they could always see the boy, making sure Aaron's arms were locked around their shoulders. Sunny Jim had seen how fast Reverend Bauxite's hand opened toward the boy when they heard the artillery coming, how fast Aaron's hand reached out and took it. Saw, too, how Reverend Bauxite looked Merry over when he met her, appraising her for how well she could protect the child, overlooking everything else. She reminds me of Aline, he said. With that single sentence, understanding why Sunny Jim loved his wife better than anyone. And then, after Aaron was gone, the way they talked about the boy, wondered what he was playing with, what he was eating, whether he was sleeping better or worse now that it was so quiet around him. Consoling themselves with the idea that he felt too safe with his aunt to miss them. They were both his parents now, Reverend Bauxite could feel it, though he had no idea how to tell Sunny Jim that.

"You think it was too long," Sunny Jim said.

"Yes."

"..."

"..."

"I waited so long because I knew my sister could handle it," Sunny Jim said. "You know that, right?"

"I know."

"I have so much faith in her. Can't imagine her ever letting anything happen to him."

"But now——"

"——Yes, now everything's different."

"..."

"Reverend? Do you believe that after the storm, there's nothing?"

"Do you?"

"I don't know."

"..."

"Ten years ago," Sunny Jim said, "whatever time I had, it was enough. Wanting more than that seemed like I was pressing my luck."

"I understand."

"But Aaron's changed all that. Aaron and the storm."

"Yes."

The Big One was making converts of us all, Reverend

Bauxite thought. Perhaps questions of faith and questions of what we had done to the planet had always been converging. Both had their deniers, people who claimed no responsibility. Things just happen, they said. But among the faithful—those who had seen enough evidence to believe that things happened for a reason, and that we were part of it—there was a sense of having sinned, and of there being a reckoning for those sins. The hope that if we changed our ways we would be saved. The paralyzing fear that we'd done too much and were already damned. It had been that way for a long time, and the planet had taken many things back from us. But the Big One was making it acute. It was an epiphany, the appearance of the divine on earth, and we could not deny its power any more than we could read its intent, or foretell the consequences. As if the war was not enough. As if, all at once, we were being forced to eat all the poisonous fruit we had been cultivating for years, eat it without knowing how to survive it. Reverend Bauxite had to believe we would survive, that something better was coming. On this mountain the Lord of hosts will make for all peoples a feast, he thought. Of rich food filled with marrow, of well-matured wines strained clear. And he will destroy on this mountain the shroud that is cast over all peoples, the sheet that is spread over all nations. He will swallow up death for ever.

But it was so hard to wait, to know what to do until then. For Reverend Bauxite, the central question of being God's instrument was the dilemma of righteousness or mercy: whether one should condemn or forgive. The crucifixion was supposed to have solved that problem—he had been told that, it was part of his training. The cross was love overwhelming justice, love in the divine destroying the need for a balancing of the scales on earth. Reverend Bauxite understood that on the page. The idea could still stir him, make him try to accept what he had seen. But there had been too much death, too many people scorched in flaming buildings, too many people blown to pieces in the street. Too many people he loved were gone for him to believe that faith demanded he abide it. Was there not a jagged stone of pride, a kind of judgment, embedded in the admonition to accept the world as it was and turn to the devotion of the divine? Was it not a small claim to know God's mind? He did not know, could not pretend he would ever have an answer. He knew only that he could not look upon so much wrong and not act, and he asked for forgiveness only in the sense of comprehending his imperfection in not being sorry for some of the things he had done. He knew, too, that he had not always been true even to the path he had chosen, that he had erred often—been too merciful when righteousness demanded expression, been righteous when mercy was needed. There were two peoples in his head, the righteous and the merciful, in conflict with each other and arguing among themselves. He would never find an agreement that satisfied them, Reverend Bauxite knew. He was not smart enough. It was the nature of his faith. And that was only the beginning, for within each position, the questions compounded, fractured, turned inward, pointed outward.

But now his only friend left in the world, the father of his child, was standing in the middle of it. Tell it to him straight, said the righteous people. Tell him Aline's dead, dead and gone, and shatter him. Then help him come together again, so he can get Aaron and deal with the world before him without ever looking back, even once. There is no time for anything else. But the merciful smiled. You do not see? they said to the righteous ones, all in unison. He needs her to live right now. She is not yours to take from him, only his to release. Reverend Bauxite could not see into his friend as well as he wanted to. But he saw something: how Sunny Jim had been pulled apart, the man who married Aline now separate from the new father who held his wailing son on the first day of his life.

Sunny Jim's wife and son were the poles of his existence, and now they were opposed, moving away from each other. The husband saying to hang on, to wait. He could suspend himself until she came back—for she had to come back, she had to, even though every word he said about her, every utterance of her name, abandoned a small part of her, and a piece of him, to the world. He was not ready for that, or for the waves of grief that would come for him afterward, but he did not know what else to do. And then there was the father, calling to the husband, laying a hand on his forehead: Get ready, for the time is coming when you will let everything go, so that you can give it all to your son, the one you love most in the world. And it will all be worth it, even when you cannot recognize what you are in the light that follows. Sunny Jim could almost see it, this better place. He did not know how to get there, but knew, just knew, that Aaron did. Thought maybe his son would let him come with him. And maybe when they arrived, Aline would be waiting.

Two hours before dawn, they felt the *Carthage*'s engine shudder beneath them, the bow push into the current. Light and sound faded, and they were moving again. Slipping past islands overrun with broad leaves, arboreal poison ivy, frogs sleeping in the trees. In a day or two, maybe, there would be rain again. Sunny Jim fell asleep, at last, in the hammock, hands under his cheek, legs at strange angles. He must have been so tired, Reverend Bauxite thought. His own ear was to the floor, and under the ship's machinery and the slide of the Susquehanna, he could hear her. Aline still there in the water, under the boat. Following them north, waiting for him to fall asleep, too. And the priest spoke to her through the floor. Your husband cannot let you go, but you can leave him alone. Let him find your boy without you. Stay out of this house. You are not wanted here, because Aaron has to live. He waited for her reply and it did not come. But Sunny Jim turned in his sleep, murmured. For it was him she had always wanted, him she was talking to now.

The Highway

THE SOLDIERS WERE APPROACHING Ravine, Pennsylvania when the monsoon, the storm before the storm, swept its arm over the countryside. Turned the curving road, the fading farms, the steep cliffs in the land ahead into water. The highway drowned in it, the convoy squealed and stopped. They observed a silence, a breath. The lantern in the truck was out. Rain battered the roof. One of the soldiers rose, muttered. Sparked an ancient lighter and lit the lantern's wick. Shuffles, scuffles, the groans of people stretching their legs. Standing up. Pissing into a bottle, screwing the top tight. They knew the storm would not stop soon, and until it did, beyond the truck's steel doors was the end of the world.

Ketcher sat on the floor, the papers from the satchel piled on his legs. Photographs, written files. Newspaper clippings, from when there was still something like newspapers, still something like police. People trying to keep the peace. He could remember them as a boy, the yellowed pages stacked and folded in his parents' basement. Already decades old. Just down the block, two militia men in the battered shell of a police cruiser, idling behind a hedgerow. In time, they moved the cruiser to the middle of the road, sat on the hood with their guns out, pointed them at the driver of every car that tried to pass. Their free hands out, reminding the drivers that they were providing a valuable service. The smart drivers knew what to do. Gave them what they had, in time stopped driving altogether. The others were beaten, a few killed, the bodies disappeared. Their families quiet at the funeral service. They knew there was no one to complain to, and killing the men with the guns would not bring their own people back.

In the newspaper photograph, there was a house on three legs leaning into the space left by the fourth. A porch sliding off the front. Two men in shabby uniforms leading a girl to a truck, her hands behind her back. Unclear if she was cuffed or she held them there herself. A red circle drawn around the face of the boy sitting on the steps of the porch, Sunny Jim's name underlined. But Ketcher's eyes were on the girl. That expression. Not angry or surly. Almost content, as if she had seen this coming, planned for it. She was having a conversation with someone in her head.

You know what to do next.

Yes I do.

You will live to see all of this fall. Everything that is left.

I can't wait.

Ketcher could not make out the boy's face. Only a certain slump in his posture. Old before his time, Ketcher thought. Bet he still does that now. He took out a pen, a sheet of paper. Began writing. Disparate thoughts at first. The few facts he understood about the man they sought. This Jim, he was part of the record once. The quiet brother to a sister who made the paper. The sister went off and came back. He stayed there the whole time. Then, a few years later, something happened. Ketcher did not know what, because the newspaper was gone by then. But there was no trace of Sunny Jim. He vanished for almost a decade, until the war, Aline—Sunny Jim, her shadow. Their son. Ketcher looked again at the clip. The boy's fuzzy expression, his fingers curled around the lip of the stairs. He was already disappearing by then.

Ketcher rose with the photograph, walked six difficult steps over prone soldiers. Stood before Tenenbaum, gave her the picture.

"What's this?" She was eating a piece of cold, fatty pork, two days old.

"The house he grew up in. It's not far from Binghamton."

"So?"

"So I think maybe he's not going to Binghamton. Maybe he's going home."

"For what?"

"Is that our problem?"

"Go tell the others," Tenenbaum said. "When we reach Binghamton, we go to the house." It was a quick decision, and seemed so clear, yet she could not think of what they would do if he was not there.

A half mile in front of the truck, a huge spear of stone sliced itself off from the rock face, where the highway swerved through the pass, and buried the road. They heard the roar through the rain, felt it through the tires of the truck. Three other trucks were lost in the collapse, thirty-six soldiers killed. Most of them died before they understood that their lives were over. Skulls fractured in a horrible tumbling off the road. Impaled on a piece of jutting metal. For the rest, death came slower, calmer. A patient crushing. Bleeding out into the cracks in the rubble. The people in the trucks to the south of them swarmed over the debris, tried to dig them out, but could not. It took them three days, first in the smothering rain, until the monsoon's arm passed and the water slithered off the road. The soldiers wrung out their clothes, peered into the heavy sky. Some tried to look for evidence of the dead. A glint of helmet, a twisted boot. Ketcher looked only at the face of the hill, the fresh fracture exposed to the air. The edge of a tooth, he thought. He turned to regard the cleft in the ridge rising to either side of them, could see it all for a moment, as if from the air, the thread of the highway darting through a trembling maw in the country. It was a mouth, aching to close. When it did, it would snap the road in two for good, then never open again, and the road would not return.

The River

WHEN THE CON ARTIST, the man with the top hat, was a boy three decades before, he sat on the shore of an island in the Susquehanna with an older kid. A fire on the stones behind them, started from driftwood just as the sun was going down. Around them, a multitude of frogs, calling for their mates. A shack perched in the trees behind them, the ladder to the door rotted away. It had been there since they could remember, but they had never gone in, for their personal mythology had peopled it with the dead. The site of a murder-suicide, a sacrifice. The bodies still in there. The shadow of a desiccated hand on the filthy window.

"Did you know the trees used to lose all their leaves?" the older boy said.

"Like in a storm?" the younger boy said. He knew, he had heard the stories, too. But he felt like playing with his friend, decided to speak with just enough disingenuousness to get the older kid going. A bit of the con artist in him already, learning how to bait people, then seeing how far he could lead them out.

"No," the older boy said. "Every year they'd just fall off. Turn all kinds of colors, orange, red, yellow, and then fall."

"Didn't the trees die then?"

"No. The leaves'd all grow back again a few months later."

"That's crazy," the younger boy said. Repressed a smile.

"My grandfather told me," the older boy said. "They'd all just come down." Tried to mime it with his fingers, millions of leaves twisting and fluttering toward the ground, but had difficulty, for he had never seen it. None of us have. "That's why they called it fall," he said.

"Well, why'd it stop?" the younger boy said.

"I don't know."

"Your grandfather's crazy," the younger boy said. Setting the hook.

"No he isn't."

"Sure is. You know what I saw him do?" the younger boy said. Then uncorked a narrative about public nudity, desecration of the state flag. All false, no fictional detail spared. Enough of a whiff of truth that he could tell the older boy was starting to believe it.

"Take it back," the older boy said.

"I can't. It's all true."

"My grandfather didn't do that."

"Sure did. Ask anyone."

"Take it back."

"No."

That was when the older boy hit the younger boy. First a fist to the ear. Then an oar to the back, until the younger boy cried and the older boy said he was sorry. Later, after the fire was out and they left the shore for the island's interior, spread blankets on the ground to sleep, the younger one smiled in the dark. The beating had been worth it, for it told him that he had sold his story. Picked up the truth and moved it, just a little, by saying it just the right way.

In the decades since, there had been good cons that gave him cars, motorcycles, a round of drinks. A small cottage on a lake, its plumbing overrun with zebra mussels. A houseboat he lived in for three years, tethered to a dock where the Susquehanna opened its mouth to the Chesapeake. The river was huge and wide down there, a vein of the world, driving water back to its heart. But his best, his longest con, had been in Danville, Pennsylvania. It was so good that he fell for it himself.

He pedaled over the bridge from Riverside on a yellow bicycle. A bright blue bowler, a striped vest, red and white. Called himself Sam Lightshaft. Said he used to be a circus performer, until a trampoline accident retired him from the ring. In truth he was fleeing from his last con, had just enough money to work out his new persona. Four bars, the town hall, a garden party. In time, the arms of Melody Juniper, widowed six years before by pneumonia.

Sam Lightshaft figured her. Knew what he needed to say to unlock her and said all of it. Their courtship took a matter of weeks. A wedding under the broad trees of the yard of her sweeping house on Water Street, on the river's bank. The sky built a wall of clouds that waited until it was dark and the guests had gone home to release their rain. They were alone in the house by then, and to this day he could recall, whenever he needed it, her face beneath him when the lightning struck. Two months later he was on the wide porch, frogs calling across the river. Two fishermen in a canoe on the dusky water. Yellow mayflies in the evening light. He could not believe his luck. Did not quite understand then that it had been so easy because he meant so much of it. That quiet evening was the peak of his life, the best that he would ever do, though he recognized it only later.

For he could not help himself. A small job at the assessor's office was parlayed into graft. An embellishment of his identity, the promise of capital from relatives upriver. Loans in a crumbling pyramid scheme. He told himself afterward that he should have known how sour it was going as his list of creditors grew, some with names falser than his own, a shuffle in their walk that suggested firearms or a bad, permanent injury from fighting. The jumpy speech of shaken minds. People to whom one did not want to owe anything. But at the time, he saw only possibility. If the plan could just spin out five more months, he thought then, it would open wide. The numbers blooming upon the page while he rose into rarer air, high enough to never need to work again, him or Melody. Then the ways in which he had bent the truth in secret, to everyone, would not matter. He could tell them all, five years later, how he pulled it off, and they would laugh in disbelief. And Melody would pull him down into a kiss, forgive him for how he had misled her, because in the end he had been so true.

But only two months later, at the beginning of the

monsoon, three creditors appeared at his house. Shouted for him to come out, and beat him when he did. Left him curled in the yard while they headed for the front door.

"Don't hurt her," he said. "She doesn't know about any of it."

"Relax," one of them said. "We won't touch her. We're just planning on telling her everything."

They were only there for an hour, but by the time they came out, Sam Lightshaft was gone, two drinks into what would become a sixteen-hour bender and failed attempt at expiation. He shook hands in barbershops, in restaurants with tablecloths of plastic and paper folded up and taped to the corners. I'm leaving, I'm leaving. Yes, all of a sudden. I've talked it all out with Melody, yes. She is so understanding. I cannot imagine what I will do without her. I know how much this hurts all of you. I'm so sorry I let you down.

He went back to the house at four in the morning. All the lights were off. The doors locked, a thing she never did. As if the house did not know who he was, told him he did not belong there. He stood in the street, wavering. He was waiting for her to open the window, tell him she was worried sick about where he had gone, then beckon him inside. He waited until dawn, when he could almost see into the house, then turned toward the river, took the bridge back to Riverside.

The con artist had told himself then that he could never go back to Danville, but now the *Carthage* was taking him there. It would force him to see the house, the porch, the broad branches. Leaves scattering the sun. She would be in the yard as they passed, turn her face to them. See him there on the rail, put her hand to her brow to shield her eyes from the light. Then, he knew, there would be a sign. A shadow across the face, an angle of the hip. A bend in the shoulder. Letting him know how much she still hated him. The *Carthage* was not a good place for him, he decided. It kept him from the bullets, but there was only so long he could stay, only so long before someone figured out what he was. He could not stay here much longer, though he had no idea where else to go. And he did not want to go alone.

No one else was awake on deck. The con artist walked among the rows of birdcages, the livestock lowing in their pens, waiting to be fed. Around him people slept sitting up. They passed through another notch the river had bored into the hills, shorn slopes towering to either side. On the eastern shore, the land had snapped the train tracks in half, pulled them into the river, heaped them with boulders. As if the water and the mountain had conspired together, called a truce in their war in order to turn on us. We were so easy to beat, a matter of a few hundred years—nothing to them, who had been fighting each other for millennia.

When the con artist thought back on what happened next, it seemed as though someone must have told him Sergeant Foote was coming. Be here on the deck at this hour. Watch that door. The fourth person to walk through it? You must do what you can to win her. But at the time, he felt only a vague anxiety. He was thinking about Melody. Leaning against the wall of the captain's quarters, fidgeting. First, two of Judge Spleen Smiley's band members emerged on deck with an erhu and ukulele, tuned up, and started playing a languid old Mississippi Sheiks number, an easy swing. The erhu had the melody covered, but the uke player could not keep from singing, When I find that river, then I'm coming home for you. Then there was a man with a beard scraggling down to his waist, very thin, wearing a shirt too big for him, collarbones jutting out of it like the edges of wings. Then her. Something shuddered in the con artist, worked his feet to propel him toward her. Filled his brain with words to say, though when he stood at last in front of her, he could not remember anything.

"Yes?" Sergeant Foote said.

"Who are you?" he said.

"Who are *you*?" she said.

Hallelujah James, John Ray Plum, Sam Lightshaft, the con artist thought. The history of his aliases flashed before him, recombining. There were so many to choose from. So little danger of ever being caught. For he had conned from Maine to Carolina, his successes clean, his failures not great enough to earn him infamy. He could afford to start repeating. It was easier to remember that way. His brain dusted off one of his favorites and sent it to his tongue. But his tongue disobeyed, ignored and betrayed. Gave her his real name.

"Really?" she said.

"Yes," he said.

"It sounds made up."

"It isn't."

"I feel like I can't trust you."

"You can't." Why was he saying these things?

"I appreciate your honesty," she said.

"But I'm not honest."

"Is this some sort of a logic puzzle?"

"Can I see you later? This evening?"

"If you can find me."

He did. By then the band was waist-deep into a set of New Orleans jazz, the drummer stomping the beat into the stage floor. Sending out a prayer to ward off mayhem. The denizens of the *Carthage* had put the tables on their sides and rolled them to the walls, stacked the chairs, and were dancing in ever-changing pairs. The con artist began with a husky woman from Philadelphia with big, comforting arms who gave a rich laugh at the end of each song. Switched to a woman with hair down to her waist who fixed him in her eyes, said almost nothing except thank you. Somewhere four bottles broke at once to cheers and clapping. A man in a waistcoat and shorts hopped on stage and bowed, hopped off again. The band counted off another number, and then he saw her, standing by the footlights, arms crossed. Peering into the crowd.

"A woman on a mission," he said.

She shrugged, wondered if somehow she was that transparent. She had been all through the ship in the past few hours, looking for a sign of the men she sought. Gone up and down the long wooden hallways, peered into open doorways at people sitting around low tables, speaking in low voices, who stopped when they saw her, squinted back. Can I help you? How long have you been on this boat? she asked. Since Drumore, they said. Since Peach Bottom. They boarded early in the war, before Baltimore, just after someone blew up the Conowingo Dam, flooded half of Port Deposit and Havre de Grace. It was like a tidal wave, they said. The water just surging over the land, taking everything. You never knew how fragile houses could be. How fast they could just be picked up and carried off. We've been on this boat ever since, and we're never leaving unless it leaves us, or one of those knives or guns takes us out.

She waved good-bye, sorry to have bothered them. Then paused in the doorway.

"How is it that the ship is so big on the inside?" she said.

One of them reached down, patted the floor. "What matters is that it's here. Blood and all, it's here."

She had gone in the library, a room made of books saved from fires, from water. Books shelved on books, laid into walls of books. The hallways just wide enough to walk through sideways. The people in there too young, too old to be who she was looking for. In the corner, a man surrounded by stacks of records, cranking a player by hand, leaning forward to press his ear against the waning speaker. She had gone into the boiler room that powered the paddles, watched the crew crawling over the machinery, carrying wood, shoveling it into the furnace. The pistons working back and forth, the turning wheels moaning in the humidity. The engine sighing every minute, a grandfather in a chair, overcome by memories of when he was young. Two men stood in the hall, sharing a thin cigarette, and she pretended to flirt with them. Been here long? But they were already lovers, had time only for each other. I hope you find whoever you're looking for, one of them said.

In the theater, the con artist made a flourish, his best imitation of courtliness, as the band kicked into "Dinah." She did not smile, but stepped forward. Took his hand in hers. Knew the steps. At first she was somewhere else, he thought, but five songs and two glasses of vinegary wine later, she was softer. Looked at him and smiled, and he thought that if the war were to come for them right that second, the boat to explode and take them all with it, that would be all right by him.

"Will you spend the night with me?" he said. How had he become so forward?

She looked away, looked at him again, as if to say she would. But an hour later she excused herself, said she thought she saw someone she knew. He said he would wait for her where he'd first found her, and he did.

The band's groove slowed as it crept toward dawn. The people wanted something to carry them off to bed. Something good, because, at last, no one had died that day. Pairs had stopped swapping, couples grew closer. Their dancing turned into swaying, arms around each other, hips and foreheads touching, eyes closed. Partnerless, standing in the middle of the floor, the con artist could feel them all breathing together, musicians and dancers, the room's pulse. They were all going somewhere, beyond the ship and the dark water, and he wanted to go with them, with her. But she did not return.

The House

WHEN MERRY WAS TEN and Sunny Jim was eight, Mr.
Dave, who fixed the electrical lines that ran through
town, was killed by a deer. He was driving a decades-
old sedan on the back road from Lisle to the highway,
found the animal standing in the middle of the road
after midnight. He laid on the horn, jammed the brakes,
and the deer turned toward him, charged the car. The
first hoof put a tight, deep dent in the hood. The next
went through the windshield, through the driver's skull.
Then the deer was up and over the roof, down the other
side, and Mr. Dave was leaning back in his seat, mouth
open, eyes staring upward. Hands draped over the wheel.
The car went another twenty yards, then listed left and
rocked to a gentle stop on the side of the road. Joe Thule's
father found him like that a few hours later, in the dusky
hours before dawn. Gleaned what had happened in
pieces. The shape the car was in. Patches of reddish
hair, a bit of skin, the strong odor. The expression on
Mr. Dave's face.

The funeral was two days later, and the people of the
town gathered around, looked at each other as the man
in the shroud went down. They were all thinking the
same thing. Almost every month the lights died in Lisle,
and every time, Mr. Dave resurrected them. That would

not happen again. The electricity lasted another five weeks, winked out at last in a strong wind that brought no rain. The fight on Owen Hill Road that night gave the kids' mother twelve stitches across her forehead, put their father on the floor, while Sunny Jim and Merry fled into the weather. The steps on the front porch were loose by then, rocked forward when they walked down them. Seven shingles flew from the roof in a gust and were never replaced. The kids walked through town, holding their jackets close against their bodies, passed house after darkened house. Saw the dim light from Whitney Point, from lanterns, torches, nurtured fires, aching through the leaves of the trees. Sunny Jim wondered how much longer he had to stay in that house, in this town. The first adult thought of his life.

"When's Dad getting up?" he said the next night. His dad had been carried to bed, was still there, shouting through the wooden door for water.

"Isn't the county fair happening now?" his mother said. Ran her finger along the rough stitches on her brow. The neighbor had done them, knew only a little what he was doing. "Why don't you go?"

Merry and Sunny Jim's seventeen-year-old cousin drove them to the fairgrounds in Whitney Point in a pickup with a plywood bed. He sat in the cab by himself, with the windows rolled up, smoking. The kids sat in the back, leaning against the rear window, their legs resting on three shot tires and a gutted jackhammer. They passed houses built close to the road, still wearing skins of Tyvek and tar paper. Clear plastic stretched across cracked windows. Then the houses yielded to rusty gas stations and empty body shops. A motel painted burgundy, defensive on the far end of a crumbling parking lot. The middle school cut in half by a sink in the land. The wound in the building exposing pipes twisting out of the floors, rusting desks, classrooms without roofs collecting dirt and cultivating weeds. The roots of trees spreading into the cracked foundation, breaking it further apart. The high school had burned to the ground for some reason no one could remember. By the time the flames came, it had been so long since anyone had used it. In the wide field beyond the school, across an expanse of dark grass, the lights of the fair were like a distant city. Electric bulbs on spinning rides streaking the air. The neon spindles on the Ferris wheel, benches in slow orbit around the blazing center.

They pulled into a clot of cars trying and failing to make rows. The truck stopped with a shudder and their cousin knocked on the rear window from the inside. He was not going with them. They walked through the lot's dried mud, past teenagers huddled in the dark. Then, at once, the fair's light and sound began together, as though they had crossed a border, entered another country. The neon running into white light that bleached the ground. Rides wheeling above them. The roar of gears and motors, hissing pistons. Riders yelling and screaming. A row of stands, painted wooden signs: THE MOLE MAN, THE DRAGON LADY. SIAMESE TRIPLETS! WHAT THE DEVIL HAS JOINED, NO MAN MAY CAST ASUNDER. Whistles and sirens, a barker's rapid patter. Try your luck, try your luck, hey there you strapping young lad, I bet your girl there would love one of these. Merry took her brother's hand and they moved down the midway, and to Sunny Jim, it was as if they floated above it. Looking down from the dark. Above them, nothing but cold clouds, invisible, eating the moon and the stars. Merry tapped him on the shoulder, pointed up to the swing ride, the chairs on long chains flying above them. The dozens of children with their arms and legs out. It was so much like flight up there. You could look out past the fair's lights, to the buildings at the intersection, to the bridge across the river. The dead stoplight swinging on a wire. The sweep of the highway beyond, the only road around there big enough to let you believe you could leave at any time.

There must have been a sound when the bolts gave way, but Sunny Jim only saw, everyone only saw, one of the swings pull loose from its mooring, chair and rider fly over the fair, rising up into the darkness. Trailing the chains behind. The passenger, a twelve-year-old girl who lived in Lisle, laughing all the way up. The police and ambulances looked for her for hours afterward, all through the fairgrounds, along the road through town. The rooftops of gas stations and old hotel buildings. The river's banks, its bed. They never found her. Her parents, who lived in a two-bedroom apartment above the arcade, succumbed to the belief that she would come back at any minute, float back down to them. This lasted until a malevolent spirit entered their house one night, throttled their marriage to death while they slept. They woke up the next morning blunted and hazy, shuffled through a few more months, then realized that they no longer saw the other in themselves, they saw only her. But that was nearly a year away.

Six weeks after their daughter left, the parents held a service for her. Another funeral in Lisle, people said. Soon there won't be anyone left, and the last one will have to bury himself. They stood in the Congregationalist church, heads bowed, hands clasped in front of them. A mountain of flowers on the altar. There was a small reception near the swimming pool in the town park, people offering weak words. Nobody knew what to say. Sunny Jim's father put his hand on the man's shoulder. Damn sorry about your kid. Sunny Jim's mother, with fresh stitches, three of them, on her arm, hugged the woman and said nothing. The embrace went on too long, not long enough. The town's kids loitered on the sidewalk, trying not to play. Cat Wallace and his two brothers sat in a row along the curb, bouncing stones across the highway. Henry Robinson and Joe Thule, who had been born on the same day and were friends since infancy, stood behind them, Henry pulling on Joe's tie to strangle him. There was a squirrel on a fraying power line. A shout from a few houses down, an old woman punishing her dog.

Then, all at once, Merry was laughing. It burst out of her as if it had been building for a year and she had gone necrotic trying to keep it in, was surrendering at last. "I knew it," she said. "I knew this was going to happen. I knew the whole time I was at the fair, before I even got there. Years ago, as soon as I saw her in school." Then she sang: Yellow bird, high up in banana tree. Yellow bird, she sits all alone like me.

That was when the mother began to wail. Merry was kneeling, clutching her stomach, her mirth asphyxiating her. The lost girl's father put his arm around his wife, rushed to take her home. Glared at Sunny Jim's father. How dare you bring her, he said, when we all know how she is. The kids stood in a circle around the laughing child, unsettled, upset. Many of them began to cry. It began to sink in that they had survived something. Get her out of here, the other parents said. Get out of here yourselves. But Sunny Jim's parents were already fighting, yet again, so it was Sunny Jim who knelt beside his sister, grabbed her arm to bring her back.

"Come on," he said.

They walked up Owen Hill Road alone. Watched their parents flash by them in the car, swerving. They could hear the shouting over the lost muffler. The fight lasted for hours, tore the house apart, scattered the aunts and cousins. Sunny Jim and Merry sat on the porch, amid the peeling paint, the boards above their heads starting to rot. The whole house, they knew, was starting to come apart, shedding wood and relations. In time there would only be them and their parents, Sunny Jim thought, and the house would be a skeleton. They did not say a word

to each other until it got dark and their parents had exhausted themselves, went to their room. No small lights
came on in the valley, no streetlights drew the line of
the main road through town. Just flashes of headlights.
Fireflies.

"What did you mean by that?" he said in the dark.

"Mean by what?" she said.

"That you knew."

"I did know," she said.

"How?"

"The shadow man told me."

"You went out in the woods again?"

"No, no. He's much closer now. He lives right over
there."

"Across the road?"

She nodded. "But not for long. Pretty soon, Jim, he'll
move in with us. Then you'll really see something."

"Merry?"

"Yes?"

"Don't let him in."

"Don't you want to see what he'll do?"

"No."

"..."

"..."

"Well, it's too late, anyway. His mind's made up."

"Can you tell me when he comes?"

"I won't have to. You'll know."

His sister was watching the road, as if the visitor
would appear out of the tall grass any minute. Take the

lawn in two steps. She leaned forward a little. She could not wait.

I love you so much, Merry, Sunny Jim thought. Please don't go.

The River

NORTH OF MILLERSBURG THE Susquehanna got wild. The water thick and slow. Islands rippling with dense trees, birds of prey skulking in the leaves. The calls and roars of monkeys. The half-submerged columns of a long-gone trestle bridge, stone and crumbling mortar, shaggy crowns of small trees. A dead bass, bloated and bleaching, bumped against the *Carthage*'s hull. In the hills and on the shore, shambling flooded farms. Houses with plywood walls and tin roofs melting into the water. A dock made of tires, a bright blue fan boat tied to a tree with dirty yellow rope. A dented gas can with a hole in the top, floating on its side, pouring greasy rainbows into the current. As if everyone had left without much of a hurry, stood outside their houses while the water rose and the sky churned to the north of them. They took a good long look. Understood that material goods didn't mean much. The blue couch in the living room, the Formica table. A kitchen full of particleboard shelves. Grandmother had made the purple pillows on the bed, but Grandmother was gone now, never sentimental when she was here, and alive in their heads besides. Those three kids in the car, hitting each other, pressing their hands into the condensation on the windows, were all that mattered.

Faisal Jenkins, the pilot, saw the rain in the water before he felt it in the air. It was a scout for the Big One, and the river was rising with it, pushing harder. The channel broadening and deepening. Soon there would be debris from upstream. A tangle of branches, broken trunks, roots grasping for ground. A signpost. Clothes. Maybe bodies, some poor people facedown, arms out. Faisal Jenkins had talked about it once with another pilot, before the war came to Harrisburg. The other pilot sitting on the floor of the bar, back against the wall, spitting out the husks of seeds.

"You know all those dikes," he said, "in Binghamton, in Scranton? Wilkes-Barre? All those towns walling in the river? I think this is the year the river breaks them all. It will put us under six, seven feet of water, and stay that way until we stop thinking of going back. Do you hear what I'm saying?" A glare in his eye. "It wants revenge."

"Revenge for what?" Faisal Jenkins said. The other pilot squinted. Spat out another seed.

"For what?" he said. "Where do I start?"

Judge Spleen Smiley was sitting on the deck at the bow, his back to the north, picking out some Delmore Brothers on a tenor guitar, that old freight train moving along to Nashville. The clouds were scudding down the valley behind him, a wall of rain.

"Hey," Faisal Jenkins said. "Hey! Get under here. Big piece of weather in about two minutes." He pointed and Judge Spleen Smiley turned, gave a low whistle. But nothing could rush him. He put the guitar in its case. Closed all four latches. Ambled up to the pilothouse just as the rain swept the water in front of them. It started pounding the tin roof as soon as he stepped under it.

"Nice timing," Faisal Jenkins said.

He patted the case. "Why they pay me the big bucks." He wanted to say something else, but the rain started hitting hard. A steady clash of thick drops on metal. Water running off the roof in ropes and liquid scarves. The river whipped into peaks of whiteness all around them, curtains of water flailing across the surface. The pilothouse got hot and damp, far too loud to talk. Then the musician smiled, produced a small silver flask, uncapped it, and handed it to the pilot, who smelled it. The stuttering burn of alcohol, wood, and caramel. Two small cups followed, filled with what the pilot first mistook for marbles, stones. Then he realized it was ice. He had not seen any in a year. Where did the judge get it? The musician poured the booze over the ice in one of the cups, smiled, and handed it to the pilot, who took a long sip. It was harsh going down, but soon a coolness spread from his stomach, soothing the heat in his clothes, pushing it away. If the river was whiskey and I was a duck. He took a second long draft and knew for sure that whiskey would never taste so good again. It made him glad, as if something had been won. A minute unwasted.

The rain slackened but the clouds thickened, bringing night early. They passed the flask eight times, were on their ninth when the musician saw the pilot's eyebrows rise, wrinkles appear on his forehead. His eyes getting watery.

"What's wrong?" Judge Spleen Smiley said. "Is it time?"

"No, no. It's not that."

Something in the river was talking to Faisal Jenkins, and he was beginning to feel bad. As though he had gone hiking and discovered the corpse of a child in a stand of white pines. No: corpses. More than five. More than fifteen. The river was overwhelming him with it, filling his head. By the time they saw the smoke on an island in the river, the pilot did not have to be told. There was a fish kill around the dock, a hundred bass decaying into porridge in the water, eyes distended from their sockets. A wall of stench and flies. Blackened streaks across the sign for the Boy Scout camp. A fire in an oil drum. A new sign swinging from the old one by a yellow rope. SAVE US.

"I don't think we should stop," the pilot said.

"We take on who we can, Faisal. Especially now," Captain Mendoza said.

"I just don't think there'll be anyone to take."

The captain watched from the rail as the first mate and two other crew members rowed a skiff to the dock. They stood up and began batting their arms at the air, swimming through insects. They disappeared under the camp sign and into the trees, were gone less than a minute before the first mate reappeared on the dock. She beckoned the *Carthage* closer until the captain could see her face. Shaking her head. Her hand on her stomach.

The captain nudged the second mate. "Go find the preacher."

The smell hit Reverend Bauxite where the dock joined the land, at the thin wooden stairs to higher ground. Rancid and gamey. The camp was in severe disrepair. A few cinder block buildings, shingles peeling off. A lawn ringed with trees, spiked with saplings. A basketball hoop jutting out of the grass, the backboard furry with moss. The last of the rain pattering through huge old trees that shaded everything. At first, Reverend Bauxite thought the ground was strewn with laundry as far as he could see in the gathering dark. Shirts, socks, pants. Red, green, yellow, blue. Stripes and checkers. Floral dresses. Then he understood. These were men, women, children, all laid down under the trees. Faces to the earth. A bright pink headband in a woman's matted hair. A man in a red jacket, hands under his head. A family, the father's arm thrown over the mother. The child between them, legs curled. Reverend Bauxite tried to be holy, decided it was better to be human. God damn it, he thought. God damn it. Then he was saying it out loud, louder and louder, until the crest of his anger passed, though he knew another was coming.

"We don't have anything to cover them with?" he said. One of the crew just opened his arms. Where would we begin?

The first mate was taking soft steps among the bodies.

Then she squinted, looked toward Reverend Bauxite, who was praying: Into thy hands, O merciful Savior, we commend thy servants. Acknowledge, we humbly beseech thee, a sheep of thine own fold, a lamb of thine own flock, a sinner of thine own redeeming. Receive them into the arms of thy mercy, into the blessed rest of everlasting peace, and into the glorious company of the saints in light.

"Father," she said, "who could have started the fire in the drum?"

She found the washtub full of poison inside one of the buildings. A pile of people in the windowless darkness, looking like they were cold, huddling together. They had died trying to comfort each other. The first mate kneeled, dug her fingers into her scalp, and let it go, a shriek that unfurled into a crying stutter. Tears dropping off her face onto the earthen floor, a girl's black shoes.

"Don't do that. They can't hear you."

A boy stood in the corner. His arms, shirt, hair, eyes, were all the same gray-blue in the half light.

"That one's my sister," he said. Pointed. "My mom's behind her."

The first mate strangled the questions in her throat. Too cruel, she thought, to make him tell her anything. Did they all just fall over together, mewling, shifting their feet in the dirt? They must have been so brave when they poisoned themselves. Did they start to lose their nerves when their limbs began to harden? Wondering if somehow they could take it all back?

The boy saw the first mate through lightning and fog. An apparition moving among the dead, speaking to him from a great distance. The past unwilling to recede, charging into the present. His home on the opposite shore, hiding in the trees at the water's edge. Crab apple trunks twisting toward the house. His father throwing him in the air and laughing, before driving south in the back of a truck with six other men, a rifle between his knees. They never see him again. A year later, his mother is counting potatoes in the kitchen. Letting the dog go. Why did you do that? the neighbor says. We could have eaten it. Then the news of the Big One coming down the road. A meeting in the road with eight neighbors, all of them turning north. Why can't we see it? one of them saying. Why can't we see it coming? The boat out to the camp. Hoping for a little dignity. We love you so much.

"Did you start the fire?" the first mate said.

"No."

"What about the sign?"

"That wasn't for you."

The first mate held out her hand.

"Do you want to come with me?"

"No. You scare me."

"Why?"

"Because you're crying so much."

"Please come with us."

"Not until you stop crying."

In the end, Reverend Bauxite took the boy aboard the *Carthage*, guiding the boy's slender shoulders with his big arm. Angry all over again for being made so small. Why did You forsake them? he thought. We would have saved them all. Why did You not let us?

The boy thought they would feed him and put him back on the island. When he realized they were leaving, he hung on the rail and screamed across the water at the swinging sign, the fading fire. The captain sedated him with Valium, put him on a roll and pallets on the first mate's floor. The first mate insisted. Lay on her cot no more than three feet from him. Now and again she stretched out her arm, put her hand on his chest. Making sure he was still breathing, as if he were a baby. He shifted and murmured in his sleep. She imagined he was reliving the final hours, the distribution of poison.

He was not. In his dreams, his family was whole again. His father sitting on the steps of their house in a white shirt, a thin green tie, a wool fedora on his head. His mother next to him in a light dress. Both of them eating fruit out of a white metal colander. Behind them, five-hundred-foot giants dug their fingers into hillsides, pulling up acres of land, the boulders beneath it. Ripping houses from their foundations. Getting closer and closer, shaking the ground with every step. The boy stood in front of his parents, jumping and pointing, trying to get them to turn around. His father smiled as his mother held out the colander, half-filled with perfect strawberries, and a monstrous hand descended from the sky.

※ ※ ※ ※

I FOUND THEM TOGETHER, the first mate and the boy, in Rainelle, West Virginia—the place where she was from, though the house she grew up in was gone. They were living in what used to be an outdoor store in a little strip mall, their belongings in a small pile on the linoleum floor. She told me then how it still stunned her, what she felt for the boy, how fast she felt it. A bond that shackled her heart to him. She had never even contemplated children, she said. Never thought she was the kind. When she was a kid, she was a hellion, always trying to escape. Could not wait to get out of that town. She took her parents' car when she was ten, craning her neck to look between the steering wheel and the dashboard. Thought she would get to Covington, Virginia, where she would sell the car and use whatever she made to get even farther away, but the car ran out of gas in White Sulphur Springs. It took her two days to walk back. She left at last at sixteen, headed east with a boyfriend. Her first time out of the mountains. She could still remember the long descent into Lexington, Virginia, as though the car were sliding down the road, the land opening out below her into yellow farms, clusters of towns, the Blue Ridge a curtain over the next horizon. Her boyfriend trying to drive and smile at her at the same time. He said they would stay together forever, did not see that when she had talked about leaving everything behind her, she meant him, too. They broke up in Richmond, and after that, she was single, solitary, with a ferocity that frightened men and women alike after only a few weeks of trying to court her. She found the *Carthage* a few months after it was built, saw in the captain the same quality she had herself: accepting the country's disintegration, the land turning to water all around them, while so many others just panicked. She was that ship's first and last first mate, and once she was afloat, she thought she would never be tied to anything again. But she knew she was wrong as soon as the boy spoke to her on that island, and she pulled him to her. She acted on the impulse before she understood it. Never questioned it. And though she was not a believer, could not be convinced there was a plan, she could not help but notice the symmetry: that she saved the boy, and he would save her, too.

So we stood in the parking lot in Rainelle, the boy coloring the asphalt with house paint from a rusting can he'd found in the next shop over. And why did you come back here? I said. She looked toward the north, then back at the boy, who did not look up. I don't know what's coming, she said. But at least I know where I am.

※ ※ ※ ※

ONCE, THE CONFLUENCE OF the west and north branches of the Susquehanna was choked with infrastructure. High floodwalls imprisoning the river, imprisoning the towns that grew up when they found coal and were left for dead when the coal was gone. A web of bridges. Dams for the ferry, for the power station, to create a lake in the summer, broad and shallow, for boats and swimmers. The river huge and serene, its push against metal and stone so quiet that it was easy to forget it was there until it took a child, a dog, from one of those places where it had been diverted and forced to show its strength. The towns faded behind the walls. The power station struggled to stay open, gave up with a final sigh. The four smokestacks on the eastern shore still rose high over the trees, but were leaning askew. Waiting for the Big One to knock them over. The electric lines hanging in a long curve over the water held out for much longer than anyone thought, long after the power was turned off, but at last, on the tail of a brittle winter, they snapped with a whipping yelp. That was the river's signal, but it did not hurry. It went over the dams and carried pieces of them off—not enough to pull everything down, but enough to flood the towns, taste the land, and recede, leaving marks on buildings, fences, telephone poles, to show where it had been. Would be again.

It was past midnight when the *Carthage* rode by Sunbury during a break in the rain, the moon through the clouds throwing gray light on black water. The crew on watch saw that the wall there had broken, the river spilling through the breach, covering the houses along the frontage road up to their knees. The water stretched across the town, turning each house into an unstable island. There were torches lit on chimneys, making sparking reflections in the water. In the glow of the fires they could see a couch resting on sheets of plywood propped up by lengths of pipe, erecting a stage across the roof. A blue tarp on poles, stretched over the couch to keep the rain off. Laundry suspended from house to house. On a tall tan garret, a bucket on a winch, half-lowered and pushed by the wind into a slow swing, tapping against the vinyl siding. Signs of lives lived outside, though not of the people who lived them. Everything silent, while on the ship, there was so much noise. The deck of the *Carthage* was packed with cries and hollers, people haggling under the lanterns, the rising whoops of young men who were getting drunk too fast, the edge in their voices of wanting to start something bloody. Wanting the kind of night they would wake up from with teeth missing. In the theater below, the band had started early, struck up a lilting, relentless rumba. The bass and drums laying down a beat that forced hips to move. Twin guitars climbing a rope of sunny notes that the singer set to swinging. Trying to ward off bloodshed. Feet tapping, legs bent, backs arched, hands in the air. They shouted and yelped when the music asked for it, and it gave them ripples of ringing arpeggios, splashes of percussion, in return. The sweating walls sent the groove through the hull of the boat, into the water, to vibrate against the banks. For a small hour, there were no couples, just a mass of humans moving together, letting everything in. The brushes with another's skin. The tang in the air from a million breaths. Smoke rolling across the ceiling from sputtering lanterns. The grainy ferment of shared beer. Each person believing that what they were feeling could spread across the ship, turn the knives outside to steam, then carry them where no bullets flew and no bodies failed, and it would not matter if the earth and sky left, for they no longer needed them.

Until one of the six young men playing Russian roulette in the back of the theater lost. He was smiling when he did it, halfway through a joke, so casual when he pulled the trigger. Later the other five would wonder if he was so loose because he never imagined it would happen, or because he was hoping it would. The sharp shot, the pained shouts from all who saw it, the smell of salt and gunpowder, killed the music, made the dancers spin and hit the floor, sobbing. A few rushing forward, trying to hold the boy's head together, shredding their throats with cries for help. The first mate ran up with bandages and alcohol, saw what had happened, and just stood there, digging her fingers into the cloth. A woman standing nearby had taken the bullet in the thigh. Another was spattered with blood. A curl of brain on a third's shoe. A small piece of skull had made it to the other side of the room.

Then all the torches on the shore winked out, and, for the people in the theater, the walls shook from the outside, as though the ship had struck something. From above, cries, shouts. Gunshots. Moans. Another shudder. The sobbing getting harder. It was the war, they all thought, the war had come for them at last. Voices rose toward panic. The second mate ran through the crowd, burst onto the stage, the spotlight gleaming off the horn in her ear. Grabbed the microphone.

"Anyone who can handle a gun, please help us now,"

she said. "The rest of you, stay here." A shock through the boat, greater than the last. The report of splintering wood.

"Where are you going?" Reverend Bauxite said.

"You heard the woman," Sunny Jim said.

". . ."

". . ."

"You can handle a gun?" Reverend Bauxite said.

Sunny Jim shrugged, was gone. Reverend Bauxite followed him up the stairs, past people running to their rooms. Saying their prayers. The ship lurched again as they reached the open air. The hiss of bullets in the moonlight. The crew scrambling, firing. On the darkened shore, shapes ran along Sunbury's broken wall. More shots. It was an ambush, an organized attack. Someone had seen the *Carthage* coming, rallied people and weapons to the river's edge, and they were all firing now, though nobody on the *Carthage* could say why or even who was doing it. It was not the army. If it was the resistance, then someone had made a terrible mistake. Seven arrows lodged in the deck's wood. A spear. There was no way to call any of it off. Andre, Elise's boy, crouched just below the rail, eyes stark, muscles locked in terror. Before Reverend Bauxite could say anything, Sunny Jim was moving. Grabbed the boy's ankle, dragged him across the deck into the stairwell. Then strode to the rail as if the bullets were afraid of him, would curve around him in the air. Picked up a rifle, loaded it, stood by the rail, and dug the butt into his shoulder. Took his time and shot. Brought the gun down and reloaded. Took his time again. Shot. Amid the shouting and stumbling, the bleeding and crying, his chest rose and fell in complete calm. More sure of himself with a gun than Reverend Bauxite had seen anyone be, even Aline.

But there were seven dead on the deck already. The second mate was sprinting from bow to stern, passing an order to all along the rail, when an arrow slid its point between her ribs, twirled into her left lung and a major blood vessel. She fell, coughing and spluttering, the horn clanking against the planks. She knew what was happening. She was bleeding out. She felt like she was drowning, though she could not say it. Lifted her eyes to the dark sky, as if she were sinking in the ocean, twenty yards down and dropping, and the clouds above were the sea's rippling surface. It was not true what they said, she thought, that the end was peaceful.

The first mate ran to her, looked once at the arrow, at the second mate's face, then got down next to her and stroked her hair. The second mate wanted to thank her. Ask her if she ever did drink a fifth of gin and then shoot eight out of ten bottles from fifty yards, like she'd said she could one night. To tell her that it was a good thing she did, taking that boy in. But she could not make the words come.

Then the sky tore open into blinding color and it seemed as if there were voices all around. The second mate felt a multitude of hands pulling her away, though she could not be sure.

In the theater, they had put out all the lights. They all lay on the floor, weeping, listening. The ship vibrated again, with less violence than before. A sign that perhaps the worst had passed. Yet the screaming, the shots, persisted, and Sergeant Foote, in the darkened theater, felt that old feeling again, the terror she was resigned to. That she would die very soon. That she would suffer a grave hurt. A limb taken off, organs loosed from their cage. It was happening on deck right now, she thought. A man on his side, legs digging into the wood, staring at his own intestines. A woman missing both legs below the knees. A man slumped against the pilothouse. Blanched skin, emptied bowels. Hands spidering across a clammy scalp. It was happening everywhere, the maw of war opened wide enough to eat a continent. They could see the flames at night to the south, from Millersburg, from Liverpool. The land on fire behind them, giving off too much light, with too much darkness ahead.

It took Sergeant Foote a minute to understand that the people next to her were huddling together, arms around each other. A hand on the small of a back. A gasp, a stuttering breath, a moan, as if of surprise. Clothes rustling against the floor.

Someone crawled to meet her, put his hand on her shoulder, his face close to hers. "I've been looking for you all night," the con artist said. Foote said nothing. But she did stand up, take his hand, pull him up to her. They stepped over the couple beside them, headed up the stairs to her room, and closed and locked the door as the ship bucked and stuttered all around them. Shutting it all out to be open with each other, as they had never been with anyone. Kicking death in the teeth.

HER ROOM WAS VERY hot after a few hours. They lay on a thin mattress, their clothes all around them in a ragged halo. He on his back, one arm behind his head, the other around her. She on her side, nestled against him, her head on his shoulder, fingers on his chest.

"So why can't I trust you?" she said.

"Because I survive by lying."

"What, like a con artist?"

"Exactly like a con artist."

"That's no different from what any of us are doing."

"But now I want to tell you everything," he said.

"I don't understand why."

"I don't either."

"I won't reciprocate, you know," she said. "There are certain things I need to keep secret. At least for a while. Until certain other things are settled."

Does this involve the pistol in your bag? he wanted to say. He had seen the glint of light off the handle even in the near dark. Like the eyes of a rat, he thought. But he knew it was not only about the gun, not even only about the war.

They could not let the Big One into their heads. What good would it have done if they did? It would be as if the war had caught them at last. They were lucky that it had not, even though they had seen so much of it, her far more than him. The black night sparked with oily fire and the screams of the wounded. The constant odors of flesh—raw, burnt, rich with fresh blood, beginning to decay. They had not had the chance to figure out why they had survived, make it mean something. Would not accept being denied that.

"I understand," he said, and felt the reply in her fingers, moving up his chest to curl around his shoulder. He could feel the air thickening with morning, the light changing through the cracks in the shutters. Someone was moaning through the wall, from love or injury, he could not tell. He would have kept them in that second forever if he could, kept the air suspended in their lungs until the dead receded far enough away that they could live with them without having to forget them.

❋ ❋ ❋ ❋

BY MORNING THE *CARTHAGE* was clear of Sunbury, and there was a service for those who had died the night before. The bodies lay side by side on the deck. Captain Mendoza managed words even for those she did not know well. Made the attendees realize she was watching them closer than they thought. They rowed the dead to an island in the middle of the river, buried them in the damp earth amid mosquitoes and poison ivy and immense ancient trees, the wrinkles in the bark deep and dark. Reverend Bauxite presided over it all. Grant to us who are still in our pilgrimage, and who walk as yet by faith, that thy Holy Spirit may lead us in holiness and righteousness all our days. Grant to thy faithful people pardon and peace, that we may be cleansed from all our sins, and serve thee with a quiet mind. Give courage and faith to those who are bereaved, that they may have strength to meet the days ahead in the comfort of a reasonable and holy hope, in the joyful expectation of eternal life with those they love.

The congregation spoke their amens, first hesitant, then stronger and stronger, until they were speaking as one, and Reverend Bauxite felt the walls of stained glass rising around him, the vaulting ceiling over his head. Was grateful for the chance to build another church, even if it was out of the air, even if he would have to tear it down again. He was at the head of a congregation, and so, at the end, looked heavenward, spoke within himself. Jesus, of late, my people have had many funerals, and they are tired. He looked over the graves, the treetops, the moving river. Trying to listen, trying to hear. His faith staggering on its feet. Knife wounds and bullet holes in its skin. Defiant, shouting at the world: Give me what you got. It made him so strong. But revealed to him, too, his smallness before the creation—and what a creation it was turning out to be.

Behind them, a charcoal line slithered into the sky over Sunbury, as if from a burning house. Only the pilot noticed it, and he did not make much of it. There were so many fires now. He could not hear the voices rising in grief. Could not see the flames framing the pyres, already taking apart the bodies who the people of the *Carthage* had killed. A father of three. A mother's only daughter. A cousin, a friend. The one who could not shoot a gun to save his life. Three girls, none over fifteen, who had fired off volleys in unison. They had attacked because they thought the *Carthage* was the war coming for them at last. The ship was too big to be anything else, the scouts had said, even though they all thought the war had passed them over, followed the highway, left their part of the river alone. They had hidden everyone who could not fight in houses away from the river and boarded the windows. The people sequestered inside saw the last light fade through the spaces between the planks, lit no lanterns to replace it. Debated in the dark what to do until the firing began, then hit the floor as one. The children mewling, held in trembling arms, parents pleading with them to be quiet. To them, the shooting was a week of no sun, no food or rest, and death racing across the water. Then a shout from outside, a voice they recognized. Come on out. A woman pried a board away, spied into the gloom.

"Is everyone all right?" she said.

The bodies were already almost consumed. The pyres were ships with riggings of fire, the wind filling sails of smoke. The people of Sunbury waited until they were sure that flesh and bone had become ash, then pushed their dead away from them with a final wail. Watched the fiery vessels wend their way into the current, where they broke into pieces, cast a long line of sparks along the surface of the water.

❈ ❈ ❈

WE TRY TO FIX our gaze on the consolations, the bread broken, the fruit shared, the kind words. The light that must be coming. But it is too easy now to remember other things instead. All that suffering. There must be something better than this world, and the world must be better than this. We want to know how it got so low, and we are angry when there is no answer. I am failing you, too, in leaving so much out, the people I cannot find, the names I cannot record, the places I can no longer go. The words I cannot say. Though if there is a plan, perhaps this is part of it, that we will look on those who suffer most, consider all that we have lost, and speak with their voices when we say we have had enough and we cannot lose any more. Speak, and then turn to act, with what the powers have put before us.

I have been to so many funerals now. We bury them in the gray soil, stand over the mounds, lean on our shovels. Say the same words again and again. But there are pregnancies too, children coming. A woman like a great egg. Another just conceived. They help us dig, then turn and spit into the earth. They will not say it, but they cannot keep it all in either. For their coming children are their hopes embodied, their faith made flesh, that all that is ending is beginning again. For the world will not be fallen to their children. It will only be the world, new as they are. And perhaps if we tell them enough, if we say the right thing, they will see a way out, and know what to do.

❋ ❋ ❋ ❋

THAT NIGHT AT SUNBURY, Elise almost died twice. First there were the two bullets through the window, hissing by her ear so fast that she could not think to duck. She looked at the shards of glass on the floor, the holes in the wooden wall. Realized that if she'd seen the shots coming, tried to get away, they would have gotten her, one in the jaw and one in the neck. Then she ran out into the hallway, looking for her boy. Found his girl-friend, standing in the hall, arms at her sides. Where is he, she said, her voice too sharp. The girl winced, just pointed up the stairs toward the deck, where the slugs and arrows were already flying. Elise yelled her son's name, scrambled up the stairs, just in time to see Sunny Jim pull her boy to safety, then start shooting. Andre lay in the stairwell, not blinking enough, then blinking too much. Her hands moved over him, pressing into him, rifling through his clothes, as though he were a child again. She was looking for the wound. When she found nothing, she crushed him in her arms. Andre, Andre. Started crying as soon as she felt his hands move, hugging her back.

At the service on the *Carthage,* Sunny Jim stood near the back, his hands clasped in front of him. Was slow to move as the service ended, only began to turn as others moved past him. The partiers comforting each other: When we get to Towanda, everything will be better. We just have to get there and we'll be all right.

He felt a hand on his shoulder. "I want to thank you," Elise said, "for saving my son yesterday."

"It was nothing," Sunny Jim said. "You would have done the same."

"Maybe. You have kids?"

"Yeah. One, also a boy. I'm going to get him now."

"Where is he?"

"Up north, with my sister."

"Whereabouts?"

"Lisle."

"I grew up in Elmira."

They both nodded. A shared understanding of the country, the fits of luck and misfortune that could bend a life. How you could start out at their mercy, though that never meant you should give up.

"You know, Andre's never even met his father," Elise said. Thought, for a moment, that she should be careful, then decided there was no time for it. "He's had people in his life before that do the job, but no one for a while, for long enough. Just me. It seems a shame, doesn't it? When it's so much easier with two."

"What's your name again?" Sunny Jim said.

"Elise."

"Elise, I have a wife." A hitch in his voice when he said that, and for an instant, she saw straight into him.

"I'm sorry."

"No, don't be. You didn't know."

"I hope you find her," Elise said. "Does she know how good you are?"

"No. Or how bad I am, either."

There was so much he had never said to Aline. They met years before the war in the basement of a house that someone had turned into a bar whose name he could not remember. He creaked down the wooden stairs and found her there with another man. They were fighting, like Sunny Jim's parents had fought, and she was winning. It ended with her splitting the man's forehead open with a green metal toolbox. He staggered back three steps to the wall, sat down as though he were hypnotized, the blood already halfway down his shirt. Both eyes still open, staring at her, the hatred settling into his face to stay. She dropped the toolbox and just looked at him. Almost fascinated by what she had done. An expression Sunny Jim had seen on Merry, before he left.

"It's not as bad as it looks," Sunny Jim told her. "Though, if I were you, I'd quit seeing him."

". . ."

"Do you have a place to be?" he said.

He had two rooms over what had once been a Chinese restaurant. Windows overlooking the parking lot in the back. Two cars there that weather and animals were taking apart. The windshield had gone on one of them, and plants grew from the seats. Fourteen cats lived in the other. They lounged on the dashboard, mated in the footwell, slept on the engine, though it had not been warm since Sunny Jim lived there.

Sunny Jim and Aline stumbled up the stairs together. He put her in the bed, then lay on the couch, hands under his head, unable to sleep, since he had given her the blanket. The cracks in the ceiling were dry riverbeds on a desert floor. He listened to Aline breathe all night and decided he needed it. In the morning, he convinced her to stay a few days. By the end of the week, they were sharing the bed. The sound of her breath was even better when it was closer.

Then there was Aaron, Aaron and the war. Their pasts and futures fell away from Sunny Jim and Aline until only the minutes close to them mattered, the bullets and bombs looking for them, their son's fingers in their hair. The three of them clung to each other whenever Aline was there, holding their little family together. There was a night two years into the war, when Aaron was only four, and it was just the three of them in a house that had been half taken apart by the fighting. The living room, the stairs to the second floor, open to the sky. Two of the bedrooms covered with broken glass. But one room was somehow still intact. A twin bed, a dresser, a nightstand. Only the lamp knocked over. The three of them got into the bed and Aaron fell asleep between them, on his side. Soon Aline was slumbering, too. Sunny Jim could hear the war, not far off. Hear the house groaning and shuddering around him. They were in danger, there was no question about it. Tomorrow they would have to move, and he did not know where they were going to sleep then. But for that hour, Sunny Jim was happy, as happy as he had ever been. And when Aline was gone, every day was a year, a year that Aaron skipped through, stringing songs together from what he saw all around him. Broken glass, broken glass, make one slip and cut your . . .

And then Aline did not come back at all.

From the night he met her, Sunny Jim knew what people thought Aline was. She was half feral to them. They looked at her teeth and her nails before they got too close, because she looked like someone who would use them. And when Sunny Jim and Aline got together, he knew what everyone they met was thinking, that someday she would eat him alive. Leave him in a pool of his blood if he said the wrong thing. One pair of eyes after another would say it: What are you doing with her? They did not see what he saw, the loyalty coiled inside her ferocity, the ferocity that made him loyal to her. Before he met her, he could not imagine living very long. He was far from home, and the storm was coming. But with Aline, he had built a temporary shelter, and wherever they went, the rain could not touch them. When Aaron was born, he felt invincible, as though the evils of the world parted before his family when they walked down the street together, the baby in his arms. He began to dream, as he wouldn't let himself before, of a new house, beneath trees on a hill, a place that could keep the rain out for years, and that he would not live to see fall over.

They first saw the war feasting on a small town in Maryland one night. They were walking along a county road that skimmed across rolling land, a wrinkled map folded in Sunny Jim's jacket pocket. Aaron asleep, strapped to his back. He and Aline thought they would round the next bend out of a stand of trees and see the lights from the windows of low houses. Instead, all the houses were dark, lit from behind by a great fire. Flares and columns of flame rose into the air. They knew what it was that they were seeing, had heard about the violence rising out of the south, and Sunny Jim felt Aline take his left hand, grip it hard. They watched the destruction for a full minute without saying anything. Did not need to. I will never leave you, Aline said, and Sunny Jim knew she wanted to believe it. But he could feel the war pulling at her even then, opening its fiery arms. Knew that he could not stop her from running toward it.

You left us, Aline, he wanted to say now. You left us to this. Why won't you come back? There was so much he wanted to tell her, because he had never said enough. About how much he loved her. About their son, the incredible being he was, the kind of man he was already becoming. Embodying what was good in his parents and casting the rest aside. He had never told her everything about Merry: enough that Aline was worried, but not enough to be scared, of Merry, of him. If she knew it all, she might have left him earlier, he thought, left and taken Aaron with her. Or maybe she would have loved him more, he never could decide which. He always imagined telling her one day when they were much older, telling her everything, about the bodies in the driveway and the deal he struck with his sister, a promise they both kept and always would. How he thought he could tell sometimes when his sister was thinking of him, feel a warmth under the scalp, spreading across his skull. I love you, Sunny Jim, even if I cannot imagine what you look like anymore. He wanted to tell Aline all these things, but could not. He was not ready.

"I didn't realize you were so good with a gun," Reverend Bauxite said later.

"Learned it hunting," Sunny Jim said.

"You must have been some hunter."

"..."

"They could have used you in Harrisburg."

"I know."

"Jim?"

"Yeah."

"Have you ever shot anybody before?"

"..."

"..."

All those nights in Harrisburg when Sunny Jim had said no guns, Reverend Bauxite thought it was because he did not know how to shoot, or would not. Believed that the willingness to hurt, to kill, was a thing that separated him from Aline. But now the priest could almost see it, the burning hand shaping his friend's life, leaving its fingerprints. The violence he was capable of. He thought of Merry, too, an hour before she took Aaron with her back to Lisle. A long rifle slung across her back at a casual angle, an obvious piece of hunting equipment that set her apart from the guerrillas, made Reverend Bauxite worry whether she'd be able to keep the boy from harm. Then a shell landed close to them, shook the floor and ceiling, brought down pieces of plaster. Sunny Jim didn't even duck, and Merry closed her eyes and smiled a little, as if listening to distant music, the voice of a beloved child in another room. A small rapture blooming in her. Reverend Bauxite studied her, the doubt in her abilities replaced by something else——he could not say what with precision. She opened her eyes again, stared at him, as though she could read him in a glance.

And then Sunny Jim embraced her, gave her and his son a long, crushing hug.

"Merry—"

"—There's no time, Jim. No time. Just know I'll do anything to keep him safe. You know I will."

"I know."

Reverend Bauxite believed her, and was afraid of her. As he was a little afraid of his friend now, though he loved him all the same.

The Highway

THE SOLDIERS COULD HEAR the fighting ahead of them for miles. Even over the truck's roar, the booming rumbled through the ground: drums, footsteps, thunder. When the truck blew another tire on the road four miles south of Scranton, they could see the war in the sky. The city's light projected onto the belly of the monsoon. Flashes of fire, then the sounds of the explosions rolling over them. The echo carried the voices of the victims, rising in surprise and terror. The soldiers on the road could feel it then. What it might be like in the valley right now.

A change came over Largeman. His ears pricked, his arms and legs grew taut, and his eyes and mouth went slack, as though something else were taking over. Ketcher saw it and a sharp, dissonant pain speared his brain. Something terrible was about to happen. It was waiting for them on the road, feet stamping the earth. Come here.

"Are we posted for combat?" Ketcher said.

"No," Tenenbaum said. "It's straight through to Lisle now." Oblivious. Whatever was waiting on the road for them smiled.

The light gathered around them, poured into the crack between the doors, as they rode into Scranton. The voices of bombs much closer, more complex, a hissing roar over the thudding shudder. The truck's engine jumped and screeched, the vehicle leaning forward. Going faster, as though the driver was trying to outrun something. Jumped again, lurched back. The tires skidding to the left and right, jostling the soldiers. Then they stopped. The engine idled, died. The sounds of war got even clearer. The whistles of shells, notes at intervals dropping together. The hoarse trill of machine-gun fire. A great shuffling, human voices yelling, complaining. Sighing, dying. The driver's head out the side window. Please get off the road and let us through. The truck did not move. A discussion in the cab, footsteps at the side of the truck. The doors swung open.

"Help us clear the road," their commanding officer yelled.

They were on the highway passing through the city. The war's incendiary edge was no more than a half mile away. Night flickered toward day with each rising fireball, the machine guns already getting more insistent. The streaked skeletons of cars stretched across the pavement, as though they had been straggling north and starved to death in their tracks. The dark buildings off the highway huddled together, trying to stay out of sight. They saw, then, what made the truck stop: a thick column of refugees, shambling across the road. Clambering over the guardrails, disappearing beyond the far shoulder. What was left of their lives tied to their backs, sometimes falling off. A path of worn clothes, pots and pans, cracking shoes under their feet. The commanding officer was yelling louder. The refugees closest to him turned their heads, gave him a quick look, proceeded as before, as though he were a spectacle they did not want to see, an accident. The rest moved along unchanged, dragging their children by their wrists. Pushed by the squall of crying babies, the fires behind them. A bomb went off close enough to feel the heat, and everyone moaned and flinched in the sudden light, the clap and roar. Coughed as the smoke swept over them and away. Too tired to stop or run.

The truck still could not get through. Another truck trying to get into the city was in the other lane, on the other side of the refugees, blasting its horn. Four soldiers tried to wedge their way in, make a wall, but the refugees flowed around them. The soldiers brought their rifles to attention. Stop and let us pass, or we cannot be responsible for what happens to you.

There was a keening in Ketcher's brain. Everything was about to explode. This had happened to him once before, when he was a kid watching three men argue in the street over a wheelbarrow. The wheelbarrow's owner was smaller than the other two men, but there was a coiled violence in the small man that the two larger men did not see. They bullied the wheelbarrow away from him, then turned their backs. A sound went off in Ketcher's ears, and the small man pulled a blue metal spade from his pack, lunged and buried it in the neck of one of the larger men. The victim jerked, five times fast, flopped to the ground, and lay there, facing the sky. For an awful second, nothing happened, then blood poured, with great freedom, from the back of his head. The third man let out a cry like a child—the sound Ketcher should have made—then a series of *ohs*, falling off into nothing. Ketcher ran, faster than he thought he could, to the railroad bridge over the river. He ducked under it, sat among the large stones by the dark green water. Decided never to tell anyone, and did not. No one ever asked.

Stop, the commanding officer called to the refugees. They did not. He ordered the soldiers to level their rifles. The soldiers hesitated. They did not want to do it. The commanding officer did not want to, either. Then the firing started, and all at once, nineteen of the people crossing the highway seemed to lie down, as though they had decided to rest there. As if the oil-stained road was a copse of sorrel and milkweed, shaded by great elms, a brook running through it to slake their thirst. They settled down, and the survivors began to scream, bolted to the nearest shoulder, dragged their kids through the tall, scraggly grass. Left behind a litter of cooking utensils, socks, photographs. A bundle of pink clothes, a shirt with daisies on it. The nineteen people who had come to the highway only to cross it, move away from this place. The soldiers would never know where they were trying to go.

"Who fired?" the commanding officer said.

The soldiers looked at their guns, afraid of them. Would not look at the bodies.

"Who fired?" the commanding officer said again.

"I did, sir," Largeman said.

"I didn't give the order."

"I'm sorry, sir. I thought you did."

Another ball of flame rose from the city. Lit the quiet highway. They all stared at Largeman. Could not read him. The commanding officer shook his head, ran his hand over his face.

"Get these people off the road," he said.

The bodies were heavy, uncooperative. One of them, a woman with streaks of white through mousy hair, lay in languid repose, as if for a painting. Tenenbaum took her legs, Ketcher her arms. When they lifted her, blood poured from her mouth and nose onto Ketcher's legs, as if she were a bag of wine, emptying. He could not look at the children. The ones who carried them had blood across their chests, all up and down their arms. They did not look down at themselves, just went back to the truck and got inside. Do not ask me to do anything more today. Ketcher gave himself one more glance at the city before they closed the doors. The night was getting brighter with all the fires. Thick smoke sparking with the light below. Another bomb going off, another, another. Spurts of gunfire, screams and cries. The seething rush of buildings collapsing. The war an invisible monster, feasting on the city.

In the first months of the war, Ketcher thought, when reports of fighting crept up from Georgia, Virginia, there had been reasons for it. He had heard it was over land, it was over water, political difficulties. Too many people fighting over too little. Some high-flown, contradictory language about cutting down or breathing life into principles that already hung from the gallows that a century of chaos built. Remember when we used to be a country? The propaganda beginning early. But it seemed by the end of the first year that the reasons did not matter so much anymore. The war was an earthquake, destroying towns and cities. Or it was a job, three square meals a day. Why are you doing this? the guerrilla by the side of the highway had said, just before they shot her. They had all joined, Ketcher knew, because they did not know what else to do. They'd been squatting in houses losing pieces with every storm. Sleeping in the backseats of abandoned cars. They were staring at flooded fields of wheat, the grain rotting on the stalk, the plants wilting and dropping into the water. They could justify it all to themselves then, putting on the uniform, picking up the gun, eating the rations and sending home whatever they could, whatever helped. The larger reasons for joining were long gone, lost in the smoke, the ruined bridges, the fires. The personal reasons, the wives, the husbands, the families, shone ever brighter. But sometimes even that was not enough.

The doors closed and the truck gained speed. The soldiers inside sat against the walls, limbs splayed. Too exhausted to do more than breathe. The truck stank with blood, thick, tangy. Ketcher closed his eyes, pinched his nose. He was shutting it out, or trying to, and then it got him and he was kicking, stomping, as if the blood would fly off his clothes if he thrashed hard enough. A bomb went off, very close, and the truck jolted, swerved. Talked about coming apart, here, in the war's jaws. He had to believe, then, that there was a place of cool, hushing breezes, unbroken glass. There had to be. Perhaps it lay behind what was coming from the north. They were all so afraid of it, would not talk about it, even as it made them frantic. But maybe it would sweep over them and make them whole again. Put all the cities back together, put the rivers back in their beds, and we would wander across the land, down wide boulevards, with open hands, like children. Marveling at the gift of the world, promising not to squander it again.

Then they were clear of the front and the light and sound faded, until there was only the fanning hum of the truck's motor, the *lum-dum* of the tires over the road, a stuttering heartbeat. Ketcher could not see who anyone was. Just a curve of shoulder, the mountainous wrinkles of a pant leg. Every few minutes someone struck a match to smoke that showed that almost everyone else was asleep. But Tenenbaum was still awake, eyes hardened into glass. Ketcher made sure Largeman was snoring before he spoke.

"Sir."

"Ketcher."

"About him, sir." A finger pointed at Largeman.

"What about him."

". . ."

"What about him, Ketcher. I'm not going to make this easy for you."

"Do we need him to be with us, sir?"

Tenenbaum squinted. "You mean that there should be a stronger reckoning for what he has done."

"Yes."

"A trial. Perhaps a hanging. Or no trial, and a bullet to the head. Because some of those he killed today were children."

"Yes."

"I'm sorry," Tenenbaum said. "We need everyone we have." Also, you are complicit, you sorry son of a bitch. Do not pretend that because you did not fire, you can go home clean.

Ketcher wanted to go back, to shoot Largeman before he opened fire. To shoot Largeman on the highway through Ravine, or kill him with a stone. To desert the army on the shore of the Susquehanna in Marysville, before they ever started north. He could have done it while they were oiling the truck. Walked through the tunnel lined with rusting beds and dying soldiers, slipped into the river, put his legs out in front of him, and floated, under the long bridge, under the broken roads and highways. Even if they saw him from the banks, the flooded spit of City Island, they would have mistaken him for a corpse, borne too fast to stop. He could have eased past Three Mile Island, toward the country. Touched ground near a swollen strand of trees, a field rising out of the flood. A new name, or no name, until the war was over, and then back to his parents. I'm so sorry I disappeared, he would say, and his parents would cry with joy. We don't care. We're so glad you're here now. But he knew there was no time for any of that, anymore.

Jackson sat facing the soldiers passed out on the other

side of the truck, his own eyes wide open. He heard everything. Thought of his son, who had died three years before the war began. The boy was four years old, rambunctious, joyful. Threw things out the windows of the house, jumped up and down when he heard the crash, then ran into the kitchen laughing. An infection had developed in his eyelid, first puffed it, then painted it red, as if someone had hit him. They had no idea what caused it. The doctor passed his hand over the angry skin with gentleness. There's nothing we can do now, he said—he had not seen antibiotics in years. Just make him rest. Give him what he needs and hope for the best. The infection spread fast, across half the boy's face, shot into his blood. He died in a wilting haze, unable to see his parents, who held his hands and wailed as one when he was gone. The years they had him were the best of their lives. Every year after, the worst. They promised not to leave each other, regretted that at first, then grasped that no one else would have them, that they wanted no one who could not share their ragged sorrow. When the war began, he enlisted. Told his wife maybe it was better for them to have a little time away from each other, then thought of her every day. Wished he had told her what he had been thinking for years: that he knew how to get past it, if only they had the courage.

The River

IT WAS A QUESTION of belief, Sergeant Foote thought. If she believed, she could forget about her mission, stay with her man, forever, on this ship. It was noon and the con artist was asleep beside her, his breath flirting with a feathery snore. The light from outside fading the room into a pale print, as if it were halfway to vanishing already. She had watched the people moving in the theater last night, the orgy, and was tempted. They all believed. They had bent their lives to the coming storm, were all going upriver for something: a grandmother with asthma, a farm, a house, the land from the road to the slope on the other side of the dry creek bed. A silver necklace in a pine dresser drawer. A great-uncle's grave. Towanda, Towanda, Towanda. It was a shared understanding, an acceptance of each other and the time they had left, even given the violence, the killing they had done, the pasts they had. And there was repentance in that, enough to hold the *Carthage* and themselves together until the war or the storm came for them.

But she did not believe yet. The storm would pass, and the war would soon be finished. She could complete her last mission, find her targets and dispatch them. There would be medals, a pension, and then no more war for her. Just a house—on a riverbank, she thought for the first time, for the *Carthage* had started to get to her. On a river, and her on a blanket under the thick shade of trees choked with vines. Her toes digging into the sandy soil. She could live herself out like that, she thought, by the water, until a stroke took her, as her grandmother had been taken. They would find her body twitched off the blanket, her face inches from a rusty bottle cap, a waterlogged plastic bag. The last images from her head still in the air above her: the light off the small waves, her wrinkled hands on the blanket's wool. Then nothing more, for the stroke would come so fast. It did not seem like so much to ask.

So she stole away from the con artist sleeping next to her. Dressed in the half dark. Began to wonder where else she might look, caught herself moving her lips, forming the words. Talking to herself, for it was getting harder to keep her mission secret. When she left the room, the con artist rose, checked her bag. Felt the handle of the pistol nestled among her clothes. He did not know what she was doing, but figured that as long as the gun was still there, he did not need to.

In the hallway to the steel door of the galley, she questioned someone who she thought for a minute might be one of her men. Brought him to tears when she forced him to recollect his wife, who had died in a truck accident in Emmitsburg, Maryland, far from the river's shore. In the hold of the ship, amid lumber, a trove of paintings, six telescopes, a pile of clothes, and a high stack of windows, she thought she heard someone in the corner. Only found two teenagers, startled, scared. His hands on her face. Her hands up the back of his shirt.

"What are you doing here?" the boy said. Too frightened to be angry.

"Sorry," she found herself saying. "I'm sorry." Felt the mission slip from her a little then, but pulled it back. In the theater she heard music, calm and light, an ambling bass, strolling piano, walking through "Night and Day." In the middle of the floor, on a steel frame bed, a woman dying of pneumonia. The first mate, the closest thing the *Carthage* had to a doctor, tending to her. Reverend Bauxite standing by, for she would not last much longer. All the woman wanted was the old songs, the ones her great-grandmother sang to her when she was a small girl, standing in the kitchen while the old woman peeled potatoes, chopped onions, skinned rabbits. Billie Holiday, Fats Waller, Dinah Washington. The band did what they could, but they knew they were doing a bad job. The woman smiled anyway, nodded after every song. Falling away, the taste of sweet fruit in her mouth already. I'm coming, grandmama. She passed two hours later.

"You're the preacher around here," Sergeant Foote said afterward.

"I am."

"Are there any others?"

"If they are," Reverend Bauxite said, "they're doing a pretty good job of hiding themselves." Unaware of what a perfect thing that was to say to keep her from shooting him. Though it only meant she would come back later, gun ready. He did not have much longer to live.

"I need to talk to you," she said.

"Confession?"

"You might say that."

Without another word, he rose, retired to the corner where the Russian roulette player had died. The floor still darker where it had happened.

"What do you want to talk about?"

"I've done a few things," she said. Though never been cruel, she told herself, never unjust. Even in Baltimore, I was never bad, though the walls were shaking.

"Like what?"

She turned for a moment. Looked upriver, where the clouds were thickening. A tight nausea gripped her abdomen, moved through her chest. Climbed up her throat. And then she was telling him, about all the people she had killed. The ones who had been shooting back, the ones who had been running. A few who did not see it coming. She had lingered over them all a little too long. Gotten to know their faces. A few times, she was sure she had seen the last of their lives leave them. Saw the muscles in the faces change, collapsing and stiffening, the eyes still open. They never once looked back at her. They were casting her aside already, pulling inward, moving out and away, and would not let her see where they were going.

"I quit the army after Harrisburg," she said. A lie, a lie, but in that moment, she wanted to believe it.

"And they let you go?"

"No."

Reverend Bauxite smiled. "Good girl."

He said a few prayers then, offered her absolution if she would take it. The Lord has put away all your sins. Go in peace, and pray for me, a sinner.

"Thank you so much, Father. I'm so glad you came aboard when you did."

Reverend Bauxite made no outward sign. Only hesitated a second, but spent it trying to stare into her. An alarm jangling in his head. Even on this boat, the war would not leave them be. How much of what she had just told him was a story? What was she here for?

"It may not look it," he said, "but I've been on this boat a long time. Every ship needs a chaplain."

"Especially now," she said.

"Yes. Especially now."

He blessed her again, let her go ahead, kept himself from running belowdecks to the room where Sunny Jim lay in utter slumber. He had not slept the night before, Reverend Bauxite knew. It was too much to uncoil from. The shock of the rifle kicking on his shoulder. The people on the river wall falling. His finger on the trigger. He must have marveled at how easy it was, Reverend Bauxite thought, how fast it came back to him. Knowing how the gun would buck, knowing to stay loose but strong, let the weapon do its work. But later it crept into him, that he had cut the wires of those lives, left the ends sparking in the air behind them. It was all for Aaron, all for his son, but that did not diminish what he had done.

In his dreams, Sunny Jim was laying on a bare mattress on a splintered pine floor. The walls moved, shimmered, broke away. He was in the shell of a warehouse in Syracuse. He was in Philadelphia. In Wilmington. All the places he had been before Aline. The Wallace brothers on either side of him, standing on his arms, looking down at him and shaking their heads. Henry Robinson crouched on his chest, his fingers in Sunny Jim's mouth.

"Soon the dreams will sweep your boy up," one of the Wallaces said. "You know what I'm saying, don't you?"

Sunny Jim nodded.

"Soon he will know everything," the other Wallace said.

Sunny Jim forced the fingers out of his mouth with his tongue. "But I want him to know everything," he said. The fingers crawled back into his throat.

"The hell you do," said Henry Robinson. "You tell him what you did to us, and he'll be terrified of you for the rest of his life."

Reverend Bauxite woke Sunny Jim up with a hand on his forehead, as he had in Harrisburg many times, and at once Sunny Jim was awake, alert, though his body was too tired to move its limbs. Still feeling the three boys holding him down.

"Jim," Reverend Bauxite said. "I think someone is looking for us."

"For what?"

"I don't know. But if someone asks you who you are, you should lie."

"Okay. Who should I be?"

"I don't know. Something easy to remember."

"How about I pretend I'm you."

Reverend Bauxite looked at him. You shot people less than sixteen hours ago, Jim.

I know.

Stop joking around. Be serious. You owe them that.

I know.

"When we see Aaron," Jim said, "we'll have some stories."

"What are you planning to tell him?"

The war raged in him. Tell him nothing, or you will lose him, him and Aline, for he will leave you when he hears what you have to say, and she will vanish in the telling. No. Give yourself up and tell him everything, and you all can live.

"I don't know," Sunny Jim said.

✖ ✖ ✖ ✖

THERE WERE HOLES IN the ship, the first mate told Captain Mendoza, from the assault at Sunbury. A good flood would sink them, the river peering in, then entering and pulling them down. The crew was moving over the *Carthage*'s hull, trying to mend the wounds. But they needed more wood, more metal. Anything to keep the water away.

"How is the boy?" the captain said.

The first mate shrugged. Dark patches under her eyes. The boy had woken her once by thrashing in his sleep, trying to tear his mattress apart. She shouted him awake, held him close. He would not say what had visited him, but she could guess. He fell asleep again, did not wake again until late morning. Came out and looked at the people tending their animals, conducting trade. A dispute near the bow that the captain broke up before there was blood. To the boy, the air around them was a boiling darkness. Greasy light spilling from everyone's skin, their souls preparing to leave them. They have all come here to mock or gawk, he thought. Rawhead and Bloody Bones. He walked over to the nearest man, smiled at him, and introduced himself. Got the man to smile back. How do you do? When the man extended his hand, the boy grabbed it, bit into the soft muscle below the thumb, then did cartwheels from bow to stern, yelping as though he was in the schoolyard, waiting for his parents to pick him up. The captain glared at the first mate. Control your new boy. He needs it bad. The first mate caught him in mid-cartwheel, her arms around his chest. He shouted and flailed as she brought him to his knees, cradled him to her. There, there. Carried him to his bedroll on the floor, where he screamed himself to sleep. She lay next to him, ready to hold him when the dreams came again.

That kid is spooking the ship, some said, as though a bad spirit from the island had followed him aboard. Had luxuriated in so much death that it had become greedy.

"You're the best thing he has," the captain said to the first mate later.

"I wish I wasn't. I wish he had better."

Against her will, the captain's thoughts became unkind. I wish my boat had no holes in it. I wish Aline were still alive. I wish I had a child. But this world was not made for wishes anymore. It was falling away around them, and soon the captain, the first mate, and everyone they knew would fall, too. That they would fall together was a comfort she did not want to pretend she was grateful for.

"Just do what you can," she said. Wondered where the sudden, maternal lilt in her voice had come from. And at once the first mate was in her arms, but only for a few seconds. Said nothing. Then extracted herself, straightened her sleeves.

"I should see where he is," she said.

She found him on the deck, cross-legged in front of the bass player, who was sitting on her bass, a rattling banjo in her hands. She was picking out a Skip James song she could only half remember the words to, though she nailed the humming, broken chorus every time. The music drained of hope, as if the man had seen these years coming, seen them and tried to tell us, but we did not understand.

"Do you know anything happier?" the first mate said.

"Not today," the bass player said. "But tomorrow? Who knows?" Then smiled at her own joke, and each of the other three musicians, in different parts of the ship, smiled with her. They had played together so long that they were always in contact with each other, and with the man they had lost. Slim Herkimer, Herkimer Slim.

They never knew which way his name went. But they all remembered the first time they heard him play. A trumpet, a guitar, a cello. A piano with rotting keys. It did not matter what he touched. Each of them swore later that they could see the air ripple around him when he played, and everyone within earshot swooned, their voices curling back in their throats. All the doors opened, the walls peeled away, and the music swelled into the space until it overflowed it and covered the world. They could hear it in distant deserts, over the waves of the sea. When Slim finished, there was a full four seconds of silence, and then a sound came from the people who had heard him, a stuttering, rising moan, as though he had given them a piece of light, a sharp spark that they held in their hands before it slipped through a seam in the sky.

After the audience left and he was putting his instruments in their cases, each of the musicians asked him if they could play sometime, if he needed a band, if he could stand a drummer. "Sure," he said. "Let's do it." His eyes pointed at them, but were almost unseeing. He hummed in the long pauses between his words, the notes still coming to him even when he could not express them.

They became a five-piece. Judge Spleen Smiley did most of the singing, but as soon as Slim started to play, nobody heard a word. He taught them all how to put their voices into their fingers, channel their souls through metal and wood. Before the war they played at fairs and dances, on outdoor stages in searing sun, under sagging awnings in the rain, under the spread of stars. Even played at the West Side Ballroom once, though Elise was asleep that night, her child curled in her arms. They played late shows in raftered rooms murky with the light from a single dim lamp. Each of them had good nights, when they were the music's instrument and they could feel the groove dig deeper, the people yell louder, dance and drink a little more. They could feel how they were bringing everything together. But none of them could touch Slim. The best nights, he played for hours, eyes closed, rocking back and forth. Fingers moving as if they were independent animals. Those who saw him couldn't talk about it for a few days, then talked about nothing else.

They traveled together on a wagon with a plastic sheet tented over the top, piled beneath it with all their instruments. Four horses in front, pulling them through the country. When it rained, they found shelter for the horses, huddled together under blankets in the wagon and dropped into sleep, one after the other, in fugue. When it did not rain, they slept on the ground. Never stopped marveling at the vastness of the sky. As if the music was opening their heads to everything, letting them step into a single moment, then stay and stay.

They heard the war before they saw it, a long tearing whine from the far side of the hill behind them. They turned and looked, saw a flash of light that Judge Spleen Smiley mistook for a meteorite, until there were too many for it to be natural. None of them slept, listening to the war dismember the town down the road. They had just played there, the bass player thought. There had been rumors, people going home early. More guns than usual. But at their show, there was a woman with purple plastic earrings, in a white blouse, dancing close with her man. Resting her head on his red shirt. Three men trying to grow mustaches, who drank too much but never got nasty about it. Sat on the bar, swinging their legs, hollering come on, honey, you know I'm worth a try. Four women ordered eighteen shots at once, to make sure they had enough for the night. The smallest of them put down eight of them herself, insisted on getting up to sing. She was good. A husky alto, knew some old country, some old jazz. Knew what the people in that room wanted and gave it to them. They cheered at the end and she curtsied, pretended she was wearing a skirt.

They did not gig as much as they wanted to after that. Played cinder-block social halls that survived the fires. Field hospitals. Weddings and funerals that both ended in breaking glass and blood in the dirt. A man passed out facedown in the road, one hand on a greasy pistol, the other on a glass bottle, the inside still shiny with a thin stripe of rancid alcohol. Baptisms frequented by white-haired grandparents hobbling forward, stretching out their arms to hold the children in shaking hands.

Two weeks before he left, Herkimer Slim—Slim Herkimer—played the best they'd ever heard from him, in a former grocery store in Harrisonburg, Virginia. It did not start well. Broken lightbulbs and snapped strings. A splinter in the top of his guitar. A wire that kept shorting. But people stayed to listen, as if they sensed what was coming. A drop in air pressure, a change in the light. Someone coughed, scuffed his shoes, and Herkimer Slim closed his eyes, did not open them again until dawn. His teeth glimmered between parted lips, fingers twisting and rushing. The notes in alien intervals, showing you the way in, then throwing you heavenward, holding your head under the water and lifting you out again, exhilarated and gasping for oxygen. He was crying for the last hour, but the notes spoke of nothing but joy. Only fifteen people heard him that night, but he changed the directions of their lives. Caused marriages, divorces, children to be conceived, raised better. Raised the best they could be. He did not sleep at all the next day, then slept for fifteen hours straight. At their next gig, it was as if the last one never happened. But as they were all putting their instruments away, he gave one long last blow into a clarinet, a high cry that spoke of grief and rapture, and then disappeared. It was only later, when his band thought back on it, that it began to seem as though he'd known he'd have to go, had some music he needed to play before he left. They told each other that over and over again, the story they pieced together to make his loss bearable. They played the music he left them as well as they could, and to those who had never heard Herkimer Slim, Slim Herkimer, it was revelatory. I love you guys, someone had told them once, always hanging back even when you rush forward. They nodded to each other, for they all knew what they were doing. Leaving room for him at the center of their sound, as if the last note he played was still going on somewhere, sustaining them through their lives, and if they hung back far enough, they could still hear it. Sometimes I think I can hear it, too, and my daughter is singing along.

※ ※ ※ ※

THEY KNEW SOMETHING WAS wrong even before they saw the town of Danville, for there were cars in the water. Pieces of roofing. The sheared-off face of a two-story house on the shore, its top tangled in trees. Half the town was in the water, the land broken off into a ragged, collapsing cliff. As if the whole place had been hollow, the first mate said. Hollow and brittle, Captain Mendoza thought. An eggshell drained of the egg, the meat taken while the mother was sleeping. She would know her child had been killed only when she crushed the shell under her weight.

They could read in the broken land that Danville had once sloped down to the Susquehanna's banks, peered over the edge of a long wall. There had been a mill under the trees, a row of factory housing, a bridge to Riverside. The river must have done its work in a single night. They could see the cracked columns where the bridge had been, the tooth marks in the earth still fresh, a few acres ripped off the front of the town. A jagged race of rocks and stumbling soil, exposed tree roots clawing at the air. The water now feasting on the debris at the hill's foot. The next row of buildings, red brick and iron, teetered on the dusty edge, ready to fall. The house where the con artist had been happiest was ripped in half, the rooms within exposed as if it were a dollhouse.

The captain had the pilot pull the *Carthage* closer to shore. She put a red megaphone to her lips, shouted out hellos. Stated their intentions, to find wood, to fix the ship. Could anyone help. A troop of screaming monkeys appeared on the crest of a roof, leapt from house to house, flailing and bantering, until one of them fell into the street with a wail that was then cut short. The other monkeys gathered at the gutter, looked down to stare. This will be worse than Sunbury, the captain thought. Worse than the camp.

Then two women and a man appeared where the frontage road dropped into the water. Held guns, but without wariness. Motioned for them to come closer. The captain turned around, asked for volunteers.

"Go," Reverend Bauxite said to Sunny Jim. "I know we're all stuck on this boat together, but I think you should make yourself as scarce as you can, when you can." Thinking of the woman who had asked too many questions.

The con artist had stayed belowdecks. Did not want to see the house that used to be his, the woman who was once his wife. But he found Sunny Jim before he left, put a note in his hands with a name on it. "Please ask how she is," he said. "If anyone has seen her."

The landing party crossed the front between the

river and the earth, a hundred yards of a slurry of roads and houses, the fractured ends of plumbing and infrastructure. Spurs of territory had been claimed by either side, a leg of rock repelling the water, a flat of ground turning to swamp. The border of the shore would be renegotiated in time, the land become a hillside again, but the town would not live long enough to see it. The people who lived there knew that. They had been there for generations, seen the iron and coal and giant hospitals come and go. At first they tried to believe that they would only lose a few blocks, a few houses, until the night that half the place drowned at once, the houses, cars, and everyone inside them. So they gave up, packed what they could carry, and moved to higher ground. Came back only to salvage, to scavenge, the needs of the living too pressing for nostalgia.

On the ridge of Route 11, the destruction ended and there was only neglect: the car dealership, buildings built for light industry that they no longer had any use for. The empty highway turned curvy, crawling over rises in the land. Then they turned onto State Hospital Drive, the bent green sign, the pavement curling as if it had been banked too tight. They passed fields washed out by monsoons, small ponds collecting in the depressions in the earth. A guardhouse, a line of barbed wire, a sign that used to be white with red letters, now peeling and faded. A new sign posted in the center: WELCOME TO NEW DANVILLE. They crossed into the hospital compound, topped the next hill, and saw how the people of

Danville were putting their lives back together. Rows of small calico shacks, pieced together from old houses. A wide scattering of vegetable gardens. Animals lowing in communal pens. People walking about the gardens on dirt paths strewn with rocks and paper, beaten into streets by footsteps. Bartering at a long table piled with clothes, parts of farm tools, the soles of shoes. Small fires, for cooking, for warmth. A woman with a banjo, tapping her foot in the mud. The grunt of a pig being slaughtered. Behind them, the high towers of the old state hospital, its wings spread wide like a giant bat, its stones black with soot. The unshattered windows were warped, the shattered ones covered in plastic. Lines of laundry hung from sill to sill, reds, blues, browns, greens, shocks of yellow and gold. The flags of their new country.

"Seventeen hundred souls left," said the mayor. "That's why we moved up here, put ourselves in one spot. Took some doing, the way the state left the place. Still parts of the building we can't use. But enough left to keep us all out of the rain."

"Does it ever bother you? Being here?" the captain said.

"You mean because of the history? I don't believe in ghosts, Captain. It's just an old building, fields, and trees. That's all." She was taking them down a long hallway through the east wing. Paint cracking off the walls, chips falling as they walked. "You find some sad things now and again. You know, the straps. But they didn't build this place out of hate. They were just trying to help. It was just that the *building*—the building, and the patients, I suppose—got away from them."

Like the castle in Binghamton, Sunny Jim thought. He had run away from Lisle to go there, go and get his sister, after what she did to her father. Ridden his bicycle until both tires blew from the rocks on the roadside, then ditched it and walked the rest of the way. Made it all the way down there and stood outside the wire fence guarding the ruined castle, the newer brick facility nearby, sickly in the street lamps' yellow light. He could not bring himself to go in, just stood out there and felt the hills moving in on him. Tried to understand what his sister had been talking about. How the shadow could get into you, at the bottom of the valley, in the places where the trees died young. After a while one of the nurses took him by the arm, made him call someone in Lisle who still had a phone. His cousin came to get him and he suffered through the ride back to his house. They could not find his bicycle on the road.

He did not go in his house for four days. Lay in the yard at night, looking at the black stand of trees across the road. Wished with all he had that he would be taken as his sister had been. But it never happened. He woke in the morning covered in dew, his father yelling that he better come inside, a plea blooming into threat.

"It's getting away from us, too," the mayor said. "But we do the best we can with it."

At the tip of the hospital's wing, building scraps lay in spiky piles. Dark beams, water-stained and studded with nails. Sheets of plywood, some sides still square, the others ragged and splintered. Flapping walls of vinyl siding. A paneled blue door half-split down the middle. A cracked glass doorknob loose and shining on the screw. A sign that once hung from a porch. A painting of a boy in a raincoat in a little red boat, fishing line in the water. Everything of their town they could pull from the Susquehanna before the current carried it off.

"Help yourself," the mayor said.

"What do you want for it?" the captain said.

"Nothing," the mayor said. "We have more here than we can use." She did not finish the thought aloud: in the time we have left.

The crew clambered over the piles, picked up boards, a sheet of wrinkled metal, hefted it all in their hands. Waved at each other. They were throwing the pieces in the hallway to sort through them when the captain put up a hand.

"Wait," she said, and picked through the pile herself. The crew looked at each other. As if on cue, rolled their eyes.

"There's no time to be sentimental," one of them said.

"There's no time not to be," the captain said. She took the best pieces from her crew's hands, put them in a small stack. Found a plank with the name of the town stamped into it, a date centuries old. The surface of the wood warped and smoothed. If only she were more clever, she thought, she might find ancient fingerprints, signs of birth and murder. The story of the dead town in the grain.

"You sure there's nothing we can give you for this?" she said.

The mayor winced, then opened her arms. Why are we still talking like this? Still pretending? "Take it," she said. "It's yours."

They were out of the building when Sunny Jim remembered the note in his pocket. He took it out, unfolded it, gave it to the mayor.

"Do you know what happened to this person?" he said.

The mayor read it, did not look up.

"How do you know her?"

"I don't. I'm asking for someone else."

"I see."

" . . . "

"She died," the mayor said. "Tuberculosis. Eight months ago. Which in some ways was a blessing. If she'd seen what the river did to her house, it would have broken her heart."

As it broke mine, the mayor thought. To see what had happened to her town after all she had done. She had been mayor for two years, elected to her husband's seat after he was conscripted, killed by a mine in Virginia. For the first year, she was in thrall to anger. First that the news had taken so long to reach her, that there was no way to mourn him right. He was cremated along with six other casualties, all the ashes scattered in the Occoquan River days before she knew he was gone. He would have wanted the Susquehanna, she thought, not something in the boiling south, the name of which she was unsure even how to say. Had they told her sooner, she could have come, just to see him off. Tied a fresh line from her to him so they could find each other later. But they did not give her this, and he was gone, into the hurricane-whipped Atlantic. In her dreams, he was drowning out there, over and over, tossed by sixty-foot waves of white brine under a black sky split by frantic lightning, and her too far away to save him. Then she was angry at the war, treated it like a dog that had maimed a child. Chased off recruiters with a pistol, shot one of them in the calf just to make a point. You are not welcome here. Then she turned to the last of her town, so many more women than men, and there was no one left to be angry at but herself. For wasting so much time. For fighting. For letting hours slip by her unremembered. For not memorizing more of his face. And at last her anger burned out, left her blackened and brittle for a month. If she went outside, the wind could have disassembled her, the gentlest touch turned her to smoke.

But her husband had not married her because she was weak. She pulled herself out of the ashes, made the town her husband and child. Did not flinch when the Susquehanna came for it. They say she saved eight lives herself, running down the hill in the night as the water was taking pieces away. Broke windows and yelled at the sleeping people. Dragged one of them up to higher ground herself, because the poor woman's legs would not work after she watched the river eat her house. Then the mayor gathered them all on the curb where Route 11 curved up the valley out of town, told them what she had in mind for them. Felt a thrill of pride that first day at the state hospital, though the paint on the walls had shredded like tissue paper and there were long puddles in the hallways. Between the highway and the river was her kingdom. They would work its land, mend its cracking walls, fix the roof before the heavy rains came, and the war would never hold dominion over any of them again.

"Melody Juniper was a good woman," the mayor said.

"I'm sure she was," Sunny Jim said.

"Do you mind me asking you a personal question?"

"No."

"Why are you still alive?" the mayor said.

"I was protecting my boy." Then saw what she was asking. "My wife did the fighting. I stopped a long time ago."

"Is your wife with you?"

"Yes. Should be back any day now."

". . ."

". . ."

"My husband, too," the mayor said. "Where's your boy now?"

"With my sister. I'm going to get him. It's why we're going north, even though . . ."

"Yes," the mayor said. "Even though."

Sunny Jim turned a small scrap of wood over in his hands. Looked at the floor, then back up. A woman in a nightgown was coming down the hall, dragging a girl in a wooden wagon behind her. The girl had her hands over her face, her tangled hair spilling over her fingers.

"Maybe you should get going," the mayor said. Keeping her voice as even as she could, hoping Sunny Jim could tell it was hard.

The woman smiled at the mayor. "So nice to see you. Who is this?"

"Someone passing through."

"Going north or south?"

"North," Sunny Jim said. He had not understood how the mayor was trying to protect him. Now it was too late.

"North?" the woman said. Turned to Sunny Jim. "Why?"

"To get my boy," Sunny Jim said.

"Say no more. I understand. This is my daughter here in this wagon. I think." Streaks of worry cutting the smile away. "How far north is he?"

"Just fifteen miles or so north of Binghamton."

"You don't have much time," she said.

"Then you've seen it?"

"Oh, yes."

"What is it? What's happening?"

She stared at the ceiling, put her hand over her mouth. "Everyone wants to know, don't they? What's happening up there."

"Please tell me," he said. "Please."

She looked at him again. "What can I say? There are no words. It's as if the land is giving up to the sky. As if it's falling asleep and its dreams are coming for us. Do you understand?"

He was backing away. "I just want to get my son."

"But you won't make it in time, and your son will see

it all. The sky peeled open, showing its true self. He'll look up into it and laugh, just before the lightning takes him."

"That's enough," the mayor said.

"And the house he was in? The wind will blow it all away. It will blow until there is nothing left. Nothing."

"I said enough," the mayor said.

"But he has to face it all soon, face it all and be done with it." She turned to Sunny Jim. "How else are you going to be good for him?"

"I don't know!" Sunny Jim said. The girl opened her hands, lifted up her head. He could not read her face, could not tell if she had one. She was disappearing into the air, the light from the windows moving over and through her. It was all loosening, coming apart, the people around him and the windows and the walls, dissolving into a thrashing darkness that rushed toward and over him. He could not find his hands, his arms, his legs. A last thought, flung to the edge of the drowning world: Aaron, I'm so sorry I failed you.

Then he was in the hall, stretched on the floor. The mayor standing over him, putting out her hand. "I think you need some rest," she said. "I'm sorry."

"Do you believe her?" he said.

"I think everything is always ending and beginning again," she said. "It's just that we all know about it this time."

"You have to believe that, don't you? To do everything you've done."

"It's not a question of whether I have to. I do."

They pointed the hole in the *Carthage* away from the current, and five of the crew spidered over it with hammers and nails, a crowbar, a bucket of glue, and a brush. The light was bleeding out of everything by the time they were done. The remains of Danville a ragged shadow, the river turning thick and oily. As if it had watched for any mistakes the crew had made, was remembering where the flaws were, the fatal weaknesses. Soon, the river thought, it would feel the inside of that vessel. There would be an explosion, and the fire would let the water in. Let it pour in and flow down the stairs, spread along the theater floor, then force all the air out, fill in all that space, until the tables were floating on the burning ceiling, legs dangling. It would creep through the flaming hallways, force its way under doors, take anyone it found. Then the river would take the ship in its liquid hands and break it against the rocks, the tips of islands. The water swelled with the anticipation of it, and Faisal Jenkins felt it, turned the boat's bow into the stream a little. We are still here, the pilot thought. But the river had not told him anything yet.

The con artist found Sunny Jim as soon as he was back on the boat. "So?" he said.

"So," Sunny Jim said.

"Did you find her?"

Sunny Jim took a good long look. Saw the hope and dread on the man's face. He did not know why, could not have guessed that the con artist's past with Melody Juniper was so complicated. But he understood that the man was looking for forgiveness. Knew, too, that the truth was too much, that the con artist was not ready to bear it, not yet, maybe not ever. They were all grieving so much for the days they would never get. Why grieve, too, for the ones they had already lost? So Sunny Jim decided to lie. Give him news that would let the man put down what he was carrying and be lighter. Even if it meant stripping away his pride. There was no time left for that anyway.

"She found someone else," Sunny Jim said. "Found someone else and then took off. For Kentucky. They say she was pregnant when she left."

It was a good lie. The con artist's lips narrowed, his eyes grew glassy. Then he was pumping Sunny Jim's hand, thanking him over and over. Sunny Jim did not know what to say. He could see Aline shaking her head. Feel her, still, reaching for him from the water.

The House

WHEN MERRY WAS TWELVE and Sunny Jim was ten, Matt Robinson, Henry's second cousin, skidded off the highway during a torrential rainstorm. His car sliced along the guardrail for thirty yards, then eased over it belly-up and took the short muddy slope down to the river. From there, it rolled three times, coming to rest on its roof in the river. The car began to fill with water, and Matt Robinson, concussed, suspended upside down with a compound fracture in his arm and a broken collarbone, could not escape it. They found him with his head submerged, his feet by the pedals, his sneakers still dry. Matt Robinson was difficult, stuck with an argument as though his feet were nailed to it. But he was also the valve in the boiler, kept Henry out of a bad fight more than once. Put his hand on his younger cousin's shoulder, said hey, look. It's just not worth it. Henry, who was twelve years old like Merry, bawled at Matt's funeral as if he were six again. Spent a month afterward wondering how he was going to stay alive.

Sunny Jim saw ever less of his sister, but he heard the stories. Your sister is crazy, the Wallace brothers told him in front of the Lisle Inn, Henry Robinson and Joe Thule nodding.

"Shut up," Sunny Jim said.

"Crazy, crazy," the brothers said again, and Sunny Jim tackled them, pinned one Wallace to the ground and hit him in the face five times before the other Wallace and Joe Thule pulled him off. Henry Robinson then hit Sunny Jim in the stomach four times, wanted blood, but Joe Thule stopped him. Turned to Sunny Jim with what Sunny Jim recognized even then as pity. "She is, you know," he said.

She was hunting more by then, much more. Stepped into the woods with a knife and a rifle, six rounds of ammunition. An orange wool hat, a thick jacket, a blanket rolled up and tied on her back. She vanished for four days at a time, when it was just cold enough to make their great-grandmother remember stories of winter. My parents told me there used to be so much snow that it was hard to believe it fell from the sky, she said. Easier to imagine it coming up out of the ground. But Sunny Jim could not picture it. Had only read about snow in books. On the fifth day, Merry always came back, a small grin on her face, with half as much ammunition. Her knife a little duller. Once, a single neat, oblong stain of blood on her pant leg, above her knee.

You have to stop going out there like that, Sunny Jim wanted to say. You don't hear what they say about you. He followed her once into the woods, watched her bed down in a pile of leaves, the rifle's barrel lying across a fallen log. He did not see the deer, just a tensing in her muscles that didn't disturb the leaves around her, a slight cock of her head. The rifle barrel pivoted, emitted a single shot, and a halting crash tumbled from the underbrush. Then a stillness, and his sister rose, the knife already unsheathed. Threw a quick glance over her shoulder, that wan smile again, and though she did not seem to see him, he understood at once that she knew he had been there all along. Knew, too, that he would not stay for the butchery.

The house was half-empty, all the aunts and uncles gone. The grandparents and great-grandmother on the second floor with Sunny Jim, Merry, and their parents. The third floor abandoned but for their cousin, who moved from room to room in the spring, trying to convince the insects that the floor was still inhabited. They were not fooled. He found a chain of spider nests in the molding along the ceiling of the corner room. They had built a city over his head while he slept. His rap on a window frame broke the painted surface, revealed how termites had hollowed it out and died, and flies infested the space. He heard a rustling in a mattress one day, saw a small ridge rise and fall under its skin. When he cut it open, centipedes streamed from the wound while a horde of arthropods swarmed beneath, turning the mattress to soil. For a year, something bigger than a squirrel lived in the attic. Only Merry would go up to see what it was, but when she came back down, she would not say what she had found.

The rage in Sunny Jim's parents was by then a demon in the house. It hid in the walls, in the cracks in the floors, then roared out and smashed chairs, upended tables. Pushed a hand through the kitchen window. Howled through the place for hours, then spent itself and withered back into the wood. Sunny Jim's father went to the veterinarian's house twice, came back once with an angry track of stitches running from his hairline to the bridge of his nose. How did that happen, the veterinarian had said. You don't want to know, the father said. Yes I do, the veterinarian said. But the father would not tell him.

At last, there was a fight that threatened them all. Sunny Jim's parents were already screaming when Sunny Jim came home. He stood there in the middle of the floor while his parents tore around him. A chair splintered, and Sunny Jim's father lifted the jagged leg high, began to bring it down. Aiming for Sunny Jim's mother, seemingly unable to see his son. Sunny Jim had time to crane his neck upward, see the club bearing down on him. Then a flash of blood, and another. The chair leg spun in the air, and his father brought his hand down, clutched it in the other one, jammed both between his legs. Long streams of red shot down the cloth of his pants toward the floor. Two bullet holes had tunneled into the wall behind him. Two of his fingers lay half curled at his feet. And Merry stepped in, the rifle on her shoulder. Did not hesitate.

"Try to hit him again, and I'll do the eyes next time," she said. Smiled as if she'd enjoyed herself, and off to Binghamton she was shipped.

Sunny Jim did not see her again for two years. His parents would not let him, tried at first to scare him with stories of the place she had been sent to. They tie the children down in there, they said. Tie you down so you can't move for hours. Your sister is very sick, they told him, but did not explain how tying her down would make her better.

His cousin left the house after he picked Sunny Jim up outside the castle, decided to depart with a flourish. Bad enough that they had to put one of your kids in the crazy house, he told Sunny Jim's father. Now your other kid's trying to get in all by himself? I have better things to do, he said. He had parked his truck facing the road, heaped the truck's bed with everything he owned. A bundle of clothes, a flapping mattress. A record player that never had a needle. A pair of hunting rifles his father had given him. Then all they could see of him were the headlights of the truck, swinging around the bend toward the bottom of the hill. They learned later that he'd made it to Atlanta, died in a knife fight over a girl, a small sum of money. No one knew what became of the rifles.

Sunny Jim only understood how long Merry had been away when she came back. He had trouble recognizing her. She had grown hips, breasts. Her face had slimmed and her eyes darkened. Her hair was shorter, perhaps a different color. It was hard to be sure. Her mother was waiting for her on the porch steps, stood when the car grumbled on the gravel in the driveway. Put out her arms when Merry opened the passenger side door and climbed out, but made her walk across the lawn to her embrace. Her father trailed behind. He had gone to Binghamton to get her, driven her back to Lisle. But it was unclear whether he had even touched her.

"What was it like in there?" Sunny Jim said.

"Crazy," she said.

Dim hallways lit by waning fluorescent bulbs. The generator coughing and grinding outside her window. A row of broken window frames covered in plastic and tape. Someone kept poking holes in it to let the rain spit in. The other patients wandering the halls, like livestock, she thought. Like geese. Until one of them lunged, attacked another, scrambled on the floor. Or threw himself into the walls, shouts rising into a keening yelp. Then the orderlies and nurses descended, pinned him to the floor. Four-point restraints were so common that the kids in the ward put their dolls in them. Merry was strapped down a few times, for defending herself from Randolph, another patient who said he liked her. She put a fork in his hand, added six months to her stay. But after that, he left her alone, and she started getting herself out. Laid low. Said the right things. I know what you're doing, a nurse told her once. You're just playing the game. Merry looked to the side, stifled a smile. If that's what I'm doing, she said, do you think it's working?

In the evenings, a clacking projector showed movies on a stained sheet hanging from the wall, the scratches on the lens fogging the picture. Someone had gone at it with the tip of a pen. Warbling sound through a crackling speaker. Once a week, a bearded man on the staff pulled out a guitar, stood in the middle of the cafeteria, and belted out old folk songs. Forcing his voice into a strength it did not have. The patients circled him in a tightening spiral, murmuring and yelling along, mixing obscenities into the lyrics. From the door, where Merry watched, it was as if the patients were coming in to feed. The music had already ended in injury twice, but the bearded man persisted. It's helping them, he said. I know it is.

"I tried to see you," Sunny Jim said.

"Mom and Dad told me. I'm glad they wouldn't let you in."

"Why?"

"It wasn't safe."

"But they told me you were safe there."

"They lied."

Her parents forbade Merry from ever touching a gun again, but they could not control her, did not realize how little she slept. Sunny Jim only caught her because she made a mistake, a noise in the hall that roused him, though he could not say what it was. A falling glass. A car crash. Then he saw her in the doorway, a finger to her lips. Don't tell Mom and Dad, she said. But you can come with me if you want. She floated down the stairs. He drafted in her wake.

The rifle was waiting for her in the shadow of a tree. They moved out into the blunted fields. It was late fall. The land was high with crisp stalks of grasses that grew and burned out, dead where they stood and surrounded by tall woods. The trees thick around them, shivering with leaves. No moon. They waded to the middle of the field and stopped. She made him sit down and he looked up at her, could tell even in the near dark that her eyes were closed.

"What are we doing out here?"

She rapped him on the head with her free hand to shush him, then raised the rifle. Cocked her head, though there was no noise he could hear. Steadied the gun at once and shot, pivoted and shot, shot, shot. Turned and shot. Sunny Jim's heart beat once. Then the sound of five birds falling, bodies thudding into the weeds.

"How did you do that?" Sunny Jim said.

She did not answer, did not have to.

"Where is the shadow man now?" he said.

She lowered the gun, put a hand to her chest.

"Right here," she said. "All the time."

The River

AFTER DANVILLE, THE TREES crowded the banks again, hung their branches over the current as the *Carthage* passed among the bones of bridges. There were towns in the hills somewhere, cracked highways following the valleys. But the people on the *Carthage* could see nothing, hear nothing. As if we had all left already, and the land was eating the abandoned houses. Reaching under the roofs to pry them off, pressing against walls and windows until they broke and the ants and spiders could swarm in. The plants and insects were marauders, come to raze and pillage, to colonize spaces they would occupy for the next thousand years, even after the Big One came and went.

That night, a thunderstorm shredded the sky, dragged knives across the river's skin, sent bolt after ragged bolt of lightning to scar the hills, a message from the north and west. From the hold, they could hear the monkeys screaming on the shore. The monsoon roaring to life again. The storm before the storm. In a few weeks, the pilot thought, the space within the ship's hull would be the only dry place around, for as long as the monsoon lasted. They would drop the anchor and repair to the theater, fire up all the lanterns, and wait, like they did every spring when the rains came. By the end of that season, strangers would be friends, friends become lovers. All the quarrels they'd had and worked out. The hands of the weather would pull them tighter together, and though it meant that the pilot's heart had been broken a dozen times, the tightening was worth the sundering later. Perhaps they could convince themselves that was all the storm was then, just a bigger monsoon.

But then the river spoke at last, told him what Judge Spleen Smiley had been asking about all the way from Harrisburg. Showed him his first glimpse of a flock of souls surging into the air, leaving the boat behind in rising water. The heart of the storm was coming, Faisal Jenkins now knew, but the *Carthage* would not see it.

In the gray mist of the next morning, six rafts piled with clothes and furniture and milling with people passed the *Carthage* on their way downstream. The people shouted and waved their arms, trying to tell the pilot something, but they were already gone before he could hear. Then, all at once, the river was filled with boats. A family of eight and all that they possessed, piled onto a raft made from the side of a garage. Another family on a piece of roof, the mother and son with long poles in the water, the daughter asleep on a pyramid of clothes. A rowboat holding three boys, a dog, and the salted remains of a half-butchered calf. Thirty-seven people crowded onto a plastic barge, taking turns standing and sleeping, sitting cross-legged on the roof, one of them blowing into a rough clarinet made from a pipe, another pattering on a plastic bucket for percussion. A lone man in a bright blue tub. It was unclear if he was wearing any clothes. They all parted around the *Carthage* as they passed, punting with metal poles and shovels. Reached out and put their hands on the *Carthage*'s hull, as if offering benediction. The *Carthage*'s children leapt from the rails to swim among the passing boats, hitch rides for almost the length of the ship, then reach for a rope thrown by a friend, wavering like a snake in the water.

"Where are you from?" Elise called.

Scranton, they called. Wilkes-Barre. Then shouts of warning, of despair. The war had come there, it was there now. Don't go. Do not go. And then they were gone, and it was only the *Carthage* and the river again, as if there were no war at all. The wave of corpses came an hour later.

※ ※ ※ ※

IT WAS NIGHT, AND still. The dark gray outlines of the hills to either side. Not a star or moon in the sky. No wind. The water in front of the ship a sheet of smoky glass, murmuring as it slipped past the hull. The river still whispering to the pilot, but too low for him to hear. It was easy to think the river was cruel, teasing him, playing with him and everyone he knew. But his mother, his grandmother, had taught him better than that. The river was just a river.

He heard the tap of boots behind the pilothouse, could tell who it was without turning.

"Hey. You have any more of that coffee left?" he said.

"Sorry, my man," Judge Spleen Smiley said. "Saving it for a rainy day."

"They're all rainy days now, chief."

"Point made, but still no coffee. Got you some whiskey, though."

"Not tonight," the pilot said.

Judge Spleen Smiley lost his smile. "You got the message."

"Yes. The *Carthage* won't make it to the end of the season."

"Ah."

". . ."

"When's it going to happen?"

"I don't know."

"But you'll tell me, right?"

"Yes."

"We have a deal."

"Of course."

"Because I want to be here when . . ." He waved his hand north. "I want to see it. Hear it. Because I have this theory, see."

"That it isn't really happening. That it's just another storm. That if we hadn't heard the news, we'd never know the difference between it and the monsoons we've always had. I've heard those already."

"No, no. I don't believe any of that. It's real and it's coming. But I think it will be beautiful."

"Are you giving up on me?"

"No, no," Judge Spleen Smiley said. "It's a good world we have here, even with what we've done to it, and I'll be sorry to see it go. I just think that what's coming might be better."

"..."

"It has to be better."

"I think your music has gone to your head," the pilot said.

"Maybe. I just want to hear it coming."

"I don't think you'll have a choice."

"There's always a choice, my man."

"..."

"Listen to us," the judge said. "You'd think we've been friends for years."

"I don't even know your real name, Judge."

"That's okay." He laughed. "Neither do I, anymore."

"..."

"So, are you staying with the ship?" the musician said.

"Yes."

"I'll miss you."

"I'll miss you, too."

But they are always here with me.

※ ※ ※ ※

THE FERRIS WHEEL CURVED high over the trees on the north bank, an arc of yellow and red, a long chain of white lights. Carnival machinery tilted toward the clouds, rose and fell, blurred in a haze of smoke colored by neon as if in a grainy film, a projection of a fair decades ago. The illusion lasted until they heard the screams and cries, straining chords. A child's long wail. A chorus of fireworks shot above, exploded into a garden of fire, illuminating the water, the ship, the five peaks around the town, in sheets of green, blue, purple.

"Is this Shickshinny?" Captain Mendoza said.

"Where else could we be?" Elise said. "But I don't remember it like this."

I don't remember anything like this, the captain thought. The sense that everything was turning to smoke, to light. Keeping its shape only as a matter of luck. She had found herself, in the last few days, touching her own forehead with three fingers, examining the texture of the skin, the hardness of the skull beneath. Thankful that it was still there. The boy from the camp seemed to understand. He was sleeping better, the first mate said, maybe too well. Ten, twelve hours. Had begun to play with the other kids on the ship. Soccer, a frantic frolic in the water. A game of hide-and-seek through the *Carthage*'s dark halls, during which one of them burned an arm in the boiler room, lay in her bed with bandages from wrist to shoulder, trying to ward off infection. The boy was lying on the deck now, faceup toward the fireworks. Eyes wide open, chest heaving. As if the blooming color was a gate opening, and something was walking through it that only he could see.

"Do you still want to go?" the captain said.

Elise looked at Andre: the ship's child, the deck his nation. The place where his girl was. She had seen them, walking back onto the deck from somewhere darker, their clothes rearranged. Trying not to hold hands. And she had seen the looks they gave each other, eyes flashing and darkening, charging the air. It was hitting him so hard, the poor boy. She understood, for she had felt it herself, that jumping spark. Still felt a little of that thrill when something her son said, something he did, reminded her of his father. It was going to hurt him to be taken from the ship, from that girl and her green eyes, her small hands. But he would survive it, and she could not let him go.

She let him say good-bye to her, then made him climb into a small boat facing the shore. The girl stood at the rail, unmoving. For the space of two breaths, the mother felt guilty, for she had broken her son's heart. Looked back at the girl, trying to communicate to her. You will see. When you have a child of your own, you will see. Then she took his hand, turned away, and did not look back.

The shore was thrown into shadow by the lights beyond it. She thought at first that it was choked with the wreckage of a building, then realized it was a pile of rafts and small craft, scattered across the rocks and mud, tangled in the exposed roots. A dozen bodies twisted into the debris. She rowed until she could not get any closer to the shore, then dropped an anchor, put a leg over the side into the water.

"Come in," she said to her son. He was looking at the bodies.

"I don't want to go. I heard gunshots."

"Those are fireworks."

"I know the difference."

"Come on."

"What do we need to find Monkey Wrench for anyway?"

If you couldn't find me, she thought, you would understand. But she knew it was unfair to say it. "Just come on," she said.

They waded to shore together through the crowd of boats, then up to the line of trees, of damp sandbags. Broke through to the marshy field between the town and the river. It was ablaze with light, thick with smoke and people. The carnival rides swung overhead, dropping rust, joints creaking, engines screaming too loud. With a wrenching hoot, a car carrying three people bent from its frame, fell seventeen feet to the ground, crushed its passengers. The crowd first dispersed, like water disturbed by a stone, then flowed back in again. The people waiting in line stayed there, brushed the rust off their shoulders. Only flinched a little when another car careening over them shuddered downward. A gun went off behind them. Another, another. A short burst of machine-gun fire. Weeping. On the midway, a man cutting a zigzag through the dirt, holding a bottle by its neck, sidled up to Elise, put his hand on her shoulder, and said, is this a party or what?

Just off the midway, still in the glow of its lights, a horde of people were hopping on one leg, shaking as if in a fit. Behind them, four bodies lay on a long white sheet, weak surprise on their frozen faces. Another carnival ride stuttered and whined, and a ripple of violence swept over the crowd, a crest of gunshots and shouting that flew through them and was gone. Three of the dancers fell, and one crawled away out of the light. His legs shuffled in the dust and then did not move.

Under the shriek of the machines, Elise and Aaron could hear wailing. They ran, then, mother and son, out of the field, until they were crouching next to a brick building, in the glass-strewn mud under the branches of a wide, old tree. The tree surveyed the chaos as if from a hundred miles away. It could wait.

"Mom, why did you bring me here?"

"It was never like this."

"It's because we're back before the war's over, isn't it. Because the war's still here."

This is not just the war, she thought. "It'll be over soon," she said.

"How do you know?"

"I just do."

"No, Mom. How do you know?"

She turned on him. I don't, she thought. I don't even know if we're going to be alive next week. I don't know anything anymore, and I can't bear the thought of watching you die. She kept herself from saying it, but her eyes sharpened with the effort, got much sharper than she had intended, and her hands shook. Andre saw it and was a small boy again, a kid who had fallen and hurt his arm, who had broken a good toy. Trying to be brave.

"I'm so sorry," she said. "I didn't mean it." She had not known she still had such power over him. Felt a flash of embarrassment that he had seen her like that. Getting away from herself.

The street leading to the center of town was clogged with tents, shacks with thin metal walls. Houses to either side with porches full of people, piles of belongings slipping toward refuse. Small fires everywhere. The smells of burning wood, burning paint, melting plastic. A blue-gray gauze thrown across the air. Three brothers standing against the side of a house, trying to sleep, their arms around each other. A corpse, swaddled in a dark blue sheet, lying on the cracked pavement. One mourner kneeling next to it, her hand on the covered forehead. She did not make a sound. They were all refugees from upstream, kept asking Elise if she had any food, a roll, a potato. A carrot for a child. There was not enough to go around, they said. When the rest ran out, things could start to get ugly.

She looked toward the low wooden buildings in the valley, the stone bank building, the white church nestled against the cliff, growing from the earth like a tooth. The houses in tight knots along roads tangled in the hills. The canal running by the school. They would take this place apart, she thought. It could not withstand their hunger.

Goodbye, beautiful town. Every Sunday, the Baptists used to cram into the church up the hill, park their cars all over the road in front, and sing loud inside. She'd kissed a man by the canal once, put her hand on the back of his head, got up on tiptoes to be closer to him. Andre still a baby, lashed to her back and dreaming, fidgeting against her. Perhaps in his head he was flying, like the birds he had seen, though he could not yet walk. You saved me, she said to the place. Me and my son. I'm so sorry I can't save you. And the town answered: Don't worry, child. I am already moving on. I always was.

The sun had not quite risen when they reached the West Side Ballroom. In the light leaking through the clouds, it was possible to imagine that it was as she had left it. The streaks left by fire only shadows across the walls that would soon be erased by the light. But the door was on one hinge, askew on the frame. The scent of charred vinyl and timber. The flames were recent visitors, harbingers.

Elise recognized nothing in the front room. The damage done in the years she'd been gone. The carpet had turned to ash, the furniture burned to bones. The ceiling half-eaten, the remaining half buckled, its seared edge hanging like a taloned hand. Andre began to cough, drew in a wheezing breath to cough again. The room pushed its way into him, into the walls of his lungs. She may have cut months off the end of his life, she thought. Then thought of what was coming, and stopped worrying.

But the back room was as she remembered. Her first night there, sleeping on the floor, the parties in the parking lot. Andre at thirteen months, his first steps goaded and cheered by a room full of drunk musicians. Come here, little dude, you can do it, one of them said. And another, to her: is this really his first steps, right here? Is this the shit right here? Andre at two years, when everyone in the world was in the third person. His small hands around her thumbs as she lay on the floor and he climbed her angled knees, stood up, then leaned into her hands and balanced there, his feet in the air. Andre at seven, the flash of the soles of his sneakers as he crawled into a drainage pipe, shimmied through to end up under a grate in the lot. Called up to the people walking by, laughed when she told him how dangerous it was. All at once, she was crying and hugging her grown boy, running her hands through his hair. He did not like it, was too old for it. She did not care.

"Mom. Mom—"

They saw the gun's barrel first. Then the man behind it.

"Are you kidding me?" Monkey Wrench said. "Are you kidding me?" He dropped the gun and ran forward, lifted them both in his arms, his big hands on their backs.

"I tried to keep it together," he said. "But I couldn't do it."

"You did do it," she said. "Don't you see? Here we are. You did it."

So they ended as they began. The Big One was almost upon Shickshinny when I found them there. I could see it beginning to fall onto the five peaks, a great wave cresting and crashing. The first rain just threads of gray drifting on the streets, the houses, the stoplights, the churches. The river flowing dark and flat. The lightning over the next hill starting fires, the smoke mingling with the clouds. A distant roar. I took the last ten miles of highway to the West Side Ballroom, past the empty supermarkets and dollar stores, past quiet houses, abandoned auto dealerships. Saw the sign for Zephyr Plaza even before I saw the rising smoke. They were all outside, Elise, Andre, Monkey Wrench, twelve others who had found their way back. They had enough food for a few more days, a fire in a wide pit. A pot suspended over the flames, the cooking warm and sweet. You could see the good coming from there, see it flowing over the land. A woman sang a slow song I could not recognize, the melody floating and swooping, backed up by a man picking at a guitar with four strings left. The talk, then, of those who were not there, who did not make it, and Elise and Andre spoke of the *Carthage*, the years they had spent aboard that ship. The captain. The revelers. The musicians. Even Sunny Jim and the priest. Just nodded when I told them what had happened to them all. The others told old jokes that they had already heard so many times, they could just repeat the punch lines, pieces of punch lines. Make them all ugly again. As soon as I get these pajamas off. They laughed all the same. It was almost upon them.

"You know you could go," I told them. "You still have time."

"We know," they said. "But we're already where we want to be."

✸ ✸ ✸ ✸

AS THEY PASSED SHICKSHINNY and neared Wilkes-Barre and Scranton, there were only trees again, trees and the cooling towers on the north bank, until the dikes rose to either side, the old grassy mounds submerged and the long ridge of concrete walls built atop them almost cresting. The hasty lines of sandbags sagged with rain. Holes and cracks from four springs ago, never fixed. Now they never would be, Captain Mendoza thought.

They all thought at first that the rippling gray ahead of them was another storm, and waited for thunder that did not come. Then the wind carried to them the whiff of char: sweet, earthy, tangy, bitter. As if ghosts were passing through the ship in turns. The smell grew until it had crawled into the lungs of everyone on the deck, and they wheezed and coughed with it, but stayed, made everyone below come up. For the valley was on fire, all of it, from the roads at the lip of the dikes to the buildings far beyond. The delis and the movie theaters, the social clubs and furniture stores. The banners stretched between the streetlights, fringed with red tinsel. WE LOVE OUR NEIGHBORHOOD. It was all burned or burning, the flames huge but taking their time, for nobody would stop them from their work, and there was so much left to consume.

In Baltimore, the captain had seen the cityscape from the bay after the fighting was through. It was a decaying mouth pried open, filled with blackened teeth. She had brought the *Carthage* in close to look for survivors. Called to the silent shore for hours. Nobody ever answered. At last she saw the corpses of three people lying on a dock, just a few feet from the water. They were charred into dark carbon, but she could see their arms around one another. They had been on fire, all three of them, and were trying to get to the water. They had al-most made it.

She looked at Wilkes-Barre, all fire before her. "How long will it take to get through this?" the captain said.

"A few hours," the pilot said. "There's a lot of debris in the river."

She looked ahead to Scranton. The heat, the flames, even brighter there.

"There's nothing here, is there," she said.

"No."

"I'm going to my quarters. Let me know when we're out."

The deck stayed crowded, for it was too much not to look at, these walls of rolling flame. The people stood there, calming their animals, trying to hush the birds, frantic in their cages. The first mate's boy sat close to the bow, letting the fire pour into his eyes, quieter than the first mate had ever seen him. Somewhere between the border of Wilkes-Barre and the place where the river turned north, the sun went down and the sky above the smoke darkened. No one noticed.

The House

AGAIN MERRY WAS IN the attic window, rifle across her lap, waiting, under a slate of gray clouds. She felt her legs falling asleep, shifted them. Then no movement at all. Her breathing too slow to see or hear, as it was when she was hunting.

Aaron sat on a mattress thrown on the planks behind her. Played with a plush monkey, a toy that had been his father's. He was bored again, had been bored for a long time, though it was leading to unexpected riches: He had become a good painter, a good plumber. She'd found him composing songs, unintelligible words riding melodies that rose and fell on a scale her ear could not decipher. But the pieces were consistent, they were as he intended, refined by repetition, unbeholden to an audience. He made them for himself. She loved it all, she had decided weeks ago, the music and the boy. It went beyond her brother now, the pact they shared. Beyond simple compassion. In her defense of Aaron, she decided, she would be like his mother. There would be no mercy.

"What are you waiting for?" Aaron asked.

She did not want to tell him the truth. "For the sun to come out," she said.

"Why do you need your gun for that?"

"I don't."

"Then why do you have it?"

"I always have it," she said, "to keep you safe."

A lone bird shot over the house, heading south. Two more. Eight. Then a giant whisper in the air, as of a wave approaching, and the sky was black with birds. Swarms of swallows, starlings, and sparrows, warblers and finches. Mobs of geese, herons gliding in pairs. Red-tailed hawks beating and keening. All of them crying at once, a general alarm sounding across the empty farms, fields turned to weeds and saplings, houses falling into the dirt. Animals ran on the ground before the wave in the air, and the earth seethed with bounding rodents and snakes. Aaron came to the window and saw the procession, gripped his aunt's shoulders with two long fingers.

"What are they doing?" he said.

"I don't know," she lied.

"There are deer and geese out there."

"Yes."

"Why aren't you shooting them?"

"I told you the gun was to keep you safe."

"Not eat?"

"We have enough food," she said.

"For how long?"

"Long enough." She could see that her answers dissatisfied him. He was starting to understand, but had not worked up the courage to ask the questions that would strip away the gauze of fiction that she had wrapped around him. In the story she kept telling, Aaron's father was coming soon, and together they would pack and go, far from this place to one where the word for war was never spoken, except in contempt. What did it get us? someone would say. Bullet holes in houses and school buildings. Bricks and broken glass scattered in the street. Empty bedrooms and unmarked graves. No more. A time of plenty was coming, a balm for the lean years they had just lived, and they would walk into them sure of step, never looking back, for deprivation's only useful lesson had been learned long ago. They did not need to know more.

The animals were still fleeing all around them, a heaving, crying darkness. They were not letting up. Merry looked at Aaron and then turned away. Soon he would be able to see how bad it was. What Merry was trying to protect him from. She could feel it herself: a magnetic pull north, a constant whisper, come away, come away. You have been on the earth too long already. She wanted to go as others yearned for children. Part of her, she knew, had left years ago, disappeared into the woods, dissolved into the fields at the top of the road's rise. Now the rest of her wanted to leave, too, with a final, ecstatic sigh. She would tell Aaron all of this, except that it would only frighten him. Would not prepare him for what was coming.

Hurry, Jim, she thought. I do not know how much time we have left.

The River

IN THE FIRST FIVE seconds that Sunny Jim was awake, he knew that Aline was there. She was on the floor with him, her legs curled beneath his, her lips at his ear, whispering to him. In his dream, her words had been so clear, but they were already falling from him, letters and sounds fading away. He would not catch them in time.

It was still night, but they had cleared the cities, turned with the Susquehanna when it cut north and the flames boiled its edges, covered it in ash. He could still smell the smoke, but only a slight tang, weakening in the eddies of cooler air. He dressed in the dark, went up on deck. The animals, which had brayed and lowed when the *Carthage* passed through the flames, were all sleeping. The cows lay in a huddle, the birds twitched in their cages. Near the bow, three women slumbered under a bundle of blankets, all wrapped together. A shirt strewn on the boards next to them.

We can never lose each other, Aline had said once. They were sitting in a corner of a tractor dealership that had become a flophouse and livestock pen. Hay about their feet, a heavy odor of pig excrement. Seven sows roaming the cement floor, knocking over children who picked themselves up without crying. Their parents joking and haggling. A woman in a pink vest boiled water over a propane stove, chopping onions and carrots on the cover of an old book. Aline was seven months pregnant with Aaron, leaning back against her husband. His hands clasped her belly.

"We won't," he said.

"No, I mean it," she said. Turned her head to stare at him. "We can't."

"I promise we won't," he had said then. But he had not seen her in so long. And he was trying so hard to remember now, but pieces of her were going already. Her face, when she tasted something sour. What she sang to Aaron when she bathed him. The feel of the soles of her feet in his hands. He could not hold onto all of it, and at once he was shaking. Aline, my girl, my darling. He rattled against the rail as though he would scream or retch, but instead dropped to his knees, hung his head. Felt the river moving beneath them, the vein from the heart of the north bleeding into the sea. He shut his eyes tight, was sure that if he looked up, he would see the life in the hills, the way they bucked and subsided under geology and weather, smothered the towns cowering in their hollows. The planet preparing for the next era without us. He would not mind going if the bullet came for him now, or the virus, or the lightning, if not for his son, his best boy.

He had not been ready for it, what being a father would mean to him. The night after Aaron was born, the boy was crying, screeching, his lungs letting out a sound that his throat was too small to bear, his will already too big for his body. He choked and gagged, the crying stuttering into a mockery of laughter. Little arms batted the air. Sunny Jim had no idea what to do. But Aline lay unconscious with exhaustion, bloodless, for the labor had been hard, and they had no medicine. In all the world, nobody awake but Sunny Jim cared about the child, nobody else even knew he was alive. So he picked Aaron up, held him close, and felt it, all at once, a wide expanse, annihilating and exhilarating, opening within him, leaping through him. The feeling would take him apart if he let it, and it was all for the infant screaming in his arms, the certainty that he loved this little boy so much that he would kill for him, die for him. It was the strongest thing he had ever felt, and Sunny Jim did not know how to use it. Could not figure out how to impart it to the child, to give him comfort. And so the son was unconsoled, and wailed until dawn.

I'm getting ready, son. I understand now. Please forgive me for taking so long.

"Are you sick?"

Sunny Jim turned. The boy from the camp.

"No. Just very tired."

"Why? It's morning."

Sunny Jim smiled at that. "Yes. But too early in the morning."

"My dad told me once that the water reflects the color of the sky."

"He did?"

"Yes. He said that the water was blue because the sky was blue."

"That sounds right."

"And it's gray when the sky is gray."

"That's true."

"But then why is the water gray when the sky is black?"

"I don't know," Sunny Jim said. "There must be light in the sky, even if we can't see it."

"That doesn't make any sense," the boy said.

Sunny Jim laughed, four short chuckles. The first time, he realized, since Aaron had left. "It doesn't, does it?"

"No. Because I see lights in the sky all the time."

"You do?"

"Yes." He pointed. "Right now."

"I don't see anything."

"Right there. And there. And there, too."

"Oh, now I see it," Sunny Jim lied. "It's pretty, isn't it."

"It's not pretty," the boy said. "It scares me."

". . ."

"I miss my dad."

"Well, I miss my boy," Sunny Jim said. He reached over, put his hand on the boy's shoulder, let it rest there. The boy did not flinch, curled his fingers around Sunny Jim's wrist. For a few seconds, they both felt it, their twin hurts finding a mate, and it lifted them up, them and the ship all around them, until the *Carthage* was rising above the river, throwing ropes of water back into the current. The Susquehanna was a ribbon of darkness unfurling itself across the Pennsylvania landscape, the hills, the first ripples of mountains, all bleached by the moon. Then they were through the clouds and they could see it all, a long wavering line to the north and west of them, a slow wave of darkness sparked by lightning, breaking across the earth. It was almost to Lisle, it had covered the towns that lay just north of the house already, and they could not see what lay beyond it. Without warning, Sunny Jim was crying again, a little. The boy pulled away, and they were back on the river, standing at the rail while the *Carthage* drew its wake in the current. They nodded to each other, as if to mark what they had seen, confirm what had passed between them, and then the boy left.Sunny Jim, went to sleep in the first mate's arms. Sunny Jim was awake to see the dawn.

❈ ❈ ❈ ❈

FOR A FEW MILES, high red cliffs to starboard, a slack beach of white stones to port. A stalled car rusting on the shore, the door on the driver's side open and falling off the hinges, the seats pooled with water. Gnats swarmed inside, two snakes curled in the passenger-side foot well. From Upper Exeter to Osterhout to Tunkhannock, they saw no one. Dogs and chickens strutting in the roads. A troop of monkeys colonizing a rooftop, the leader clambering to the top of the chimney. Garages open, patrolled by feral cats. Front yards littered with cardboard boxes, sagging suitcases, picture frames, instrument cases. The things people decided, when it was time at last to choose, that they could live without. Then the valley widened and the river flooded into the farm-land, became a plain of water divided by lines of trees where the underwater fields began and ended. The clouds thinned and the sun broke through for the first time since Harrisburg, and in the miles of water before Towanda, it was as if they were harvesting light. Everyone came out on deck to see it, tilted their faces sunward, smiling, threw out their arms. They could not help themselves. The revelers were bringing up their bags, multicolored canvases, painted wood, circular hat boxes lined with fur. They were milling about, kissing everyone. So wonderful to be with you, so wonderful to meet you, they said, and they meant it. The valley rose again and the plain diminished, the ship rounded the bend to Towanda, and Faisal Jenkins blinked. Once the river had washed away the bridge, but the people of Towanda had rebuilt it, made it into a drawbridge, a contraption of felled trees, steel beams, a metal grate. There was a blast from a horn, low and nasal, when the townspeople saw the *Carthage* coming, and the drawbridge rose, shuddering but secure, to let them through. Then there was the waterfront, the line of brick buildings, the cluster of roofs. The octagonal green dome of a church. Boats in the water, ferries and fisherman, riding the high current. Voices calling across it. To all but the revelers, it seemed a halluci-nation, a delusion. No holes in attics, no rows of shattered windows. No funeral lines or bells tolling. Only the death wrought by years and weather, the kind that sweetens the time we have once we become aware of it.

The horns at the drawbridge sounded again, answered

by more from the shore. People emerged from streets and alleys to mass at the town pier. The revelers clamored at the *Carthage*'s rail, shouting out names and waving. The captain could see already how it would be. As soon as the gangway was lowered, bodies would surge together, commingle on the pier in kisses and laughing. I'm so glad you made it. I'm so glad you're here.

The man with the green beard was on the deck, herding people, livestock, birds down to the pier. Captain Mendoza stood behind him, let him finish a chain of instructions, greetings, embraces, then took him aside. She could not contain her amazement.

"You told me it would be good," she said. "I had no idea it would be like this."

"Do you see now?" he said. "What's coming? We're not afraid of it here. When it sweeps over us, there will be no pain, and what's on the other side will be marvelous. So we're preparing for it, with food, with drink, with festivities."

"But how can you believe that?"

"Because we don't want to live any other way." He came in closer, softened his voice. "What's coming doesn't matter, see? It's how what we believe makes us live our lives now."

"..."

"You could join us, you know."

She could see it when he said it. They could tie the *Carthage* to the pier with chains, take it apart for the wood, the metal, build the foundations for the new city that was coming. There would be weeks of joyful anticipation, of gathering grains and pressing grapes, taking instruments from their cases. Dances in the streets that began slow, as the sun went down, and ended in a mad whirl of shouting and stamping, then a long sleep until noon. And when the edge of the storm passed over them and away, they would find each other and this world, grayed with war and weather, transformed in a swarm of color, everything that was and would be revealed to them at once. They would see the plan before them, drawn from the lines of the past and crackling with ecstatic shock, the final moment and the beginning that followed, the ragged ends of joy and sorrow, transcendence and dissolution, fused together, so that it no longer mattered which was which.

But she had people to take north, a duty to them, promises she'd made. There was her ship all around her, the crew skittering over the hull, spiders who never slept. The last years of her life, the history of the river, were all bound together in the ship's wood and glass. The people who came aboard and left, the parts of them that stayed forever, the spirits she brought back with her every time she saved a scrap of the world from destruction, were all talking to her all the time. She could not understand what she was, why she was here, without them.

"Do you want to come with us?" the man with the green beard said.

"I'm already there," the captain said.

The man with the green beard nodded, looked toward the shore. "We'll miss you," he said.

"See you soon," the captain said.

I love you.

I love you, too.

The musicians saw them off with a triumphant Dixieland number, hot stepping and hollering. It was the happiest stuff the captain ever heard them play. It was music made of laughter, the clarinet giggling and wheezing, the guffaws of the tuba, the chuckling accordion, everyone working too hard to catch their breaths. They were saying good-bye, pulling everything they could out of the minutes they had before their best audience was gone. Already, they could hear more music, rising in chorus from the shore, among the brick buildings, the ornate towers, the narrow streets. For the rumors were saying there were only a few days left, a week at most. There was no more need for labor, for hardship. Only time for the things they always wanted to do, the words they always wanted to say. When it came for them, they would turn their faces to it, smile, and open their arms wide. As they were doing for one another now.

As the *Carthage* rounded the next bend in the river and left Towanda behind, Sergeant Foote and the con artist looked across the flooded valley, the tips of rooftops peeking from the waves, colonized by cranes, and each of them wondered why they had not left the ship, joined the parade to shore. Lost the mission and the manipulation in the teeming crowd. After all that they had seen, they wanted to believe. But they did not know how to talk to each other about it.

But the man with the viola, the one from Clarks

Ferry Bridge, talked to me. He had been on the *Carthage* the whole time, from Millersburg to the camp to the attack at Sunbury, the fires at Wilkes-Barre and Scranton. He had seen what the storm wrought, what it was doing to everyone around him, and threw in his lot with the revelers. Got off the *Carthage* with them at Towanda. And he was there when the Big One came. It was like a vertical ocean, he said. The rain and lightning first seething in the sky, a few miles off, then falling over everything, the houses and cars, the brick buildings and churches, the dome, the courthouse. The rumble escalating into a roar. The party was huge by then, it was in the shops and the streets, in the basements and on the rooftops. And over the music and pounding feet a raging cheer tore from every throat, of thrill or panic, the man could not say. It was defiance. It was a prayer. They turned toward the wind and opened their eyes as the wave of rain swept over them, and some of them saw something in the storm, something beyond it, a lifting up, a deliverance. They were already going, part of them was already there. But all the man with the viola saw was the darkness, the lightning, and he thought of his sister, of the land farther south. He tucked the viola case under his arm and ran through the streets as the lightning chased him, found a car someone had left running and pointed it south, hit the gas until the rain stopped. Then he got out and looked back. There was no sign of Towanda, or land, or river. Only the storm was there, all the water and electricity in the world moving in on him. He thought of all those people back there, with envy and with dread, and kept driving. I still haven't found my sister, he told me later. I'm still looking.

✶ ✶ ✶ ✶

THAT NIGHT REVEREND BAUXITE was up, insomniac, witness to the ship's every creak and groan. How imperfect the vessel was. How ready it was to stop sailing. It was just waiting for something to break against. Something was coming for him, too, climbing out of the water. He could almost hear it, a gathering of voices, rushing forward. The roar of his church collapsing, the screams of those inside. He moved through the hallway, was halfway up the stairs to the deck when he closed his eyes, turned around. Was not surprised at what he saw when he opened them again.

"I was hoping I'd see you again," he said.

"They came in so quiet, the bombs," Talia said. "I didn't hear anything. I was praying. Then I was on fire. Now I'm here. I have news for you."

"What's that."

"I saw everything that is going to happen to you. Everything that's already happened to you on this ship. I saw it all, months before the war even started, and never told you. Should I have told you?"

"What would I have done with it?"

"That's why I never said anything. Forgive me, Father. There's still a place for our own desires and dreams in the plan, isn't there? I didn't know what you would do. And still don't, even with the news I have for you now."

"What do you want to say?"

"You won't live much longer," Talia said. "I mean, within three days."

"Will I see Aaron first?"

"No."

"Ah."

". . ."

". . ."

"Are you angry?" Talia said.

"No. I don't have any more time to be angry."

". . ."

"I just wish I had more time."

"I understand," Talia said. Then pointed up, toward the open door at the top of the stairs that framed the night sky. "The rumors about the storm are true. Yes, they are."

Clouds ripped across the sky. Beyond them, it was brighter. No, darker. No. He did not know. A rushing in Reverend Bauxite's ears. Something coming for him.

"Is that it?" Reverend Bauxite said.

"What gets you? No. Your death is much more mundane."

". . ."

"I'm sorry," Talia said.

"Don't be. You're only telling the truth."

The sound from the sky was already getting louder. The screams of multitudes from far away. Begging him to join them, though Reverend Bauxite did not want to go. Not yet. So he went back down to the cabin, where Sunny Jim was lying on his stomach on the floor. He shifted when Reverend Bauxite opened the door, sleep leaving him, too.

"Jim."

"What."

"We need to talk."

"Is everything all right?"

"It will be, I think," Reverend Bauxite said. "I just need to tell you some things."

He did not begin at the beginning. There was no need. For Reverend Bauxite, the things that mattered about his life, the things he wanted Aaron to know, were clear notes, as from chimes, sounding through white noise. The conditions of his epiphany, the way the door had opened in the trees. Being ordained on the banks of the river, the veins in the bishop's hands, the hitches in his voice. Talia, all his parishioners, and all he learned from them. How he thought he could hear God's voice the most in the hum of their everyday lives, the miracle of creation shown to him in glimpses and glimmers, the cracks between the smallest acts, fragments of imperfect glory. He was in awe that people could be so good, and through the fall of his church and the atrocities that followed, he kept that tiny revelation safe. He was sure, he told Sunny Jim, that believing it allowed him to see it, pull it out of others, and if he could give one thing to Aaron, it would be that. The ability to cast a circle, to build a house and gather friends, wherever he went.

"Why are you telling me this?" Sunny Jim said. "You can tell Aaron yourself."

"Jim. I'm not sure I'm going to make it."

"Of course you will."

"Just promise me you'll tell him."

"You're going to make it," Sunny Jim said.

"Promise me," Reverend Bauxite said. "He's my son, too. The closest thing I'll ever have."

"I promise," Sunny Jim said. Forgive me, Aline, he thought. I should have told you so much more.

The Highway

THE FRONT WAS LONG behind them, and for Ketcher, it was as if they had launched from a beach into the open ocean, from the ground into the sky. The road to Binghamton moved through close, steep hills, choppy swells in the land, and the truck did not like it. It was beyond complaining. The engine gave out a constant, sonorous grumble, now and then a long, wavering whine. Even the soldiers who knew nothing about cars could tell it was dying.

There was no resistance, no volley of fire from the highway's shoulders, no bombs planted in the pavement, but the road was coming apart anyway. Maybe it had been bad from the beginning. The winters, when there were winters, the shifting earth, broke the infant road's back as it was laid down. Years of patching with pebbly asphalt could not cover how it had been crippled, could not repair it anymore, and the land began to pry it apart. Trees crept closer, forced their fingers through the dried tar. The big rains floated sections of it away on a hillside softened into a wave of mud. The truck winced on every crack. For the last fifteen miles, the driver and commanding officer shared a conviction that they would not make it to the forward camp. Were relieved to be wrong.

The camp was a clot of wet, tattered tents around the broken building of the former welcome center at the state border. Five soldiers, slumped in the dawn behind a wall of sandbags on the highway, waved their rifles to usher the truck through. Buckets on the ground to catch rain. Trenches carrying water to the parking lot, sheened with three inches of brackish runoff. Six feet into the pond, a boot, lying on its side, as if trying to drink. The boys in the camp were thin, stooped. Not boys anymore. They shuffled in the mud, seemed not to notice the skin of dirt crawling up to their knees. They lay down on the patches of dry ground, appeared asleep but for their open eyes. Almost no speaking. Two of them led Tenenbaum to their commanding officer's table. Its legs rickety on the tile floor of the old building. Shattered glass and crumbled cinder blocks all around, uncleared.

"You're here," the commanding officer said.

"Yes," Tenenbaum said. "Are you?"

The commanding officer opened his mouth, but did not speak. Could not say how the last weeks had been. The hours, days, of waiting, of meaningless operation, before the coming push up the highway into Binghamton. The things they had seen in the sky at night. What they thought they'd heard. Eight of his men had killed themselves over it, the latest one just two days before. Slit his own throat with a piece of jagged metal he must have found in the trashed bathroom. They buried him the day after, the commander presiding. He watched the boy go down, wondered how he'd had the will to finish the cut. Realized, in a moment of revulsion, that he understood how he'd had the will to start it.

"No," he said. "We're not all here."

"I see."

"Do you? Do you really?"

". . ."

"Do you have any sense of when my men and I move?"

"A day," Tenenbaum said. "Two at the most."

The commander sighed. Something seemed to leave him that he did not want to go. "They'll be glad to hear it," he said. "We've been up here too long. Do you know what I'm saying to you?"

"Yes."

"Do you now?"

"No."

The four soldiers slept for five hours, walked out of the camp in the late afternoon. Left the highway behind for the small roads that followed the rivers. Joined a branch of the Susquehanna where it curled south from Binghamton into the steep, huddled hills. It took them another day to skirt the city, where the shooting was already starting. Ropes of smoke rising, chased by flares. The fading lights in the valley behind them, the darkness to the north. The wound in the firmament above them their compass needle. Then they were walking along the highway again and it was dark, darker than it had been for any of them in a long time. They walked off the road into the tall grass to put themselves down for the night, but it was too quiet to sleep. At first light they moved again, departed from the interstate to a road where all the houses leaned, sagging as if knocked out in a fight. Barns missing teeth, missing jaws, waiting for the final breath that would push them over. Cars in the driveways with their doors open, rain-soaked seats rank with mildew. Abandoned fast, as though their owners had always been ready, as though their parents had taught them how. They were on the long arm of Appalachia, its shoulder in Georgia, its fingers buried somewhere under the miles of pines stretching to the Canadian border. The people that lived on it had always been hidden, were always disappearing. Towns and cities vanishing under collapsing mountains, rising rivers. All those houses at the bottoms of reservoirs. Porches and living rooms thick with muck and algae. A brood of snapping turtles lumbering across the dining room floor. A school of perch shimmering up the stairs. Curtains wafting in the current through the open windows, as if blown by a subtle breeze. This thing that scares us so much, they lived with it for generations. The land rejecting them, the rivers coming to get them. Their kids covered in black dust, sliding into holes in the ground and never coming out. They saw all of this coming, put it in their songs, songs with thin stabbing voices, melodies angled like broken glass. They tried to tell us that what had happened to them would happen to us, too, but we could not hear the message. Mistook it for nostalgia, when they were speaking prophecy.

Six miles to Lisle. The last stretch of road through

Whitney Point, past the school, the motels, the fairgrounds. The antique tank on a slab of concrete, painted green from the caterpillar treads to the end of the barrel. All mottled with rust. The long cyclone fence bowing in the middle. The clouds in the sky moving north in an unnatural pattern, streaking toward a focal point, as if being pulled there.

"It'll all be over soon," Tenenbaum said. "The war, I mean."

"Do you think so?" Ketcher said.

"Here we are on the northern end of it," she said. "They say it stops in Binghamton. And look around you. This place doesn't even know about it."

"What do you think you'll do?" Ketcher said. "When the war ends."

The other three stopped, turned, looked at him. Up at the clouds.

"Come on," Ketcher said. "We can't live like this, the way we are now. Just for a minute, pretend it's not happening, will you?"

"…"

"…"

"I'm going to go to the beach," Tenenbaum said. "The longest one I can find."

"All the beaches are gone," Jackson said.

"There must be one somewhere," Tenenbaum said. "I know there is. And when I find it, I'll just stand there. Put my feet in the water and stare at those waves coming in. Like it'd look if I were on a ship, right? Heading out to sea."

"And then what?" Jackson said.

"I don't know," Tenenbaum said. "That's the whole point."

Jackson nodded. "I want to have another kid," he said.

"Thought your wife said no," Tenenbaum said.

"When she sees me at the end of all this," he said, "there's no way she'll refuse me." His dreams the last few nights had been full. First of his wife, carrying a pregnancy while they hoed, planted crops in long furrows, sat on the porch and prayed for rain. Then the child, a girl. Always with black hair, tan skin, bright blue eyes. A firecracker, where the boy had been cautious. Patient, where the boy had been impetuous. As if the boy were still alive and the siblings were defining themselves against each other, carving their own spaces into the world. Yet she was still the best of her parents, just like the boy had been, and in the dream, they stood behind the girl, arms around each other, marveling that people such as they could create a child like that.

Largeman was walking point, his back to them. The request hung in the air: Ask him, ask him. But they did not want to do it, did not want to know what his plans were. He'll take a job at a farm, Ketcher thought, shooting cattle in the head. Drowning the barn cats in the pond. Or find another man like him, and each will goad the other until they cut a stripe of chaos across the neck of this country that ends with a shoot-out against the chipped wall of a schoolhouse. Each of them with three dozen bullets in him, but not before they create nine corpses, put two women in a coma, take off a boy's foot.

Or maybe, Ketcher thought, Largeman has become too much the war's creature to outlive it. There will be a month of vagrancy, an abandoned attempt to fix the axle of a rusted truck. A string of splintering hallways, the wind purring through the cracks in the windows. Then a gun under the chin, the caliber high enough to paint the ceiling. Yes, Ketcher thought, for a man like that, there is no other way. And then Largeman stopped, turned. Looked at Ketcher, his face stricken, terrified. He barked out four sobs, coughing on the last one's tail. As if he had seen what was in Ketcher's head, and knew, with a certainty that Ketcher could never have, that the private's final vision was about right. He had only a little time left, and so much to be sorry for.

They knew where Sunny Jim's family house was from the papers in the satchel. Turned off Route 79 to follow the bent sign pointing to Owen Hill Road, Killawog. The houses around them, the paint half sanded off by rain, were all empty. Things on the lawn, big pieces of furniture, three chairs. The doors left open, a few jammed open with scraps of wood. Notes pinned to ripped screens, half unreadable, unable to hold the words against the weather. We are going south on 17. Meet us in Livingston Manor. Meet us in Monticello. We will wait for you there. Please find us, please. We love you to the sky and back.

The soldiers left the houses behind, walked over the rise in the road and over the dike, followed the pavement's curve through tall grass shaded by huge trees closing in over the swelling stream. It was almost dark again, and under the long branches, darker still. A heavy mist in the air. The shapes of houses hiding among the trees. The road rose into the gloom, and the four soldiers went quiet, ascended in a staggered line. Then they were out of the gully and there was a little more light. Enough to see the house before them, a black hulk spiking into the sky. They each paused for a breath, began to flash each other hand signals. Tenenbaum surveyed the grounds, the pitched lawn, the gravel driveway. Then she raised her hand, pointed at the front door, and each of them took a step forward. They did not know that the first bullet from the attic was only four inches from Tenenbaum's skull, the second bullet halfway to Ketcher's eye. The third in the chamber, the fourth in the cartridge, tiny lugs of buzzing metal, jumping, ready to fly.

※ ※ ※ ※

I FOUND JACKSON IN northern Virginia. A small man, husky, nimble, a wrestler. A wide blast of scar tissue across his cheek that made one eye squint. His wiry wife just beginning to show. I think it's a girl, she said. It feels like a girl. They both ate everything I gave them, too fast. They had not eaten enough of late.

After his wife slipped off to sleep, I asked. "Do you mind telling me what happened?"

"Mind? No. I tell everyone what happened."

He had found Ketcher's family, told them what he knew of their son, so they could grieve and grieve right.

Tried to find Largeman's family, too, learned that they'd all been killed in the first year of the war. He liked to think he understood the man better after that, though he could never be sure, for Largeman had said so little. Then he took my hand in his, turned it over, studying my palm. Smiled a little as his wife and unborn child stirred in their slumber.

"If only we all knew each other a little better," he said. "Maybe all this would have been a little different."

They were going to the shore next, he said, to wait for the Big One. A place with fish and shade, a pail to catch rain. He would take the war in his head and push it below the surface, sink it to the bottom and never let it come back up. For his wife and child needed him there, for whatever time they had left, and he wanted nothing more.

The House

IN THE END, THERE was only the mother, the father, Merry, and Sunny Jim in the big family home. The mother and father still in the same room, too tired to fight anymore. Sunny Jim slept on the couch in the living room, woke his father every morning with the creak on the stairs when he went back to his room for clothes. He heard his father shift in the sheets, let out a sighing groan. His mother off hours ago. Every spring the father and mother hauled everything into the hallway and painted their room a blinding white. They let the rest of the house go. Boards fell rotting off the side. The walls ran with the tracks of water damage. Nobody except Merry had gone to the third floor for years. Once, Sunny Jim had not seen her in a week, heard something moving up there. Went to the bottom of the stairs and called up into the grayness. Merry, are you there? Please say something. He heard movement again, and just stood there, calling her name, until the movement stopped. Late that night, she sat on the rug next to the couch, woke him with a hand on his shoulder.

"I heard you calling," she said.

"Why didn't you say anything?"

"You wouldn't have been able to hear me. I wasn't in the house."

"How did you hear me, then?"

"..."

"Merry. Tell me you're all right."

"..."

"You're my only sister. Don't go."

"I won't. Not without telling you first."

But the people in the valley were still talking about her. How they saw her going into the woods, coming out again. There was blood in her hair, they said, a streak of it on her cheek. What's she doing out there?

"Deer," she said. "Almost always deer. Sometimes a grouse."

"You have to stay here now, Merry," Sunny Jim said. "They're scared of you."

"I didn't hurt anybody."

"Just Dad."

"I was protecting you, Jim."

"I know."

"That was for you."

"I know that. But nobody outside of this house does. They only know that you shot your father, and that we don't know how to keep you in the house."

"What are you trying to say?"

"Merry..."

He was seventeen, could not tell her what he heard, on the sidewalk in front of the Lisle Inn, on the green metal bridge across the river. If someone ever goes missing, ever turns up hurt, they said, we'll know where to look. The Wallace brothers, Henry Robinson, and Joe Thule all remembered how she'd acted at the funeral of the girl who flew away. Heard all about what she'd done to her father, though they did not know why, thought it didn't matter. Sunny Jim knew that one day they would be on the lawn of her house with guns in their hands. Come out, Merry. Come on out, now. They could not see how they had made it inevitable, but Sunny Jim could. He knew even then how the town lost its young. When they were children, they vanished into the sky. They were taken to hospitals forty minutes away and never came back. When they got older, they climbed into cars and buses, and the road took them, mangled them in ditches, drowned them in rivers, flung them far away. One house after another lost its people, then the trees swarmed over the timbers and glass, knocked them down and buried them. It had been that way since the flood, and nobody seemed to speak of it. It was just a thing the people left behind knew, that in time the town would be gone for good, and all of us, too. But we have to go somewhere, do we not? Even if we do not know where?

Two weeks later, Earl Granger, six and a half years old, with a thick lisp, walked out the back door of his house. The people at the end of the road saw him enter the woods, holding one of his sister's dolls. They thought his sister was right in front of him, they said, could have sworn they saw someone with him, or they would have stopped him. Instead they watched him step into the trees. Even waved. The next day, the panicked parents ran from house to house, rapping on doors. Have you seen my son? Staggered stricken through Lisle's streets that night, shouting the boy's name. Spent days in the woods, joined by parents with bigger children who felt they owed a debt to the world since their own kids were still with them. And Merry vanished herself, for days longer than usual, came back to Sunny Jim yelling at her, the first time she had ever seen him angry.

"For God's sake, stay in the house," he said.

"I'm trying to help," she said.

"Don't, okay? Just don't."

For nine days there was a truce, an attempt to stave off mayhem. There was no sign of Earl at all, and it was easy to believe that, in the next second, or the next, the boy would scramble out of the woods, doll in hand, looking just as he left. Asking for a jelly sandwich. As though he had fallen asleep on the ground just a few hundred yards in, been in the safe hands of vivid dreams and local deities, until hunger woke him. But then they found the doll by the plane in the woods, darkened by mud and water, half-sitting on a piece of bright white metal. There was still no sign of the boy, but it did not matter. Something had happened to him out there, they said in town. He was there and then he was gone. And they knew who knew those woods better than anyone. A few years ago, Cat Wallace's father said, he'd come across Merry while hunting. He'd gotten lost, asked her to draw him a map back to the road and she did, too fast, too detailed. As though she carried that space around in her head all the time. The Wallace father showed the map around at the Lisle Inn, and they shook their heads. She's spent too much time out there, they said. She's not done with whatever it is she started.

"Well, she's done now," Cat Wallace said. Fetched his brothers, a just-opened bottle of rotgut moonshine from the cabinet, and the rifles from the garage. A handgun for Joe Thule. Henry Robinson was waiting in the road for them. Together the five of them stood in the road, passing the bottle, except for the youngest. Then they walked up Owen Hill Road, guns in their hands, across their shoulders, in plain sight. Letting everyone know what they were up to without saying a thing. They were all courage at first, until Cat Wallace began to talk about the details. I'll take the first shot, he said, but I need someone to cover me. Who's taking the second? The other four boys looked at each other, and Joe Thule felt a beam of harsh light through the alcohol's haze. He did not want to be there. Could not fire a gun that day. Was afraid of what Merry could do.

"Hey guys?" he said. "I'm staying here."

They all stopped. Cat Wallace stared hard at Joe Thule. Joe Thule stared back.

"You pussying out, Joe?" Cat Wallace said.

"I'm just not doing this."

"She's dangerous."

"What do you think we are right now? Look at us."

"..."

"Go on and do it, Cat," Joe Thule said. "I'm just saying I'm not going."

"Me neither," the youngest Wallace brother said. He was having trouble standing still. He was six years old.

Cat turned on him. "You chickenshit."

"Hey." Joe Thule again. "He doesn't want to do it."

He was still holding the pistol. The youngest Wallace wobbled, extended his arm, offering the rifle.

"Keep it." Cat Wallace said. "You're no good with it, anyway."

The paint on the house was half-gone, the angles on the walls beginning to slacken, as though the house was a book, lying on its spine, and the covers were opening to the mold and rain. They really let this place go, Henry Robinson thought. Merry was in the front yard, digging a small furrow. Burying a mouse she had found on the porch the night before. She heard them coming, stopped and turned her head.

"Hello, boys," she said. They expected her to ask if they were going hunting. She did not. She looked Henry Robinson up and down. The boy realized at once that they were all in trouble, but there was no way out.

"Did you hear about the Granger boy?" Cat Wallace said.

"Yes," she said. Looked down again, covered the mouse with earth. "They're not going to find him. It's very sad."

"You don't think it's funny?" Cat Wallace said.

"That was a long time ago," she said.

"Not that long."

She stood, picked up her rifle. The boys had not seen it next to her.

"What have you come here for?"

Henry Robinson was about to speak, but Cat Wallace interrupted him, raised his gun and fired. He was nervous and missed. He got off two more wild shots before she brought up her own rifle and shot him in the left eye. For the middle Wallace brother and Henry Robinson, the next two-and-a-half seconds were a smear of terror. They hit her twice, the first bullet drilling into her thigh, the second one grazing her ear. She got the middle Wallace in the chest, aimed at Henry Robinson, knew before he did that his next bullet would go right in her forehead. Thought of the shadow man, first in the woods, then on the other side of the road, and now in her, and was confused. This is not what you had in mind for me, is it, she thought. You had not counted on what those boys can do.

But then Henry Robinson fell, two shots in him. A third scored the air where he had stood. Sunny Jim was on the porch, his own rifle at his shoulder. Stared at his sister, helpless.

"He would have killed you," he said.

"Yes," she said.

The bodies of three young men lay in their driveway, limbs in a tangle, as if they had been dancing. Birds peeped in the trees. A bright blue day. Just down the road, they heard shouting, recognized Joe Thule's voice. They were running back down Owen Hill Road, would go to the nearest house, fling the door to the kitchen wide. Something awful has happened. Sunny Jim staggered off the porch to his sister, and they held each other close, whispered in each other's ears the promises neither of them would ever break. We will never lose each other. Never. We will always be there, each for the other. Then he was tearing through the woods with her rifle, stopping only to vomit. Shooting small animals, foraging from trash. Ditched the rifle at last in a pond on a farm just south of LaFayette, dug into the muck at two in the morning and buried it, under the silt, under the water. Then it was soup kitchens in Syracuse, odd jobs in Buffalo. A long trip south in a shambling wagon, following the farm work in the fall. The Wallace brothers and Henry Robinson sitting next to him, close, boys of eight again, as they had been at the funeral of the girl who flew away. He never slipped, knew Merry never would either. Only had to remember the deal they made, that he would disappear, and she would say it was Jim who killed them all. There was no one to dispute it. And he would never speak of it to anyone. Maybe never come back. But they were bound to each other then, no matter how far apart they got, and he could count on her for anything, until he let her go.

So was Merry thinking of her brother as she took her third shot from the window under the roof, Aaron on the other side of the attic, wanting to know what was going on. Wanting to see.

"Stay there and be quiet," she said. A razor in her voice to make him obey. She shot again. Now three of the soldiers had stopped moving. The fourth, whom she had hit only once, was crawling backward, back down the road. He had left his gun behind, was only trying to get away. She could not say where she had hit him, but she knew it was bad, bad enough that she did not have to shoot again. She could feel their thoughts rising around her. A warm, sunny place, a beach. A couple old enough to be grandparents, their arms out. Welcome home, boy. The interring of a pile of guns in a field, a shovel working with purpose to cover them good. Then a wad of spittle from the laborer's mouth on the fresh dirt, goodbye to all that, and a quiet decade raising sheep, shearing them in the spring, letting them go in the summer. Largeman could have survived it after all.

She would move them into the woods before dawn, so that Aaron would not have to see. Would bury them the best she could the next night. The war still had not yet touched the boy, and she would not let it now. She had only a few bullets left, but it did not matter. She left her perch, pulled the crates and blankets away from the boy. Looked out the window on the other side. The rip in the sky was wider, longer. It lay open above their heads, plunged behind the trees. She knew it reached the horizon. Touched the earth. She could hear it, a rushing whisper, almost make out words. Somewhere north and west of them, the storm was a curtain parting. She knew what was pulling it open and wanted, with a yearning she had not felt in years, a keening like swooning love, to step through. But would not do so until she saw her brother again, gave him his boy back. Told them both everything they needed to know.

She turned to Aaron. Put the rifle on the floor.

"There," she said.

"What are you doing?" he said.

She looked at the gun. "We don't need it anymore."

The River

AFTER TOWANDA, THERE WERE broken hills, fields of water. Derelict houses sliding under the surface. The *Carthage* half-empty, a brittle shell. The musicians settled into skulking blues, country ballads sung in soft falsetto, as if a loud note would crack the ship in half. They passed from Pennsylvania into New York. There was nobody in Athens, nobody in Waverly. From over the ridge of the crumbling dikes, they could see sagging roofs, shingles like rotting teeth. Then the monsoon draped a downpour onto the river that melted the town away, and it was just the *Carthage*, and the water touching her hull. The drops rattled against the pilothouse until Faisal Jenkins could conceive of nothing else. But the river was speaking loud and clear. This is your last rain. Do not miss it, as your grandmother missed the snow. He closed his eyes, listened as Judge Spleen Smiley had told him to, to the spaces between the raindrops, the groans of the ship beneath him, the thunder sweeping the sky. Began to tap his foot, his finger against the wheel, to the pulse he was sure he could feel. It was easy then to believe that it was all arranged, the work of an unseen orchestra. That the river, sky, and land were speaking to each other. He waited until they gave him an opening, then raised his own voice, to his mother, his grandmother, for teaching him so much.

Down below, the con artist and Sergeant Foote lay side by side on the mat in their room. They had been spending more and more time in there, closing the door to the fights, the music, until the voices and sounds were just dusty signals, half-heard reports from far away, and they pulled their own gods and myths from the room's walls, their own history, of a dissolute people coming to move in the same direction, walking toward a goal they could not see but had to believe was there.

"Let's get married," the con artist said.

"What?" Sergeant Foote said.

"Let's get married."

She turned to look at him. His eyes were big and deep, the patterns in his pupils the map to an unexplored territory, the promise of fertile fields, rich forests. Enough to sustain them for their lives.

"Come on," he said.

"..."

"Why not?"

The mission. The end of the war. Then the river's bank, under broad leaves. She had not imagined anyone else there with her. And yet it seemed he could be there, a ghost, a trick of the light. He would come if she let him.

"We could do it right now," he said. "Go find the band and bring them all on deck. Have the captain blow the horn and gather everyone around. They could salute us with rifles."

"No rifles."

"Fine, no rifles. But there could be a party afterward, just a small one. And that priest could do the ceremony. I've always liked him, you know. Ever since I met him at the Clarks Ferry Bridge."

"..."

"What?"

"Say that again," she said.

"I've always liked—"

"—No. Where did you meet him?"

"At Clarks Ferry Bridge."

"When."

"Just before I got on. We were all up there together, me and the priest and the man he's always with. . . . Where are you going?"

She was putting on her pants, her shirt. An expression on her face he had never seen before, could not read. It made him afraid to speak. She was out the door without another word, closed it too fast. He sat up, looked across the room. She had taken her pistol.

On the deck, the captain and the first mate were squabbling. The bass player sat against the pilothouse tuning a zither, a wrench and a screwdriver lying next to her. The pilot drove with one hand on the wheel, serene, squinting into the straining sun. None of them noticed the gun. But the boy from the camp did.

"I know what you're doing." Standing on his hands, kicking his feet in the air. "I know what you're doing! Rawhead and Bloody Bones!" He sprang off his hands, rolled into a stand. Took a huge breath, planted his feet, and screamed until he ran out of air. Breathed in and screamed. It was all coming for him again. The giants were destroying the landscape, reaching down from the firmament and dragging his parents into the sky. He had spent two days surrounded by corpses, trying to wake them up. Hallucinated for three hours that they had, but all they would talk about was taking him with them. They crawled around on the ground, pointed to the poison. It is so easy. All you have to do is drink. But he could see through them, was starting to smell them, and pushed himself against the cinder block walls, covered his nose and mouth.

The first mate ran to him, but he thrashed away, slashing at her with his fingernails. Don't come near me, don't come anywhere near me. The musician put down her instrument.

"Hey," she said to the boy. "Don't treat her like that, after she's been so good to you." Then she sang a song, slow and sweet, to quiet him. The first thing she thought of.

I never can forget the day
When my dear mother did sweetly say
You are leaving, my darling boy
You always have been your mother's joy.

He screamed through the first two lines, but it got to him on the third line, began to calm him down. She kept on.

Now as you leave in this world to roam
You may not be able to get back home

But remember Jesus Who lives on high
Is watching over you with a mighty eye.

Later, the bass player would wonder why she thought of it then, this old hymn. She was not a religious woman, respected those who were too much to pretend otherwise. But somehow it was the only song that seemed right. She hoped those who had come before her would forgive her for not sharing their conviction, could hear that she shared their hope. Hoped, too, that she could convince the boy that the earth was worth staying on.

⸎ ⸎ ⸎ ⸎

SERGEANT FOOTE MOVED THROUGH the *Carthage*'s halls, tracking down the few passengers who were left. Have you seen the reverend? They had not. Not for hours. At last she found them both in the theater, sitting alone at a table, speaking too low for her to hear. There was no one else there.

"Father," she said.

Reverend Bauxite turned. They both looked at her.

"Can I help you?" Reverend Bauxite said.

"Tell me again how long you've been on this boat."

The two men both looked at the floor.

We tried, didn't we.

Yes, we did.

Almost made it, too.

Almost.

"I'm the man you want," Sunny Jim said. You have to get my boy now, Reverend.

I will.

Don't die on me first.

I won't.

I need you.

I know.

Reverend Bauxite got up.

"No way," Sergeant Foote said.

He sat down again.

"I know who you are," she said to Sunny Jim. Then recited his full name, the name of his wife. Their place in the resistance. The things they had done, the people whose deaths they'd been charged with. The accusations arrayed against him, a litany of crimes that had curdled into judgment, a sentence.

"Do you deny it?" she said.

"No," Sunny Jim said.

"Then you understand why I am authorized to use any force necessary against you."

"Yes. Like your people did in Baltimore."

"This is different."

"If you say so."

She pulled out her pistol.

Sunny Jim looked at Reverend Bauxite. Don't die on me.

I won't.

You have to live.

I will.

For Aaron.

Yes. For him.

He looked back at Sergeant Foote. "How good a shot are you?"

"What?"

"I said, how good a shot are you? Because if you're going to do this, I want to be hit clean."

"You want this?"

He sighed, and the word floated in the air—*yes*—down through the floor, the planks of the hull, into the cold current. "You seem to know a lot about me. Don't you understand yet?" he said. "I just want my boy back. If I can't have that, I don't want to be here a second longer than I have to."

Then Sergeant Foote saw everything. The war was over, and the criminal and saboteur she'd been looking for was gone. There was just a man here, his wife in the water right below their feet, whispering to him. Growing impatient with him that he had not yet gotten their son. And he was not alone in being so haunted: All through the halls and rooms of the breaking vessel, the masses of the remembered dead lingered over the living, waiting for that livid second when all would be set free, and all could reunite.

"I see," she said. "I just needed to know."

She married the con artist six hours later. It began with a small ceremony, a flourish of strings, ended with a shower of broken glass, cuts on their ankles, bleeding dancers laughing and stumbling as the musicians lurched through another tango, the only thing they could think of to play. Then a violin string broke and they all cheered, rolled down into their rooms as though impelled there. And with her new husband asleep beside her, she at last pictured him with her on the riverbank, the sun flooding them with heat, then sinking into a final serenity in the blinding orange light off the water, and her laying down her arms for good.

※ ※ ※ ※

THE SUN WASHED THE world in green and yellow light. The river narrowed again, straightened, a line pointing east. Low trees to either side, fields and train tracks beyond. The *Carthage* passed under the broken arch of a metal bridge, and they were in Owego. Brick buildings, ramshackle wooden balconies tilted over the water, chipping paint and bared splinters. It was easy to imagine that there had been a waterfront once, docks like piano keys, a bustle of people carrying lumber and barrels, lines of laundry strung long and bowing. There had been a bookstore in an old mill, a florist. A boy who played the violin, drove three towns over for lessons. A winter night when the houses all along the tree-shaded streets were under two feet of snow, and the cars crept through it, wipers squealing. Dropping off kids who would be gone in less than a decade, to cities hours away, for there was not enough for them there. But they were all ghosts now. Not a soul on the rickety wooden steps, or in the buildings, the streets beyond. Though two sheets shimmered in the wan wind, tied high over the current. I LOVE YOU SO MUCH, C.J. LOOK FOR ME read one.

DON'T WAIT MAGGIE I'LL FIND YOU read the other. There were already holes in both signs, tears at the corners. Only time and the river will bring my love to me. . . . Two hours after the *Carthage* passed, one of the sheets gave out and fell into the water. Five days later, he found her anyway.

They had not yet cleared the town when Faisal Jenkins let out a sharp, rising whistle across the deck. Judge Spleen Smiley was sitting under the birds, blowing soft notes into a clarinet. He stopped, looked up. Faisal Jenkins only had to nod once. The judge took the instrument in his hands apart, put it back in its case. Walked below deck. The pilot kept the *Carthage* moving upriver, past the brick buildings downtown and into a stretch of water bordered by houses of wood and stucco, long green lawns that rolled, overgrown, to the river's edge. He brought the *Carthage* closer to that bank, and the entire band emerged on deck with cases under each arm, lashed to backs, hanging off shoulders by straps. Trumpets and banjos, mandolins and trombones. A clattering of drums. The big shell of the upright bass. Then Faisal Jenkins gave the signal, a long, low sound on the horn by the wheel, and the crew scurried to drop the anchor. The *Carthage* leaned back on the chain, hung suspended in the current.

They were loading their instruments into the rowboat when the first mate and her boy ran up to them.

"You're leaving?" she said.

"Looks that way," the judge said.

"Here?"

"Good a place as any." He reconsidered. "Every place is good."

"But there's nobody here."

"That's not the place's fault."

"You know what I'm saying, Judge."

The judge leaned on his guitar case. I'm trying to protect you. You and the boy. But I can't if you keep asking questions.

"No, I don't," the judge said. "I don't know what you're saying."

The first mate looked down at the boy. Felt the river swell, as if taking a breath.

"Do you want to go with them?" she said to the boy.

"What?" the boy said.

"Hey now," the judge said.

"I don't mean just him," she said. "I mean me, too."

The other musicians had everything in the dinghy. It rocked on the current, the cases creaking in unison. The boy looked toward the shore, back at the first mate's cabin, the open door.

"What do you think?" the first mate said.

"You want to go?" the boy said.

"If you do," the first mate said.

The boy clutched the first mate's hand, took a step toward the boat.

"All right," she said. "Come on."

The musicians rowed the instruments to shore, unloaded the boat, and sent it back. She got in the boat with the boy and pulled on the oars, held it in the stream while the boy jumped out, ran across a tangled lawn, toward a dark house. She turned to the *Carthage* as if she might row back. Instead, she jumped out into the shallow water, kicked the boat into the current. The crew tilted their heads, jumped into the water to fetch it. And the first mate was first mate no longer. She would sleep on land that night for the first time in four years. For all that time, it was as if the *Carthage* had been a spider on the river's silver thread, the earth around it smoke and darkness, heavy hills. People crawled out of it, vanished back in again. She had gazed around the ship and decided she needed nothing more. But now she was seeing it through the boy, and the ship and the land changed before her, unfolded. The *Carthage* was no place to grow up, she thought, and somewhere in the miles in front of them, there must be somewhere for him to track out his years. There had to be, and she would help him find it, even if it meant losing some of her self. For she did not want the time left anymore if it was only for her. The days only made sense if he was in them.

Sergeant Foote and the con artist were on the deck watching the musicians, the first mate, and the boy bustling on shore, arranging cases, getting ready to go. It was Towanda all over again. Smaller, quieter, but the same thing. For a moment, she did not know what she was feeling. She had not seen it coming, but now it was cresting, moving across her, subsiding. Leaving her changed. Later, she would see that the wave had snapped the ropes that held the war to her and carried it off. But in those seconds, she felt only the release, the impulse to act. She turned to her husband, took his hand. "Coming?" she said.

"Ready when you are."

Together they ran to the rail, stepped up, and planted their feet on it, jumped into the water. Swam toward the people on the shore as the musicians cheered, ran to the water's edge, extended their hands, and pulled them out. They lay for a minute in the cool grass, catching their breath, staring into the sky. His hand found hers. Then they stood up, took off their clothes, wrung them out in their hands. Put them back on again and nodded. Let's go.

The group would only be together for a little while. In time, after a final party with three families they met on the highway, the musicians went west, the first mate and the boy south. And Sergeant Foote and the con artist to me. She was already sick when I met her, and if the broken chair was not a riverbank, it was warm and quiet, the words from her lover the last she heard.

※ ※ ※ ※

HE DID NOT KNOW what woke him at first. Sunny Jim had been dreaming of smoky trees, mist rising from water. A multitude of voices rushing forward, pulling away, too many words at once, each one trying to pour itself into his ear. He was flailing his arms, swatting the air in front of his face. Then he was awake. Purple light drifted through the shutters, night hanging by a finger. The room was almost too dark to see, and there was nothing. Then the three boys, but they said nothing, just huddled in the corner with their faces in their hands. Sunny Jim understood that they were scared.

"What's happening?" he said.

"No," they said together. "Don't make us speak."

And then there was Aline, her face ragged, hair straying from her scalp. She was crouching over him, her face so close that he could smell her, her sweet scent, algae, ash. Her hands on the sides of his face. He longed to touch her but was afraid.

"I knew you were still here," he said. "I knew you would come."

She took her hands away, stood up.

"Don't go," he said. She shook her head, raised her arm, beckoned with a wave, and he rose, moved through the quiet halls, until he was on deck with her. She pointed ahead at Binghamton, the darkened city spilling into the river. Three flares shot from its center, a short burst of machine-gun fire on a distant shore. The war was here already. They thought they had beaten it.

Reverend Bauxite was there, too, scanning the opposed banks. He had been watching all night, seen furtive soldiers taking their positions, the dark lines of guns being put into place. It was happening on both sides of the river, the *Carthage* slipping up the current in between. When he understood what was happening, he had a weak impulse to rouse the pilot, the captain, get them to turn the ship around, go back downstream. Then realized it was far too late for that.

"What are you doing up here?" Reverend Bauxite said.

So many more questions buzzing between them. No chance to ask them or answer.

"Time to get off this boat," Sunny Jim said. He looked down the *Carthage* to one of the last lifeboats, swinging from a chain. The priest was gazing from shore to shore, to a new flare rising over the city ahead.

"Do you think the pilot can bring us in closer?" Sunny Jim said.

"I don't think we have that kind of time," Reverend Bauxite said. Sunny Jim, were you just talking to her?

No.

Answer me.

No.

Sunny Jim lowered the boat with Reverend Bauxite in it, jumped into the water, and climbed in. They both took up oars and were rowing again, as they had in Harrisburg, the war all around them. A tangle of corpses jammed on the columns of the bridges. A building exploding in a flower of fire. A woman stooping to give a limbless man a cool, damp cloth for his sweating forehead. The army's soldiers slumped in their uniforms, one of them playing a concertina and singing in a faltering tenor, a dying song. Back then, Sunny Jim, Aaron, and he had been phantoms passing through it, Reverend Bauxite thought. As if God had heard the promise they made to Aline to keep the boy safe, and so they were safe with him as well. Someone, he could not remember who, had told him that. He had not been able to see it at the time, that the war had been looking for them, sent grenades to the Market Street Bridge, bombs to the pulpit where he spoke in church. Never found them. Then they were on the river and the war was behind them, eating every town. But now the war was here and the boy twenty miles away, and Reverend Bauxite saw everything. The sky flickered from a luminous blue to orange to black, and the water around them wrinkled with rising waves, telling the history of the current and how it had carved its way through the mountains to the sea. Its history and all that was coming.

It's beautiful, he thought. Asking pardon for his pride, for there was no one to do it for him, he prayed. "Into your hands, O merciful Savior," he said in a low voice, "I commend myself as your servant. Acknowledge, I humbly beseech you, a sheep of your own fold, a lamb of your own flock, a sinner of your own redeeming. Receive me into the arms of your mercy, into the blessed rest of everlasting peace, and into the glorious company of the saints in light."

He looked over at the *Carthage* as they moved away from it, then at Sunny Jim. Thought of Aaron. Kept praying. "You led your ancient people by a pillar of cloud by day and a pillar of fire by night," he said. "Grant that we, who serve you now on earth, may come to the joy of that heavenly Jerusalem, where all tears are wiped away and where your saints for ever sing your praise."

The guns at the shore were arming all around him, pointing out across the water. He could almost feel, then, the force that had kept the bullets away turning toward him. He was their beacon, drawing them to him, so that he might be transformed.

"Get down," he told Sunny Jim. "Down in the bottom of the boat. I can row us in from here myself."

Sunny Jim drew in his oars, lay them down, trying to be quiet.

"Hurry," Reverend Bauxite said.

A long volley of gunfire from the nearest shore spat into the water, rang off the boat's metal hull, and Reverend Bauxite leaned forward and smacked Sunny Jim down, until he was stretched under the bench. The bullets scorched the air around them. Reverend Bauxite picked up his oars and kept rowing in strong, steady strokes, a short *ha* barking from his throat at the end of every pull. A bullet burrowed into his back and he gasped but did not stop. Another one in his arm made him wince, but could not slow him down. Sunny Jim lay there in the bottom of the boat, staring up at his friend, and with each of the priest's mounting breaths in the early morning light, it was as though he were getting bigger, stronger. As though when they reached the shore, he would walk along the bank, bending trees, crushing the guns beneath his feet. Then a bullet passed through his gut and Reverend Bauxite shouted, turned his head in time to catch a final shot from temple to temple that toppled him into the boat alongside his friend. The two men lay there, face to face, and Sunny Jim swore he saw the priest's eyes looking at him, then through him. A trail of ecstasy that took away the anger, for he had been a best friend, a father to his child. Pulled a dozen churches from the air and one from stone. Been ordained in the same water that carried him now. Years ago, felt God's breath through the trees, knew He was there, with a certainty he had never quite forgotten, and never would now.

The boat glided to shore, nestled against the land, and Sunny Jim leapt from the boat, dragged Reverend Bauxite up the bank. Together, they saw three rockets ride streaks of smoke into the *Carthage,* the house of pilgrims, the priest's last congregation. To Sunny Jim, the ship gave birth to a sphere of fire that split its mother in two, burst into a rising column of rolling flames and smoke that lit river, islands, and shore together. To Reverend Bauxite, the ship bloomed, released a swarm of souls, all who were there and had ever been there, from the mouth of the river in Chesapeake Bay to the drowning fields north of Binghamton. They spun outward from the opening vessel, across the flat of the shining water, over the land all around. And the country followed, blossoming into streams of light and color, voices and music that moved through the priest, bore him aloft over the changed earth, and took him in.

✳ ✳ ✳

THEN THE SHOOTING STOPPED. No more rockets flew. The wreck of the *Carthage* was marooned in the river, breaking apart. Sunny Jim sat on the shore, his best friend in his arms. The hour was coming when it would hit him, just how much he had lost. When it did, it would knock him to the ground and then spill out of him, a flood of words. But he had no time for it now. All along the walled banks, tracers were drawing quick stripes over the water, rockets flying again. A tower a few blocks from the bridge to Front Street took a missile, and the upper half teetered on a hinge of flame and fell into the city. He put Reverend Bauxite back in the boat, pushed it out into the current. Watched it go, waited until he could not see it anymore. Then he was sprinting down Riverside Drive to Front Street, hiding in the shadows of the doorways of abandoned stores whenever he saw soldiers or guerrillas make stuttering steps into intersections, close together, bristling with gun barrels like giant metal porcupines. They crept down the streets, dispersing in a flurry of hand signals, cringing when explosions nearby made the ground snap beneath them. Four times they saw him, shot when he ran, the bullets like poltergeists, kicking up rocks and breaking windows behind him. He ran under the empty overpasses for Route 17, I-81, out onto Route 11, past a string of asphalt plains and corroding buildings, until the road broke from the city and the trees rushed in around him. In the weak light, he could see the broken hills, the road heaving and falling, a rusting green trailer set back from the road, the earth cleared around it going to weeds and seed. The tear in the sky pushing ever wider, howling and murmuring. The wave of the storm about to crest. He was almost home, and Aline was with him, and something hot and hollow was pressing against his ribs, as if he were taking her home for the first time to meet the family.

The House

ONCE AARON WAS ASLEEP on the mattress in the attic, Merry climbed onto the roof to gaze into the sky. It was opening like the skin of a fruit, speaking to her with a clarity her parents, even her brother, had never had. She looked across the horizon from the north to the west and could see it, the land becoming indistinct, as if pieces of it were rising, breaking apart without a sound. Constant flashes of electricity. It was beautiful. Only a day or two more, it said to her, and she could go.

She recognized her brother by his gait alone, though he was slower than he had been years ago. Aaron was on the second floor, in her parents' old room. She ran and got the boy, almost bore him aloft by his left wrist as she flew down the stairs with him. Your father's here, your father's here. Then they were running down the porch steps and across the lawn to him, and he broke into a hobbled sprint toward them. The boy almost knocked his father over, and Sunny Jim stumbled and laughed, harder than Merry had ever heard. That was what the boy had wrought in him, she thought. Made him into more. He had run twelve miles past Binghamton before collapsing midstride into the ditch on the roadside. Slept through a light rain. Woke up terrified of how long he might have been there, ran the last nine miles, paused when he saw what remained of the house. But even that vanished from his sight when the people he loved best came out of it. There were no gunshots for him then, no torn muscles, no burnt lungs. No one lost. He spun Aaron around and around until the boy couldn't stand it anymore. Sunny Jim could have stayed that way forever, his boy's face fixed before him, the rest of the world blurring away. You were right, Reverend, he thought. You always were. The light was coming, it would come soon, if he'd just let everything go. He was almost ready.

"Where's Mom?" Aaron said.

Sunny Jim brought his son closer, chin to shoulder, held him until the boy's legs started kicking.

"Put me down."

"No," Sunny Jim said.

"Come on."

"Put him down," Merry said. "We need to talk."

"Aaron," Sunny Jim said. "Go in the house and get your things. We're leaving in a few minutes."

"Is Aunt Merry coming with us?"

"No," he said, and Aaron hugged Merry's waist. She bent down to put her arms around him, too, and he kissed her cheek.

"Remember all the things I told you?" she said to him.

"Yes," he said.

"You'll tell your dad, right?"

"Yes."

"All right. Now listen to your father." He was up the stairs and gone, back into the house.

"Hello," she said to Sunny Jim.

"Hi."

"And hello to you," Merry said. Smiled. "She's pretty. I see why you fell for her."

" . . . "

" . . . "

"How have you been?" he said.

"We don't have time for this," she said. "He'll be back any minute." She turned a little to look over her shoulder. Now Sunny Jim could almost hear it, too, crawling across the land.

"I want to go," Merry said. Her voice broke, ached, on the last word.

"I know."

"Will you let me?"

All the years he had carried her with him, down the spine of the country and back again. She had been with him in the old apartment above the Chinese restaurant, in the back of the purple van with Aline, heading south. The day that Aaron was born, and he first held him screaming. All through the crackling guns, the whispering bombs and mortars. The night the Market Street Bridge fell. Merry, I need you so much. Don't go. Don't go.

"Go," he said. "Before Aaron comes back."

She stepped forward, put her hands on his shoulders, then got up on tiptoes and kissed him on the forehead. I love you, baby brother. Then spun north, started walking. Quickened her step as soon as she broke into the fields. Almost broke into a run. He thought he heard her chuckle then, though he would never be sure.

For three minutes he was alone in front of the house where he was born. Half the shingles were off the roof, scattered around the yard. Long strips of siding in clattered piles. Paint peeling off in long tails, curling claws. Windows cracked from the warping of the frames around them. He could almost see the beams, the bones. See his family when he was a child storming through the house, his grandparents, uncles, aunts, and cousins. The shadow man in the tall grass at the edge of the trees on the other side of the road. The downed plane in the woods. The sparkling swings at the fair. His cousin's truck, kicking up gravel. The bullet hole in the wall, his parents with bandages and stitches. The long ride on a purple bicycle. The three dead boys in the driveway. His sister had kissed him then, too. It's what she did when she was sure she would never see him again. This house was falling. Soon it would kneel into the ground, and the earth would rise to take it. But it was in him, too, every plank, every nail, and Aline with it, until the day he gave them all away.

Aaron came out of the house at a run, jaunted down the stairs, a small pack on his back.

"So where's Mom?" he said.

He was almost ready, ready at last. But there were more important things to do first.

"You have to tell me how you are," Sunny Jim said.

"What do you want me to tell you?"

"Everything," Sunny Jim said.

And he did.

❊ ❊ ❊

IT TOOK A LONG time to find Aaron and his father. They were living in the shell of a boat that had washed aground where the river met the highway, fifty miles south of Harrisburg. Sunny Jim was in a wheelchair by then, too weak to speak. Aaron talked for him while his father looked on, pride swelling in his eyes for the man his boy was becoming. We were together for almost a month, and while I was with them, it was as if a message went out. People came with pigs and vegetables, and there were dinners, animals roasted and eaten, under the crashing sky. A woman with an accordion sat on a crate along the highway's broken shoulder, stamping her foot in the dust, and a man put on his boots and danced in the road. There was clapping and cheering, and we all looked at the ground, the cracked rock, the dark soil, around our moving feet. I have not seen any of them since, and cannot recall them when I try. Yet sometimes they revisit me: I catch a glimpse of them, of their fleeting faces, as from the light of a spark. The way a woman's scarf fanned in the air around her when she turned. A piece of a man's laugh. His chipped tooth. A thing an older woman said to me: Do not forget us. Say that what we did here was good, even with everything that came before. Say it.

Can you see it? We are here, all that was left, that I

could bring together in the flashes of these pages. We are here in the curves of every letter, in the curl of a comma. In the spaces between the words. We are all here, all of us, and the towns and cities we knew, the ones that we lost, to water and fire and water again. We are a parade along the road, of funerals and parties, weddings with one witness. A birth in the shelter of a house half-occupied by animals, the child held up to the sky. And the river, the river, filled from the depths of the sea, flowing to the ends of the earth.

It is too much. It is not enough. There are not enough pages, and there was never enough time—I should have known that, but I am still trying. I am trying to reach you, wherever you are, wherever you have gone, because we all have to find each other somehow, even if the words are all that is left when we do. Perhaps now we can tell you the things we could not say then. How much we love you. How we are sorry. How we know it will get better, even if we are only here to see it through you.

Good-bye. Hello.

ACKNOWLEDGMENTS

To The Reverend Drew Bunting, for so much guidance. To Chuck Wall and Tara Duffy, for taking the canoe trip with me. To Laura Bean Kelley, for all the stories about mental hospitals. To the Pasquales, for telling me a few things about Binghamton. To James Leva, for writing the tune. To Jacob Curtz, Joseph DeJarnette, and Liz Toffey, for making the book happen. To Cameron McClure and Liz Gorinsky, for making the book better. To Central New York and Pennsylvania. To Steph. To Leo.